MURDER
at the
BRIGHTWELL

MURDER
at the
BRIGHTWELL

Ashley Weaver

MINOTAUR BOOKS

A Thomas Dunne Book
New York

A THOMAS DUNNE BOOK FOR MINOTAUR BOOKS.
An imprint of St. Martin's Publishing Group.

MURDER AT THE BRIGHTWELL. Copyright © 2014 by Ashley Weaver. All rights reserved. Printed in the United States of America. For information, address St. Martin's Press, 175 Fifth Avenue, New York, N.Y. 10010.

www.thomasdunnebooks.com
www.minotaurbooks.com

Design by Molly Rose Murphy

Library of Congress Cataloging-in-Publication Data is available upon request.

ISBN 978-1-250-04636-9 (hardcover)
ISBN 978-1-4668-4653-1 (e-book)

Minotaur books may be purchased for educational, business, or promotional use. For information on bulk purchases, please contact Macmillan Corporate and Premium Sales Department at 1-800-221-7945, extension 5442, or write specialmarkets@macmillan.com.

First Edition: October 2014

10 9 8 7 6 5 4 3 2 1

To my parents, Dan and DeAnn Weaver,
for their unfailing love and support

ACKNOWLEDGMENTS

THERE ARE SO many people without whom this book would not have been possible. I would like to thank my fabulous agent, Ann Collette, for her belief in my manuscript and her tireless efforts on my behalf. I am grateful to my excellent editor, Toni Kirkpatrick, for her support and guidance in making this book the best that it could be. I would also like to thank Jennifer Letwack and the wonderful teams at Thomas Dunne and Minotaur Books for all their hard work and their patience with my endless questions.

I am blessed to have a host of friends who have encouraged me and offered feedback on various drafts of this manuscript. Thanks to my cousin, Allison Dodson, who has read my stories for as long as I've written them; my friend and fellow writer Sabrina Street, who pushed me to take the first steps toward trying to get published; my writing buddies Rebecca Farmer, Stephanie Shultz, and Angela Larson; as well as Caleb Lea, Haley Guillory, Amanda Phillips, Denise Marquiss, Victoria Cienfuegos, Candace Hamilton,

Faith Johnson, Amanda Hussong, and all the others who have cheered me on along the way.

Many thanks to the staff of the Allen Parish Libraries for their support and enthusiasm throughout this process.

And last but certainly not least, I am forever grateful to my amazing family. Mom, Dad, Amelia, and Danny, your love, encouragement, and faith mean the world to me. I couldn't have done it without you!

MURDER
at the
BRIGHTWELL

IT IS AN impossibly great trial to be married to a man one loves and hates in equal proportions.

It was late June, and I was dining alone in the breakfast room when Milo blew in from the south.

"Hello, darling," he said, brushing a light kiss across my cheek. He dropped into the seat beside me and began buttering a piece of toast, as though it had been two hours since I had seen him last, rather than two months.

I took a sip of coffee. "Hello, Milo. How good of you to drop in."

"You're looking well, Amory."

I had thought the same of him. His time on the Riviera had obviously served him well. His skin was smooth and golden, setting off the bright blue of his eyes. He was wearing a dark gray suit, lounging in that casual way he had of looking relaxed and at home in expensive and impeccably tailored clothes.

"I hadn't expected to see you back so soon," I said. His last letter, an offhanded attempt at keeping me informed of his whereabouts, had arrived three weeks before and hinted that he would probably not return home until late July.

"Monte Carlo grew so tedious; I simply had to get away."

"Yes," I replied. "Nothing to replace the dull routine of roulette, champagne, and beautiful women like a rousing jaunt to your country house for toast and coffee with your wife."

Without really meaning to do so, I had poured a cup of coffee, two sugars, no milk, and handed it to him.

"You know, I believe I've missed you, Amory."

He looked me in the eyes then and smiled. Despite myself, I nearly caught my breath. He had that habit of startling, dazzling one with his sudden and complete attention.

Grimes, our butler, appeared at the door just then. "Someone to see you in the morning room, madam." He did not acknowledge Milo. Grimes, it had long been apparent, was no great admirer of my husband. He treated him with just enough respect that his obvious distaste should not cross the boundary into impropriety.

"Thank you, Grimes. I will go to the morning room directly."

"Very good, madam." He disappeared as noiselessly as he had come.

The fact that Grimes's announcement had been so vague as to keep Milo in the dark about the identity of my visitor was not lost on my husband. He turned to me and smiled as he buttered a second piece of toast. "Have I interrupted a tryst with your secret lover by my unexpected arrival?"

I set my napkin down and rose. "I have no secrets from you, Milo." I turned as I reached the door and flashed his smile back at him. "If I had a lover, I would certainly inform you of it."

ON MY WAY to the morning room, I stopped at the large gilt mirror in the hallway to be sure the encounter with my wayward husband had not left me looking as askew as I felt. My reflection looked placidly back at me, gray eyes calm, waved dark hair in place, and I was reassured.

It took time, I had learned, to prepare myself for Milo. Unfortunately, he did not often oblige me by giving notice of his arrival.

I reached the door to the morning room, wondering who my visitor might be. Grimes's mysterious announcement was a reflection of my husband's presence, not the presence of my visitor, so I would have been unsurprised to find as commonplace a guest as my cousin Laurel behind the solid oak door. I entered the room and found myself surprised for the second time that morning.

The man seated on the white Louis XVI sofa was not my cousin Laurel. He was, in fact, my former fiancé.

"Gil."

"Hello, Amory." He had risen from his seat as I entered, and we stared at one another.

Gilmore Trent and I had known each other for years and had been engaged for all of a month when I had met Milo. The two men could not have been more different. Gil was fair; Milo was dark. Gil was calm and reassuring; Milo was reckless and exciting. Compared with Milo's charming unpredictability, Gil's steadiness had seemed dull. Young fool that I had been, I had chosen illusion over substance. Gil had taken it well and wished me happiness in that sincere way of his, and that was the last that I had seen of him. Until now.

"How have you been?" I asked, moving forward to take his hand. His grip was warm and firm, familiar.

3

"Quite well. And you? You look wonderful. Haven't changed a bit." He smiled, eyes crinkling at the corners, and I felt instantly at ease. He was still the same old Gil.

I motioned to the sofa. "Sit down. Would you care for some tea? Or perhaps breakfast?"

"No, no. Thank you. I realize I have already imposed upon you, dropping in unannounced as I have."

A pair of blue silk-upholstered chairs sat across from him, and I sank into one, somehow glad Grimes had chosen the intimate morning room over one of the more ostentatious sitting rooms. "Nonsense. I'm delighted to see you." I realized that I meant it. It was awfully good to see him. Gil had kept out of society and I had wondered, more than once in the five years since my marriage, what had become of him.

"It's good to see you too, Amory." He was looking at me attentively, trying to determine, I supposed, how the years had changed me. Despite his claim that I was still the same, I knew the woman before him was quite different from the girl he had once known.

Almost without realizing it, I had been appraising him as well. Five years seemed to have altered him very little. Gil was very good-looking in a solid and conventional sort of way, not stunning like Milo but very handsome. He had dark blond hair and well-formed, pleasant features. His eyes were a light, warm brown, with chocolaty flecks drawn out today by his brown tweed suit.

"I should have written to you before my visit," he went on, "but, to tell the truth . . . I wasn't sure you would see me."

"Why wouldn't I?" I smiled, suddenly happy to be sitting here with an old friend, despite what had passed between us. "After all, the bad behavior was entirely on my part. I am surprised that you would care to see me."

"All water under the bridge." He leaned forward slightly, lending sincerity to his words. "I told you at the time, there was no one to blame."

"That is kind of you, Gil."

He spoke lightly, but his lips twitched up at the corners as though his mouth could not quite decide if he was serious, could not quite support a smile. "Yes. Well, one can't stop love, can one?"

"No." My smile faded. "One can't."

He leaned back in his seat then, dismissing the intimacy of the moment. "How is Milo?"

"He's very well. He returned only this morning from the Riviera."

"Yes, I had read something about his being in Monte Carlo in the society columns." I could only imagine what it might have been. Within six months of my marriage, I had learned it was better not to know what the society columns said about Milo.

For just a moment, the specter of my husband hung between us in the air.

I picked up the box of cigarettes on the table and offered one to him, knowing he didn't smoke. To my surprise, he accepted, pulling a lighter from his pocket. He touched the flame to the tip of his cigarette and inhaled deeply.

"What have you been doing these past few years?" I asked, immediately wondering if the question was appropriate. It seemed that some shadow of the past tainted nearly every topic. I knew that he had left England for a time after we had parted ways. Perhaps his travel since our parting was not something he wished to discuss. After all, there had been a time when we had traveled together. In the old days, before either of us had ever thought of marriage, our families had often been thrown together on various holidays abroad, and Gil and I had become fast friends and confidants. He had good-naturedly accompanied me in searching out scenic spots or exploring ancient ruins, and our evenings had been occupied by keeping one another company in hotel sitting rooms as our parents frequented foreign nightspots until dawn. Sometimes I still thought fondly of our adventures together and of those long, comfortable conversations before the fire.

He blew out a puff of smoke. "I've traveled some. Kept busy."

"I expect you enjoyed seeing more of the world. Do you remember the time we were in Egypt . . ."

He sat forward suddenly, grounding out his cigarette in the crystal ashtray on the table. "Look here, Amory. I might as well tell you why I've come."

Years of practice in hiding my thoughts allowed me to keep my features from registering surprise at his sudden change of manner. "Certainly."

He looked me in the eyes. "I've come to ask a favor."

"Of course, Gil. I'd be happy to do anything . . ."

He held up a hand. "Hear me out before you say yes." He was agitated about something, uneasy, so unlike his normally contained self.

He stood and walked to the window, gazing out at the green lawn that went on and on before it ended abruptly at the lake that marked the eastern boundary of the property.

I waited, knowing it would do little good to press him. Gil wouldn't speak until he was ready. I wondered if perhaps he had come to ask me for money. The Trents were well-off, but the recent economic difficulties had been far-reaching, and more than a few of my friends had found themselves in very reduced circumstances. If that was the case, I would be only too happy to help.

"I don't need money, if that's what you're thinking," he said, his back still to me.

Despite the tension of the situation, I laughed. "Still reading my mind."

He turned, regarding me with a solemn expression. "It's not so hard to read your mind, but your eyes are harder to read than they used to be."

"Concealment comes with practice," I replied.

"Yes, I suppose it does." He walked back to the sofa and sat down.

When he spoke, his tone had returned to normal. "Have you seen anything of Emmeline these past years?"

I wondered briefly if he had decided not to ask me the favor, reverting instead to polite conversation. Emmeline was Gil's sister. She was younger than me by three years and away at school in France during much of our acquaintance, but we had been friends. After my engagement to Gil had ended, however, Emmeline and I had drifted apart.

"Once or twice at London affairs," I answered.

"Was she . . . do you remember the chap she was with?"

I cast my mind back to the last society dinner at which I had seen Emmeline Trent. There had been a young man, handsome and charming, if I recalled correctly. Something about my memory of him nagged at me, and I tried to recall what it was.

"I remember him," I said. "His name was Rupert something or other."

"Rupert Howe, yes. She plans to marry him."

I said nothing. There was more to come; that much was certain.

"He's not a good sort, Amory. I'm sure of it."

"That may be, Gil," I said gently. "But, after all, Emmeline is a grown woman." Emmeline would be twenty-three now, older than I had been when I married.

"It's not like that, Amory. It isn't just that I don't like the fellow. It's that I don't trust him. There's something . . . I don't know . . ." His voice trailed off, and he looked up at me. "Emmeline has always liked you, looked up to you. I thought that, perhaps . . ."

Was this why he had come? I had no influence on Emmeline. "If she won't listen to you," I said, "whatever makes you think she will care what I have to say?"

He paused, and I could see that he was formulating his words, planning out what he would say. Gil had always been like that, careful to think before speaking. "There's a large party going down to the south coast, a little village outside Brighton, tomorrow. Emmeline and Rupert and several other people I'm sure you know. We'll be staying at the Brightwell Hotel for a week. I came to ask you if you would go on the pretext of a holiday."

I was surprised at the invitation. I had not seen Gil in five years, and suddenly here he was, asking me to take a trip to the seaside. "I still don't understand. What can I do, Gil? Why come to me?"

"I . . . Amory," his eyes came up to mine, the brown flecks darker than they had been. "I want you to accompany me . . . to appear to be *with* me. You understand?"

I did understand him, just as easily as I once had. I saw just what he meant. I was to go with him to the seaside, to give the impression that I had left Milo. That my marriage had been a mistake. Emmeline had seen the society columns, the reports of my husband gallivanting across Europe without me; she would believe it.

I suddenly comprehended that there would be good reason for me to talk to Emmeline, how I would have authority when Gil didn't.

Gil had said he didn't trust Rupert Howe. I knew he was right. I knew Gil had seen in Rupert the same thing that had caught my attention when I had met him.

Emmeline's Rupert had reminded me of Milo.

My decision was almost immediate. "I should be delighted to come," I said. "I should like to keep Emmeline from making a mistake, if I possibly can."

Gil smiled warmly, relief washing across his features, and I found myself returning the smile. The prospect of a week at the seaside in the company of old friends was not an unappealing one, at that.

Of course, had I known the mayhem that awaited, I would have been more reluctant to offer my services.

GIL LEFT IMMEDIATELY, declining my offer to stay even for lunch.

I walked him to the door, and there was an easy silence between us, the companionability of shared conspiracy.

He took my hand as we stepped out onto the drive and into the warm morning light. "If you don't want to do this, you have only to say so. I have no right to ask anything of you, Amory. It's just that I knew at once that you would understand." He offered me a slightly unsteady smile as the past resurfaced. "And I seem to recall that you were always keen on a bit of adventure."

I had been once. Gil had teased me for my sense of daring, my daydreams of great exploits. However, life so seldom became what we expected it to be; adventure had been very sparse these past few years.

"I am happy to do what I can, Gil. Truly."

He brushed his thumb lightly over my hand. "What will you tell your husband?"

"I don't know that I'll tell him anything." I smiled weakly. "He probably won't notice I'm gone."

Gil's eyes flickered over my shoulder. "I'm not so certain of that."

I didn't turn around, but instead leaned to brush a kiss across his cheek. "Good-bye, Gil. I'll see you soon."

He released my hand as he turned toward his motorcar, a blue Crossley coupe. "Yes, soon."

I watched his car as it drove down the long driveway; I didn't turn around, even as I sensed Milo behind me.

"That was Gil Trent, wasn't it?"

I turned then. Milo was leaning against the door frame, arms crossed, his pose as casual as his tone had been. He was wearing riding clothes, a white shirt under a black jacket and fawn-colored trousers tucked into shining black boots. The picture of a country gentleman.

"Yes. It was."

One dark brow moved upward, ever so slightly. "Well. Did you ask him to stay for lunch?"

"He didn't care to."

He tapped his riding crop against his leg. "Perhaps he hadn't expected me to be here."

"Yes, well, you do flit about, darling."

We looked at one another for a moment. If Milo was waiting for more, he was going to be disappointed. I had no desire to satisfy his curiosity. Let him wonder what I was up to for once.

"Going riding?" I asked breezily, moving past him and into the shadowed entryway.

His voice followed me into the dimness. "Care to join me?"

The invitation stopped me, and I was instantly irritated with myself. I turned. The light behind him in the doorway turned him to shadow, but I could tell he was watching me.

I wanted to go, but I knew that it really mattered very little to Milo if I did or not.

He waited.

"All right," I said at last, weakening. "I'll just run up and change."

"I'll wait for you at the stables."

I went up to my room, preoccupied by the morning's strange turn of events. Fancy Gil Trent coming to see me, after all this time. There had been something a bit mysterious in his manner. I wondered if things were as straightforward as he had made them seem. Could there really be something so very wrong with Rupert Howe? I tried again to remember the young man but could recall only a fleeting impression of suave attractiveness. I hoped that Gil was merely playing the role of overprotective brother, but I knew that he was not inclined to exaggeration, nor would he have judged Rupert Howe harshly without good reason.

Good reason or not, I reflected, our intervention was likely a lost cause. I was not under any illusions that I would somehow be able to deter Emmeline from her course if she had truly determined to wed the man, but I supposed it wouldn't hurt to try.

However, if I was honest, I had to admit that I was partly compelled to accept Gil's proposal for motives that were not entirely altruistic. The truth was that I was finding it more and more difficult to ignore that I was terribly unhappy. Perhaps I had not admitted it completely, even to myself, until today.

It was as if Milo's homecoming, Gil's arrival, or some combination of the two had ignited in me the sudden realization that my lifestyle had become dissatisfying. Though I stayed as busy as possible, there was only so much for which involvement in local charities could compensate. London had felt stifling these past few months, but I was still too young to have settled seamlessly into quiet country life. In short, I was unsure what I wanted. Perhaps aiding Gil would help alleviate my recent malaise and allow me the satisfaction of usefulness, however temporary it might be.

There was, of course, my reputation to be considered. I had agreed to accompany Gil with little thought to any possible consequences, social or otherwise. Now that I had time to reflect, I was perfectly aware of how it would look for me to accompany him to the seaside, no matter how many of our mutual acquaintances would be there. If I wasn't careful, scandal could quite conceivably ensue. Yet I found suddenly that I didn't really care. It was no one's business but my own what I chose to do.

I had changed into my riding costume, ivory-colored trousers and a dark blue jacket, and I stopped before the full-length mirror, noticing the way that the trousers and well-cut jacket outlined my figure, how the color of the jacket seemed to breathe a bit of blue into my gray eyes. Milo had, in fact, bought these clothes for me. His taste was impeccable, if expensive, and the costume's overall suitability to my shape and coloring were indicative of his affinity for detail when it came to the fairer sex.

I wondered what Milo would think of my little holiday, but I pushed the thought away. He did as he pleased. There was no reason why I should not do the same.

My mental reservations systematically overruled, I went downstairs to meet my husband for our morning ride.

I arrived at the stables as he was leading out his horse, Xerxes, a huge black Arabian with a notorious temper. Only Milo could ride him, and the horse seemed excited at the prospect of a jaunt with his master, stamping his feet and snorting as he walked into the sunshine.

I watched my husband as he spoke to the horse, patting its sleek neck, the glossy black mane the same color as Milo's own coal-dark hair. There was a smile on Milo's face, and it remained there when he saw me approaching. He was happy to be home again, if only so that he was near the stables. If Milo genuinely loved anything, he loved his horses.

Geoffrey, the groom, led my horse Paloma out of the stable behind them. She was a smooth chestnut with white forelegs and face, and she was as sweet as Xerxes was temperamental.

I patted her soft nose as I approached. "Hello, old girl. Ready for a ride?"

Milo turned to me. "Shall we?"

We mounted up and set off at a brisk trot.

I felt some of the tension of the morning slip away as we rode in comfortable silence. The weather was warm, with a soft breeze, and the sun beamed down, unhindered, save for the presence of the occasional fluffy white cloud. Really, the scene was almost idyllic.

Milo looked at me suddenly and flashed me a grin that I felt in my stomach. "I'll race you to the rise."

I didn't hesitate.

"Let's go, Paloma." A slight nudge with my heels was all it took, and she was off, racing across the open field as though she had heard the opening shot at Epsom Downs.

Xerxes took no prodding, and we flew, side by side. It had been a long time since we had done this. The rise lay across this field, as the flat land gave way to a set of low wooded hills. By crossing the field and riding upward along a path that angled to the north and then westward like a horseshoe on its side, you came to an outcropping that looked out across the estate. Milo and I had shared many an evening on that rise in the very early days of our marriage. It had been at least a year since I had set foot there.

The race was a close one. Xerxes had brute strength, but Paloma was lithe and sure-footed. Xerxes outpaced us across the field, but the path upward allowed Paloma to overtake the lead, and by the time we reached the rise, I was a length or two ahead.

I reined in Paloma as I reached the giant oak, our finish line, just as Xerxes charged up behind us.

"I've won!" I cried. The exhilaration of it all hit me, and I laughed. Milo laughed, too, a sound both strange and familiar, like hearing a melody you once loved but had forgotten existed.

"You've won," he conceded. "You and that blasted docile horse of yours."

He dismounted in one fluid motion, tossing Xerxes's lead across the low-hanging branch of a tree. He moved to my side and reached up to help me dismount.

His hands remained for a moment on my waist as my feet hit the ground, and we looked at one another. There was a momentary flicker of heat lingering between us, and the uncanny sensation that things were as they once were and that we still loved one another.

But, then, I was not sure that Milo had ever loved me at all.

I stepped past him, securing Paloma's lead, and then began to walk up the slight incline to the tip of the rise. Below me, Thornecrest, the imposing country house and manicured grounds that had been Milo's father's sanctuary, spread out before us. It was a large, grand property, and Milo kept it up beautifully. The neglect he demonstrated as a husband did not carry over to his estate.

Milo walked up to stand beside me, not quite close enough to touch. Standing here, looking out across the land with my husband at my side, brought back memories of times here that I would rather have forgotten. No, that was a lie. I didn't want to forget. But it hurt to remember.

I was not sure what had brought on this fit of melancholy, but I suspected it had something to do with Gil's visit. Though I had tried to suppress such thoughts, I had remembered Gil more than once over the past few years and wondered what might have been.

"A lovely day for riding," I said. It was true, but the words sounded flat, and it seemed they hung heavily in the air.

If Milo noticed the strange aloofness that had arisen between us, he gave no sign of it. "Yes, though the paths up the rise are a bit overgrown. I'll speak to Nelson about it."

I said nothing. For some reason, I could not seem to conjure my usual equanimity where Milo was concerned. We were usually so easy with one another; even the distance that had grown between us had developed into an artificial joviality. However, I felt there was something different about this moment, as though it was building to some climax of which I was unsure.

I was uneasy, but my disquiet, the way my heartbeat increased in peculiar anticipation, appeared to be lost on Milo. He was never uneasy. He was always so calm, so very sure of himself, and because of this Gil's visit had had no impact.

"The Riviera was beautiful," he continued with characteristic nonchalance, plucking a leaf off a nearby tree and examining it disinterestedly before tossing it away. "Though not as warm as I like. I thought perhaps we might go back in August, when it's warmed up some."

"No." I said it so suddenly, so forcibly, it took me a moment to realize that I had spoken. And then I knew what else I would say.

Milo turned. "No? You don't want to visit Monte Carlo?"

"No. Because, you see, I'm taking a trip."

"One of your little excursions with Laurel?" He smiled. "Well, I dare say you'll be back by August."

"You don't understand, Milo," I said. I took a breath, smoothed my features, made my voice calm and sure. "I'm going away, and I'm not sure when I shall be back."

WE DID NOT dine together that evening.

Milo had been surprised, I think, by my proclamation on the rise, but he had not protested, had not even really questioned me. I had said what I had to say, that I was going away for a time, and then I had mounted Paloma and ridden back to the house alone. He didn't follow me, and I didn't know what time he had come back.

I spent most of the day laying out my things for the trip and drawing up a list of details for Grimes to tend to in my absence. Though it gave me something to occupy my time, the list was really unnecessary. Grimes was a treasure. Without my requesting it, he brought a tray to my room, and, mostly to please him, I ate a little and drank a good deal of strong tea.

I would be traveling without the assistance of a lady's maid. Eloise, who had been with me for three years, had recently and somewhat unexpectedly left my service to be married. I had not yet had the opportunity to interview for someone to fill her position, and now it appeared I would be unable to do so until my return. Grimes had suggested one of the housemaids might assist me at least in my packing, but I said I would do it for myself. It was no matter, really. Packing allowed me time to gather my thoughts. As for traveling unaccompanied, I thought it was just as well. Eloise, sweet as she was, had never been terribly discreet.

It was nearly dark when the knock sounded. I knew instantly that it was Milo. Grimes's knock was softer, much more deferential. Milo's confidence came through in his rap at my door, as though it was a mere formality and the door would open with or without my consent.

"Come in." My back was to him, and I continued to pack as he entered and shut the door behind him.

The irony of our being here together in my room was not lost on me. We had not shared a bedroom for several months. He had come back from one of his trips quite late one night and slept in the adjoining room to keep from waking me. Late coming home the following night as well, he had slept there again. Neither of us said anything about the arrangement, and he had stayed there. We had become adept at not addressing the steadily growing distance between us.

"Packing, I see," he said, when I didn't acknowledge him.

"Yes." I folded a yellow dress and set it in the suitcase on my bed.

"You didn't say where you're going."

"Does it matter?"

He was beside me now, leaning against one of the bedposts, observing my preparations in a disinterested sort of way.

"How long will you be gone?" His tone was indicative of total indifference. I was not even sure why he had bothered to come and inquire.

I straightened and turned to look at him. He was closer than I had expected. His eyes were so very blue, even in the poor light of my room. "So much concern, so suddenly," I said airily. "I'm quite grown-up, you know. You needn't worry about me."

"Are you sure one suitcase will be enough?"

"I'll send for my things if I need them."

He sat on my bed, beside the suitcase, absurdly handsome as he looked up at me. "Look here, Amory. What is this about? Why all the secrecy?" His tone was light, and I wondered briefly if it would even matter to him if I should leave for good.

"You needn't overdramatize things," I said, deliberately evading his question. "You travel about as you please. Why shouldn't I?"

"No reason, I suppose. Although I hadn't expected you to leave as soon as I arrived home. The house will be rather empty without you."

I resisted the urge to roll my eyes. It was typical of Milo to behave as though I were the one who had little interest in our marriage. It was also typical of him to do what he was doing now: inserting himself into my life with the full force of his charm when it was convenient for him and inconvenient for me.

"I didn't know you were arriving home," I said.

"Yes, I know." His eyes came up to mine. "And I don't think you knew you were leaving either."

"Meaning what?"

He picked up a black silk nightgown from my open suitcase, absently rubbing the fabric between his fingers. "This has something to do with Trent, doesn't it? With his visit today."

"You haven't the faintest idea what you're talking about."

"Has he been coming here often?"

"Not very," I answered, only a little ashamed of my purposefully vague answer.

He favored me with a smirk that somehow managed to be becoming. "Whatever you may think of me, my dear, I am not a fool." Languid amusement played at the corners of his mouth. "So Gilmore Trent rode down here on his steed and swept you off your feet, victorious at last. He took rather a long time about it."

"Don't be an idiot, Milo," I said, snatching the nightgown from where his fist had closed around it.

He let out a short laugh. "For pity's sake, Amory. You can't seriously mean to run off with him."

I shut the suitcase, pressing the clasps into place with a unified click, and looked at Milo. "I am not running off with anyone. I am taking a trip."

He rose from the bed, his features a mask of wry indifference. "Leave me if you must, darling. But don't go crawling back to Trent, of all people. Surely you must have some pride."

My eyes met his. "I have been married to you for five years, Milo. How much pride can I possibly have left?"

I HAD OUR driver drop me at the station early the next morning. I'd had a wire from Gil saying that he would take the morning train from London and meet me when I changed trains at the next stop so we could ride down to the coast together.

I hadn't expected Milo to see me off, but I was a bit disappointed that I saw nothing of him before I left. Then again, I hadn't anticipated a fond farewell. My comment about the state in which our ravaged marriage had left my pride had been rude, if true.

Of course, he had taken it in stride. He had laughed and said in that terribly cool and indifferent way of his, "Very well, darling. Do as you wish." And then he had risen and left the room, and that had been that.

I stopped on my way to the station to bid farewell to my cousin Laurel and to explain to her the reason behind my sudden departure. Laurel and I had grown up together and were the closest of friends. She was the single person in whom I felt I could freely confide.

"A trip to the seaside with Gil Trent?" she asked, brows raised as we sat in her parlor. "I didn't think you had it in you, Amory."

"I may just surprise us all," I answered. "Perhaps I have a reckless streak none of us has foreseen."

We were joking, of course, but her final assessment of the situation was accurate. "Helping an old friend or not, this certainly can't improve things between you and Milo."

"I sometimes wonder if anything will," I said.

The thought troubled me as I reached the station, but I did not allow myself time for further reflection as the train moved over the landscape. First and foremost, I was to help my friend. Gil was depending on me. My marriage woes had lasted this long; they could wait a bit longer.

I switched to the southbound train at the Tonbridge station, and a few moments later Gil found me in my compartment and dropped onto the seat beside me as the train set back into motion.

"Hello," he said. He smiled then, brightly. "I'm glad you've come, Amory."

"I told you I would come, Gil."

He removed his hat and tossed it on the empty seat facing us, brushing his fingers through his hair. "Yes, I knew you had every intention of coming." He spoke ruefully. "But one must never underestimate the persuasive powers of Milo Ames."

"Let's not talk about Milo, shall we?"

"I have no desire to talk about your husband," he said. "But I don't want you to be hurt. Was he angry with you?"

"No," I answered with a sigh. "Milo doesn't get angry. I don't think it much matters to him that I've gone."

Gil was silent for a moment. "Have you left him?" he asked at last.

"I hadn't realized how inclined to melodrama men are," I said. "No, I haven't really left him. Not completely, I suppose. I told him I was taking a trip."

"Did you tell him you were going with me?"

I picked up the magazine I had been reading and flipped it open to a random page, ready to be done with this conversation. "Milo's very clever, really. He just pretends to be glib because others find it charming. Naturally, he made the connection between your visit and my going away."

"And he didn't try to stop you from coming?"

"No. He didn't."

Gil shook his head and smiled wryly. "Then he really isn't as clever as you believe him to be."

THE TRAIN PULLED into the station that afternoon, and the weather was lovely. The sun shone brightly, and the warm air smelled of sea and salt. Standing on the platform, I breathed deeply and felt, for just a moment, that sense of well-being I had felt as a small child at the seaside, perfect happiness and contentment.

"Here's the car." Gil led me to the sleek blue automobile that the hotel had sent to collect us. We pulled away from the station and followed a road that led gradually upward, passing through the thriving village as we went.

"There it is," Gil said a moment later, pointing to the top of the hill.

The Brightwell Hotel sat on a cliff overlooking the sea. It was a lovely white building, sprawling, sturdy, and somehow elegant at the same time. There was something stately yet welcoming about the place. It looked as though it would be equally suited to princes or pirates, the sort of place one could be proud of visiting without being perceived to be too fond of squandering one's money. These days, a good many people frowned upon unnecessary lavishness.

Gil and I emerged from the car and moved together up the walk, stepping through the door into the hotel. The interior was as pleasing to the eye as the exterior had been. The lobby was a large spacious room with a desk directly facing the doors. The floors were of gleaming white marble, and light filtered in through the numerous windows, bouncing off the yellow walls, infusing the room with a warm glow. There was a good deal of furniture in white and various shades of blue scattered artfully about with very deliberate carelessness. A potted plant or two, strategically placed, added to the overall effect.

As Gil collected our room keys, I felt I could spend quite a happy week in this place.

"Why, if it isn't Amory Ames!" A high, almost shrill voice called out across the lobby. I turned and saw a woman in an outrageous hat and brightly colored clothes soaring toward me like a parrot in flight.

"Oh, dear," said Gil and I in unison.

Yvonne Roland, terror of London society, descended upon us.

"Amory, Amory darling!" She clutched my arms and brushed kisses an inch away from each of my cheeks, the scent of talcum powder and roses enveloping me. "It's been ages . . . Since before my last husband died, I think . . . Or maybe just before . . . Poor dear Harold . . . And how are you, dearest?"

She didn't wait for me to answer before turning on Gil. "And Gilmore Trent! How delightful to see you. But you've come together." She turned to me, grabbing my hand. "How delightful."

A thought suddenly seemed to strike her. Her eyes narrowed

and darted from me to Gil and back again. "But, my dear, I thought you had married... What was that fellow's name? The wickedly good-looking one?"

"I've just come to visit the seaside with some friends," I said vaguely.

A rather sly smile crossed her face. "Ah! I see. Well, you can count on me as the soul of discretion... If you only knew the secrets I've kept... never revealed I knew all about Ida Kent, even after she'd run off with that butcher." She wrinkled her nose in distaste. "Sordid business... but you and Gil? I'm delighted. Now, if you'll excuse me, I'm taking tea on the terrace. I'll be seeing you both later." She winked ostentatiously and was gone.

"Good heavens," Gil breathed.

I nodded. Mrs. Roland was a wealthy widow who flittered about society like a flamboyant and excessively chirpy bird. She had been widowed three times, accumulating successively more wealth as each husband faded beneath her bright and tiresome exuberance. I was inclined to believe her husbands had gone to the grave for the sheer peace of it. Still, she was harmless enough.

"At least things won't be dull at the seaside," I said with a smile. "Mrs. Roland may not exactly be with us, but she will certainly be *among* us."

"Well, then," he said, lightly touching my elbow, "I suppose we may as well go up and prepare ourselves to join Mrs. Roland and the others for tea on the terrace."

I followed him to the lift, which sat to the left of the front desk. We rode up in silence to the first floor, both of us lost in our own thoughts.

As we stepped out of the lift, Gil turned to me and handed me the key to my room. As his hand brushed mine, I suddenly felt that there was something rather clandestine about all of this. Separate rooms or no, we had just checked into a hotel together, and I felt a bit unsettled about the fact.

We looked at one another. I wondered if the thought had occurred to him as well.

"My room's just three doors down," he said. "I'll meet you here in a quarter of an hour?"

"All right."

He left me, and I entered my room. It was good-sized and decorated in an understatedly elegant manner: gleaming wooden floors with thick rugs, silk flocked wallpaper, and smooth, heavy bed linens, all in pale, tasteful colors. The sitting area had a fashionably modern sofa and two silk-upholstered chairs. A writing desk sat against the wall. As in the lobby, the furnishings seemed to say, "Don't mind us. We will just sit here and be expensive."

I took off my hat and gloves, dropping them on one of the chairs, and went to the window. My room faced the sea, and I pushed aside the filmy, ivory curtain, admiring for a moment the smooth expanse of blue. It was a decidedly romantic view, and, coupled with the vague feeling of wrongdoing I had experienced in the hallway, I began to wonder if I had made the right choice in coming. I quickly pushed the doubts away; there was nothing wrong in it, after all.

I changed from my tailored dove-gray traveling suit into a flowing white and red flower-printed chiffon dress with a soft belt that tied in a loose bow at my side. I then went to the bathroom and splashed cool water on my face, reapplied what little makeup I had worn, and combed my hair, smoothing the dark waves that were a little mussed from the journey. Putting on a white, lightweight cloth hat with a jaunty brim and red grosgrain ribbon, I was ready to take tea with Gil's sister and whoever else was in the party.

The sudden realization that I had very little idea who exactly was sharing our holiday made me feel a bit silly. Undoubtedly, I had rushed into this seaside trip with very little forethought, but I supposed it was too late to do much about it now.

Gil met me in the hallway at the designated time. He had freshened up as well, and we made a handsome pair walking down the long, golden hallway together. For a briefest of instants, I wondered what life might have been like had I married Gil. Would we have been happy? It was impossible to know.

"I would rather have had a good nap," he said as we entered the lift. "But I suppose tea is as good a time as any to make our entrance."

"Indeed," I answered. "It will give the scandal time to build until dinner."

He smiled, but I could sense his hesitation. "You don't mind a bit of scandal, do you, Amory?"

The last of my doubts dissipated, and I returned his smile. "What's a little scandal? One only lives once, after all."

We exited the lift and walked across the gleaming lobby, through a comfortable sitting area, to French doors on the west side of the building. Stepping out into the bright light, I admired the spacious terrace. Gil explained that it extended all along this side of the building, wrapped around across the south side, overlooking the sea, and then continued around the east side. There was another terrace, he told me, a short way down the cliff, accessible by a winding flight of white wooden stairs. "It's rather a scenic spot, but the wind is high today," he said. "I expect most of the guests will have tea on the main terrace."

"Gil!" We looked to see Emmeline Trent waving to us from a

bit farther down. With Gil's hand at my elbow, we made our way to where she had risen from her seat to greet us.

Emmeline hugged her brother, then turned to me. Like Gil, Emmeline seemed to have changed very little since I had seen her last. A thin, pretty girl, she shared her brother's coloring, the dark blond hair and brown eyes. She smiled brightly as she extended her hand to squeeze mine affectionately. "Dearest Amory. I'm so happy to see you again. I didn't know you would be here. How delightful."

"It was something of a last-minute decision. It's lovely to see you, Emmeline."

She turned then, her eyes alight with happiness and pride, stretching out her hand to the gentleman beside her. "You've met, I think? You remember my fiancé, Rupert Howe. Rupert, Amory Ames."

The young man standing by her side was as I remembered him: tall, handsome, and impeccably groomed, with dark brown hair and eyes to match. Bright teeth formed what seemed a practiced, too-polite smile. There was no warmth in his eyes, not for me, and certainly not for Gil.

"Charmed, Mrs. Ames," he said.

I was not at all charmed. I could tell at once that he was too polished, too aware of his own appeal. Perhaps he did not remind me of Milo so very much, after all.

As if our thoughts had taken different routes to the same location, Emmeline asked, "Is your husband here?"

I paused, allowing a slightly awkward silence to settle in our midst. "No," I said at last. "No, Milo and I are . . . well, I've come at the invitation of your brother."

Emmeline colored. "Oh, I'm sorry." She gave her brother a rap on the arm. "You didn't tell me, Gil! Do forgive me, Amory. I didn't realize..."

"Think nothing of it," I said lightly. "All water under the bridge."

I noticed then that Rupert Howe watched me speculatively. I had no time to guess what he was thinking before a voice spoke from behind us.

"It's too windy to take tea out of doors."

We turned to see Olive Henderson, a young woman I had known for many years more than I cared to. She was the daughter of a well-known banker, and we had frequently come into contact with one another at social occasions, though we really weren't well acquainted. I had always taken her for a thorough little snob, though she was pretty when her smile warmed green eyes and softened her naturally petulant expression.

"It would have been much better in the indoor sitting room, I'm sure," she said. "I've just had my hair waved."

"Calm down, old girl," said Rupert. "It won't blow you away."

She looked at him through narrowed eyes as she patted at her perfectly coiffed dark hair but said nothing further. I was prepared to greet her, but she shot a glance at Gil and me before she sat down without speaking to us.

Slowly the party began to collect, and I found that the Trents' friends were none of the same group with which we had often associated five years before. I supposed I couldn't have expected that things would remain the same, but I still found that I was vaguely disappointed.

"Amory, meet Mr. and Mrs. Edward Rodgers," Gil said, introducing me to a couple that just reached our table. They greeted me, and I was struck by the contrast between them, which was, visually, something akin to a cinema star on the arm of a parish priest.

"How do you do?" Mr. Rodgers said unenthusiastically. He was young and solemn, a solicitor by trade I would later learn. His brown eyes scanned me in a cursory way, and he appeared to have found little to interest him, for he soon seated himself and poured his tea.

Anne Rodgers was a platinum blonde, and though her features were somewhat plain, she possessed a way of moving that had attracted the attention of every man in the vicinity when she had walked out onto the terrace in a dress of clinging rose-colored silk.

She greeted me warmly, her eyes moving over me in an appraising yet not unfriendly manner.

"I adore your dress. Schiaparelli, isn't it?" she said, sinking down into a chair beside her husband and stirring four sugars into the cup he set before her. "Thank you, darling," she told him, reaching to pat his hand, and he smiled warmly at her. They seemed something of an odd pair, but I was far from an expert on what made a happy marriage.

Next to arrive at the terrace were Nelson Hamilton and his wife, Larissa. They walked directly to where Gil and I stood, Mr. Hamilton's quick strides leaving his wife behind. As Gil made the introductions, I tried but failed to recall ever having seen them at any events in London.

"Pleasure, Mrs. Ames," Mr. Hamilton said, grasping my hand in his very warm one. He gave me a thorough going-over with his eyes, and I felt justified in examining him in turn. He was older than the others of our party, perhaps in his midforties, with graying dark hair, a ruddy face, and a well-groomed mustache. He was the jovial sort, I perceived immediately, with a ready smile and an easy, almost too friendly way of talking to people. He was, I thought, the sort of person one liked at once, but for whom the fondness fades after a short time.

"My wife, Larissa," he said gesturing perfunctorily to the woman who stood a bit behind him. That introduction deemed sufficient, he moved off to engage Rupert in an earnest conversation about some business deal, the particulars of which soon became lost in the jumble of conversation. Mrs. Hamilton's gaze followed him for just a moment before returning to me.

"I'm pleased to meet you, Mrs. Hamilton."

"And I you," she replied.

As so often happens, Mr. Hamilton's vibrant personality had attracted a partner without his effusive joie de vivre. Larissa Hamilton was quiet and soft-spoken. She was at least fifteen years younger than her husband and attractive in an unassuming way, pretty without realizing that she was. There was something forlorn about her, and I was unaccountably reminded of one of Waterhouse's Ophelia paintings. She had a nice smile that warmed her expression but not, it seemed, a great deal of confidence. She was, if I judged correctly, thoroughly cowed by her husband. More than once, I saw her start when his hearty laughter broke out behind us.

Another gentleman approached our cluster of tables, and I recognized him at once as Lionel Blake, a rising star of the British stage. His Hamlet had caused quite a stir and was perhaps the most talked-about interpretation of the character since John Barrymore had come over from New York to play the role several years before. He was very good-looking, with dark hair and piercing eyes that were an unusual shade of green.

"I've long planned on attending one of your performances," I told him when we had been introduced. "I've heard you're marvelous."

"You're too kind, Mrs. Ames," he said. "But I'm afraid the reports may be exaggerated."

He pulled out my chair for me, and I sat. There was an easy grace in his movements that I would imagine translated well to the stage, and I noticed that he spoke carefully, as if pronouncing lines.

The last to arrive was Veronica Carter, a woman I knew by reputation, if not by actual acquaintance. She was the daughter of a well-known industrialist, and, despite rumors of cracks in the family's financial empire, my impression of her was that she fed on her father's wealth and had no further aim in life than her own amusement. A vibrant redhead, she was dressed flashily and excessively made up, overemphasizing a beauty that would have been more striking had it not been so heavily accentuated. She made a name for herself in the gossip columns, the most recent scandal, so the story went, involving a very married member of Parliament. Nothing I had heard of her gave me any incentive for liking her.

She did not take long in cementing my initial impression. As we all settled down to drink our tea, she fastened me in her cold blue eyes, which matched the china of her teacup. "Miss Ames, is it? Your name is familiar. Have we met before?"

"Mrs. Ames," I corrected. "And no, Miss Carter. I don't believe we have."

She bit her scarlet lip artfully, as if in contemplation. "Where have I heard that name? Let me think. I'm sure I . . . Ah, yes. I met a gentleman called Ames only last month. On the Riviera. A deliciously handsome gentleman."

"My husband, Milo." If my tone sounded bored, it was because I truly was. It was embarrassingly obvious that she was attempting to create some sort of awkward scene, as though I would be surprised to learn Milo had been behaving badly.

"Oh," she said, a thin, penciled brow arching, her features conveying mock surprise. "Excuse me. I didn't realize he was married."

I smiled coolly. "You mustn't feel bad; he sometimes forgets it himself."

There was a moment of silence. Veronica Carter looked genuinely astonished at my flippancy. No doubt she had expected a harsh reply from a jealous wife. Gil cleared his throat uneasily, and Lionel Blake openly smiled.

Conversation descended into trivialities and generally pleasant small talk as we were lulled by the sounds of the sea and the clinking of china. Nevertheless, there was a strange sort of tension in the group, despite the fact that these were people who spent a good deal of time together, people who had willingly agreed to meet at this seaside hotel for a mutual holiday. Then again, perhaps it was just that none of them liked each other very much. That was the way it often was with the affluent: birds of a feather did flock together, friends or no. Such a gathering was by no means my ideal way in which to pass a week, but I was doing it for Gil. And, really, it was always nice to spend time at the seaside.

We all sat on the terrace, enjoying our tea and tolerating one another's company. None of us realized, of course, that within twenty-four hours, one of our party would be dead.

4

THE HOTEL WAS aglow that evening. Dinner at the Brightwell Hotel was, it seemed, quite the affair, with black tie, dancing, and champagne all par for the course.

I wore a fitted gown of mauve silk with sheer flutter sleeves and flowing tulle panels inset into the skirt, the cut quite flattering to my thin, tallish frame, if I may say so myself. Gil looked dashing in his dinner jacket, slim and broad-shouldered. He was of that class of men that was bred for evening wear.

The dining room was both elegant and elaborate, without any accompanying flashiness. The walls were a striking shade of salmon with settings that managed to walk a surprisingly successful line between formal Victorian and sleek, modern art deco. The round tables, clothed in white silk, glittered with crystal, silver, and silver-edged porcelain.

There was no formal seating arrangement, and Gil and I sat at a table with Mr. and Mrs. Hamilton on my left, and Emmeline and Rupert on Gil's right.

Emmeline bore all the markings of a woman madly in love. Her bright eyes followed Rupert Howe's every motion. She touched him at every opportunity, brushing her shoulder against his, her hand pressing his arm. She was clearly proud that this handsome, charming man was hers. Lovesickness was a disease whose symptoms I knew well.

For his part, Rupert seemed to pay her the majority of his attention. He would smile at her, lean and whisper things in her ear. Yet, for all that, there was something restless about him. He seemed slightly ill at ease, as though his heart wasn't entirely in the performance. I wondered how deep his feeling for her truly ran.

"Lovely evening, isn't it?" said Larissa Hamilton in a soft voice beside me. I turned to greet her. Her light-blue gown with ruffled skirt and sleeves was lovely, and I told her so.

"Thank you. Nelson picked it out," she said, smoothing the skirt. "He's got quite an eye, really."

I had noticed as much. At the moment, his eye was on Anne Rodgers as she sauntered into the room in a beaded lavender gown that was cut just high enough to avoid absolute scandal. Mr. Rodgers followed, apparently oblivious to the effect his wife's appearance was having upon the gentlemen present.

"Nice crowd here tonight, eh, Rupert?" Mr. Hamilton asked when the Rodgers had reached the table and seated themselves. He pulled a cigarette from his pocket.

"Very nice, indeed," Rupert agreed, offering Mr. Hamilton his lighter, before turning his attention back to Emmeline and adding in a tone still loud enough to be heard by half the table, "Though it would be nicer if it were just the two of us. I look forward to the days when we can travel alone."

Emmeline blushed and smiled, and Gil stiffened ever so slightly beside me. He tried to hide it, but it was perfectly apparent how little he cared for Rupert Howe.

"Nelson likes blue, but I love the shade of your gown," said Mrs. Hamilton, suddenly picking up our conversation where it had dropped off several moments ago.

"Yes, you look quite stunning, Mrs. Ames." It was Lionel Blake who spoke as he approached and took his seat at a neighboring table.

"Thank you both. And call me Amory, please. I wish you all would."

"Anne-Marie. Such an uncommon name," said Veronica Carter from across the table, looking at me through the smoke of the cigarette she held carelessly between two fingers. It was the first time she had spoken to me since I arrived at dinner, and the mispronunciation, combined with the somewhat sneering tone in which she said it, led me to believe it was not a mistake that she had misheard my given name.

"It's Amory," Gil corrected her.

She did not reply but descended again into silence, a sulky expression marring her pretty features.

"Amory Ames. Such a striking name," said Mrs. Hamilton. "There is almost something musical about it. What a happy coincidence your husband's name so complemented your Christian name."

I began to give her the long answer but decided against it. "Thank you," I replied simply.

The truth was that I didn't take Milo's name, per se. In actuality, I was born Amory Ames. I had met Milo Ames, who was no relation of mine, and had been amused by the coincidence. We married, and I had been stuck in limbo, bearing a name that was not entirely my own yet not truly my husband's. It was, somehow, strangely indicative of our entire relationship.

Dinner was delicious: light soups, impeccably cooked sole, roast lamb with mint sauce, a fresh salad, followed by a pudding that melted in the mouth and cheese and crackers with sweet, rich coffee. Conversation was light, superficially pleasant. Afterward, everyone began breaking off into pairs for dancing.

In the style of many of the more prestigious London hotels, the Brightwell had engaged an orchestra for the summer. As they struck up the opening strains of "All of Me," Gil stood and held out his hand. "Dance with me, Amory?"

"I would love to."

He led me to the dance floor. There was an instant of hesitation before he pulled me toward him and our bodies touched. For a moment, my mind drifted back to one of the last times we had danced together: our engagement party. I had been so in love that night, so very sure of the future. What fools the young are, so full of confidence and blissful ignorance.

The orchestra was really very good, and the music flowed sweetly over the room, the lyrics of this particular song hauntingly appropriate. We did not speak but danced, lost in our own memories. I felt oddly happy, happier than I had for a long while.

The dance came to an end, and Gil and I stepped apart, but only just. Our eyes lingered. "Amory . . ." he began.

"Do you mind, old boy?" It was Rupert who had ambled over to us. He turned to me and held out a hand, brows slightly raised in inquiry.

I took his hand as Gil stepped out of the way, annoyance barely perceptible in his eyes, and I allowed myself to be pulled into Rupert Howe's arms.

The music started up again, and a young man stepped to the microphone and began to sing. Rupert, as much as I hated to admit it, danced beautifully.

"The music is very good," I noted, to break the silence.

"They're no Henry Hall and his orchestra, but they're passable," Rupert replied. "Something to dance to, at any rate. I've seen the men here looking at you, Mrs. Ames. You're going to be a popular partner tonight."

"I can't imagine why I should be," I answered, immune to his flattery, "with so many ladies from which to choose."

Rupert let out a short laugh. "Thorough bores, most of them. The married ladies are dowdy frumps." He smiled. "Yourself excluded, of course. Mrs. Rodgers fancies herself a society beauty, but she's well past her prime, and Mrs. Hamilton is too much of a mouse to make any long-lasting impression. As for the unattached ladies, Veronica Carter is not so grand as she thinks she is, and Olive . . . well, let's just say Olive and I don't get along as well as we used to."

So discreet, I thought irritably. If he and Olive had a past, it was unkind of him to flaunt it, especially given the circumstances. I glanced at Olive Henderson, who had been sitting quietly at our table, making very little conversation throughout dinner. I certainly didn't know her well, but it seemed to me that something was troubling her. Perhaps her tender feelings had not been forgotten as effortlessly as Rupert's apparently had.

"And what of your charming fiancée?" I inquired.

The briefest flash of something crossed his eyes, as though he had momentarily forgotten Emmeline. Then he smiled, and I was surprised at the warmth in it. "It goes without saying that I adore Emmeline."

"Do you?" I asked breezily. "I should think you would. She's a lovely girl."

"Very lovely," he replied, unaffected by my pointed remarks. "How nice that you find the same admirable qualities in her brother."

So it was to be a game of verbal sparring, was it?

"Gil and I have been friends for a very long time."

"And more than friends, I understand," he went on. "It's admirable, really, that you have been able to remain on such good terms ... despite your unfortunate marriage."

I smiled, unwilling to be bated by his audacity. "We are not all possessed of your good luck in finding a mate."

The music ended, and I stepped back. He leaned slightly forward, a smirk marring his handsome features. "It was a pleasure, Mrs. Ames."

I found myself unable to return the compliment.

I WAS SPARED the overbearing charms of Rupert Howe for the rest of the evening. I danced in turn with Mr. Rodgers, Lionel Blake, and Mr. Hamilton.

I learned that Mr. Rodgers was a solicitor, the majority of his experience in criminal court. He talked unenthusiastically of his work while we danced, and he seemed to find his stories as dull as I did.

"Not many imaginative crimes these days," he said as the dance came to an end. "Mainly stupid people doing stupid things."

"Really?" I asked. "I somehow thought that criminals were getting cleverer as time went on."

"Nonsense. It's almost impossible to get away with things these days, with all the modern advancements. Take the Crippen case. Even twenty years ago, the fellow couldn't escape the law. Caught him by wiring the ship he was trying to get away on. Things are far more advanced now. You would think criminals would learn, but they don't. I suppose that's because it's as I said: stupid people doing stupid things."

I danced next with the polite and very well-behaved Lionel Blake. His natural gracefulness translated well to dancing, and I had the fleeting thought that he might have a career in musical cinema should he tire of the stage. As we moved around the floor, he told me of the play in which he was soon to appear, a murder mystery set in a country manor.

"I'm afraid it's not a terribly good play," he said with a rueful smile. "But the chief backer is rather a good friend of mine. When he asked me if I would do it, I felt that I could not really refuse."

"The play may not be very good, but you'll be wonderful," I said encouragingly. "I've heard marvelous things about you. I'm certain the play will be a great success with you in it."

His eyes dropped from mine, as though he was embarrassed by my compliment, and he quickly began to speak of the weather. This apparent timidity was not at all what I expected of a handsome actor, especially not one as well-received as Mr. Blake. But perhaps I was unfairly typecasting.

Mr. Hamilton was my next partner. He was his jovial self, and I noticed his gaze travel admiringly down my neckline more than once.

"Have you known the Trents long?" I asked, in an attempt to draw his eyes upward.

"We got chummy with Rupert and Emmeline in London. It seemed we were always turning up at the same events. Rupert is from my part of the country, you know. Mr. Trent I don't know well. What I do know is that he and Rupert don't care much for one another. That's always been apparent." He laughed, as though he had a made a joke. I had not, it seemed, been the only one to notice the tension between Gil and Mr. Howe.

"Have you been to the Brightwell before?" I asked, as his eyes wandered once again.

"No, never. We came at the invitation of Rupert and Emmeline. When they invited us to join them, we thought it sounded nice. Larissa's got some foolish fear of the sea, but I told her that was all nonsense. I knew she'd enjoy it once she got here."

I glanced at Mrs. Hamilton and saw her watching us. She didn't seem to be enjoying herself much at all to me. I couldn't help but wonder how aware she was of her husband's wandering eye. I hoped that she would begin to relax and have a nice evening, but a moment later I saw Rupert Howe asking her to dance, and she looked as uncomfortable as ever.

"You look simply divine this evening, Mrs. Ames," cried Mrs. Roland, as she appeared beside me from out of nowhere. She was dancing with a gentleman perhaps a foot shorter than she, but they were managing to keep an excellent rhythm to the orchestra's rousing rendition of "Between the Devil and the Deep Blue Sea."

"Thank you, Mrs. Roland," I said. "You look quite striking yourself." It was true. She wore a long gown of bright blue bedecked with silver beads that clicked together as she swayed to the music.

"So many handsome gentlemen here, don't you think?" she asked me with a wink, before her partner whirled her away. "I shouldn't wonder if there was a trail of broken hearts left after this week."

I hardly thought that likely. From what I had seen thus far, it was only Emmeline who was in danger of being brokenhearted.

Our dance seemed to have worn Mr. Hamilton out, for back

at the table, he wiped his face with his handkerchief before he pulled a cigarette from his pocket. Rupert Howe, returning to the table with Mrs. Hamilton, offered him his lighter, and Mr. Hamilton puffed contentedly on his cigarette, his gaze traveling from one attractive woman to the next while his wife sat silently beside him.

The night was spent pleasantly enough, but as the evening drew to a close, I was more than ready for bed. It had been a long day, and I was tired in mind as well as body. I bid everyone good evening, and Gil accompanied me to my room.

"I'm happy you're here, Amory," he said, as we stopped outside my door. The hallway was deserted, and we were alone in the soft yellow glow cast by the sconces against the striped, yellow-papered walls. There was something intimate about the setting, and I felt that I should avoid what Gil was leaving unsaid as he looked down at me with those warm brown eyes.

"I think you're right about Rupert Howe," I said, by way of a subject change. "He doesn't seem at all trustworthy. There is something about him . . ."

"Yes, I'm glad you noticed."

"You'll need more than a feeling to convince Emmeline, I'm afraid. I can tell she's rather taken with him."

"I wish there was some way to send the fellow packing," he said, his eyes flashing suddenly.

"I'll have a heart-to-heart with her tomorrow," I said, "tell her the woes of married life to serve as a warning."

His eyes met mine, both sympathetic and hopeful. "Do you think it will do any good?"

"I don't know."

He nodded, suddenly brusque. "Well, I guess we shall find out. I'll see you in the morning."

"Good night, Gil."

I entered my room, shut the door behind me, and stood there for a moment, lost in thought. I had a feeling that Emmeline Trent was not going to be convinced by me or anyone else to give up Rupert Howe. His charm was transparent enough, but the veil of love could do wonders to even the most reprehensible character. It was, as I had predicted, a lost cause. I think Gil knew it, too. But I admired his wanting to try.

Sighing, I moved into the bedroom, kicking off my shoes as I went. The thick rug was soft beneath my feet.

I stepped out of my dress and threw it over the back of a chair, then peeled off my stockings, letting them fall where they lay. They would keep until morning. I would tidy up the room then. For the most part, I was enjoying not having a lady's maid at the moment. Even if I had had the time to find a replacement for Eloise before my trip, I should have hesitated to submit my current movements to a near stranger's scrutiny. There was too much potential for gossip.

I put on my black satin nightgown and pulled a loose negligee over it. I found, despite my weariness, that I was not exactly sleepy. I picked up a book and moved to a chair near the window. Pushing the window open to feel the breeze and better hear the sound of the sea, I began to read.

The chair was comfortable, and the lulling noise from outside combined with sodden prose to do just the trick. I drifted off to sleep but awoke suddenly a few moments later to voices below my window.

"I mean what I say." I recognized instantly that the hushed, angry whisper belonged to Gil.

"I have no doubt you do. But what do you expect me to do about it?" The languid insolence convinced me that the second voice was that of Rupert Howe.

I realized that the two men were likely standing at the corner of the building, their voices carried up and into my room by the wind. Closing the window would only draw unwanted attention, so I sat very still, attempting not to listen but doing a very poor job of it.

"I want you to leave my sister alone. Get out of here and don't come back."

This was met with a harsh, disdainful laugh. "You really think I would do such a thing?"

"Oh, I'm sure you would. Men like you always have a price."

"Save your breath . . . and your money. I'm not going anywhere."

"I'm warning you . . ."

"And I'm warning you," Rupert interjected smoothly. "I have those letters you've written me, trying to get me to break it off, threatening me with direst consequences." His voice dripped with mockery. "I'm sure Emmeline would be very interested to see them."

"Howe . . ."

"And as for the charming Mrs. Ames, I'm sure she'd be interested to know a thing or two as well."

"Leave her out of this."

"It's you that brought her into it, not I."

"She's none of your business . . ."

The voices stopped suddenly, and I surmised another hotel guest had appeared on the terrace, perhaps a couple taking a stroll in the moonlight. Rupert and Gil must have walked away then, for the conversation faded into the wind.

I found their exchange to be troubling, to say the least. No doubt Gil had been trying his best to help his sister, but I was not certain that I would have chosen that exact method. He had sounded so very harsh. Then again, there had been something very ruthless in Rupert Howe's tone, and they did say that fire was often best fought with fire.

I waited a few minutes to be sure they had gone and then pulled the window closed and switched off the light, still lost in thought.

I made my way to the bed, removed my negligee, and slid between the smooth sheets. I lay there for a long while, turning their words over and over in my head. What had Rupert Howe meant when he said there were things I would be interested to know? Matters were becoming increasingly perplexing, and I couldn't shake the sensation that there was more to this seaside holiday than I had originally assumed. Despite the sensation of uneasiness that had settled over me, my exhaustion eventually won the day, and I drifted off into a fitful sleep.

MORNING DAWNED, BRIGHT and cheerful. I had not slept well and had been troubled by unpleasant dreams, the details of which I could not recall upon waking. As I readied myself for the day in my warm, sunlit room, however, the events of the previous night seemed very far away. Perhaps things had not been as dire as I had imagined them. It was no secret that Gil and Rupert disagreed on the subject of Emmeline, after all. Their discussion might not have been of any special significance. By the time I went downstairs to meet Gil for breakfast, I had managed to recapture my feelings of optimism regarding our stay at the Brightwell.

I came down into the lobby and made my way to the breakfast room. It was at the south side of the hotel, a sunny, golden space that looked out over the terrace, with a sweeping view of the sea. The sky was a vibrant shade of blue, and our dining was accompanied by the sound of gulls and the waves on the rocks below. It was a lovely view for a lovely morning.

Gil stood and smiled as I approached his table. "Good morning. You're looking fresh and lovely this morning."

"Thank you." I was pleased with the compliment. I wore a cheerful yellow silk dress that was in keeping with my attempt at good spirits. The color seemed to brighten my pale skin, which I was certain could benefit by a few days in the sun. Though naturally fair, I hoped to have time to improve my complexion a bit while here.

I filled my plate from the overflowing sideboard. The food was excellent, as it had been the night before. We were served the full spectrum of breakfast fare, including sausage, bacon, eggs, baked beans, an assortment of puddings, fried bread, kidney, kippers, tomato, mushrooms, and a variety of fruits. I ate more than could have conceivably been healthy.

I could not help but feel very much pleased with the Brightwell Hotel. I thought it was a place I should like to visit again, perhaps under less strenuous circumstances. For, despite the loveliness of the morning, there was still a tension that seemed to hover in the air.

As we ate, I noticed that a change had come over Gil since last evening. He looked as though he hadn't slept well either. His eyes were tired, and there was a very definite tightness about his mouth that remained there even when he smiled. No doubt he was still troubled by his conversation with Rupert Howe. I decided that it would probably be best to avoid bringing up the fact that I had overheard the conversation. If he wished to tell me about, I had no doubt that he would do so in his own good time.

"You look as if a long walk along the beach would do you good," I said as I pushed my plate away, unable to consume another mouthful.

He smiled, wearily it seemed. "As lovely as that sounds, I'm afraid I have things to attend to this morning. But soon. Soon I would like to have a walk and a long talk."

"It will be all right, Gil." I said. "I'm sure of it."

He looked up at me, but there was something vague about his expression, as though his mind was not completely on our conversation. "Yes, I'm sure you're right."

I picked up the coffeepot and poured the steaming liquid, refilling his cup.

He held up his hand as I picked up the sugar tongs, preparing to give him two lumps. "Just milk, please."

"Oh, yes. I had forgotten."

GIL LEFT ME after breakfast, the air of preoccupation still hanging over him. I would have liked to help, but I could think of no way to prove useful at the moment. I was his partner in this, yes, but I was no longer his confidant as I once had been. The easiness that existed between us was fragile. Once again I contemplated how rottenly I had treated him. Happily, he seemed to have forgiven me, and I hoped that we could one day be real friends again.

With nothing to do for the moment but amuse myself, I went to my room and changed into my backless peach-colored maillot, over which I wore beach pyjamas of flowing white trousers and a loose crêpe de chine jacket with wide stripes of peach, white, and teal. I topped it off with a white straw hat and matching bag. A glance in the mirror confirmed that I looked suitably turned out, and I made my way downstairs. I exited the side entrance of the building, which wound around to the seaside terrace, from which the long flight of steps led down to the beach.

I reached the seaside terrace and saw Mrs. Hamilton sitting alone at a table, taking a cup of tea. There was something of the little lost girl about her, as though someone had forgotten her.

"Hello," I said, stopping near her table.

"Hello." When she smiled she seemed much less retiring, as though the simple upturning of her lips brought her confidence.

"It's a lovely day."

"Yes, quite." Her eyes darted out toward the sea. "Though the sea seems rather rough today."

The water did not seem overagitated to me, but perhaps the pronounced sound of the waves echoing up from the base of the cliff had given her that impression. I remembered what her husband had said about her dislike of the sea.

"You're all alone here?" I asked.

"Nelson has gone down to the beach." She nodded her head toward the stretch of ground below. I imagined that, by leaning slightly in her seat, she would be able to make out the guests there at the water's edge. I wondered if she liked to keep an eye on her husband. "I don't care for it myself. I thought tea on the terrace would be lovely. Then perhaps I shall find a nice quiet place to read. I'm told the hotel has a comfortable sitting room. I rather like to be alone."

So I had surmised correctly that Larissa Hamilton was not enjoying her holiday at the seaside. No doubt her husband had convinced her to come. Nelson Hamilton was undoubtedly the decision maker in their marriage. And he seemed more than happy to indulge her in her proclivity for solitude.

As if she could read my thoughts, she smiled. "I don't mind. Really. I'm happy to sit alone reading. I've the latest Warwick Deeping novel to keep me company."

"Sometimes it's rather nice to have a bit of time to oneself," I agreed.

"Yes. I've been accused of being unfriendly, but it's really just that I'm not very good with people, especially those I don't know."

"That's perfectly understandable," I told her.

Her smile returned, as though she was glad to have found someone who understood her. "Well, I hope you enjoy your time at the beach," she said.

"And I hope you enjoy your tea and reading," I said sincerely as I continued my journey toward the water.

A set of white wooden stairs at the end of the terrace led downward toward a little landing at the top of the cliff. From there two steps of staircases led ever downward, the steps on the right leading toward the path to the beach, the stairs on the left coming to the terrace partway down the cliff, the one about which Gil had told me yesterday.

I took the steps to the right, which led downward until they ended in a pebbled path that snaked its way down to the beach. There were other hotels, I supposed, that offered visitors easier access to the water. However, an establishment such as the Brightwell was not one to make apologies. Indeed, the private beach it offered its guests was well worth the slight inconvenience of access. The beach at the base of the cliff was cut off on either side by cliffs that extended farther into the water, creating its own secluded beachfront. There was no access except by the Brightwell steps or by boat.

A good number of Brightwell guests were at the beach, and I saw several members of our party. Emmeline sat in a chair not far from the path. Beyond her, Lionel Blake sat reading, his lips moving silently. I wondered absently if it was a script he was memorizing.

Veronica Carter lay in the sun, posing in a rather small bathing suit. She seemed to be tanning nicely, and I suspected that her red hair might not be natural; her skin tone was certainly not like that of most redheads I had known. Olive Henderson sat beneath an umbrella in striking green and blue printed beach pyjamas, looking out with disdain upon the proceedings.

Beyond them, I saw Nelson Hamilton talking to Anne Rodgers, who stood in her figure-hugging pink bathing suit, hands on her hips, bright blond hair shining in the sunlight. I wondered briefly where her husband might be but decided that he didn't seem much the type to enjoy lounging by the sea.

The only other person I recognized was Yvonne Roland, who was walking along the surf much farther down the beach, her gaudy red robe flapping in the wind like a brilliant cape.

I stepped off the path and into the shingle beach, walking toward the others, enjoying the warm wind whipping at my hair beneath my hat. The walls of the cliff caught the sound of the sea, and the crash of the waves echoed around us.

Emmeline was alone for the moment, as Rupert was frolicking in the surf, trying to show off his good figure to the best advantage. She looked up as I approached. "Hello, Amory. Come and sit with me." She indicated the empty striped beach chair beside her. "Unless you plan on going for a swim . . ."

"Oh, not yet, I should think. I like to warm a bit before I plunge into that icy water." I sank into the chair and, kicking off my shoes, pressed my toes into the warm pebbles.

A sudden burst of laughter turned our attention to where Rupert had been knocked down by a large wave. He stood, dripping, and wiped the water from his face.

Emmeline smiled, her eyes not leaving her fiancé. "Rupert's very handsome, isn't he?"

"Yes, very." I decided for the direct route. "When I first met your Rupert, he reminded me of Milo."

She seemed surprised. "Really? How so?"

"Dark good looks, easy charm, elegant manner, that sort of thing."

She looked down at her hands. "I'm sorry to hear about your marriage . . . It makes it somewhat awkward since I'm also happy to see you with Gil."

"I should have thought you would both be angry with me after what happened."

"Oh, no! Gil could never be angry with you, Amory. Not really." She looked up at me then, sincerity shining in her face. "And I felt sorry for him . . . but I was happy for you. I remember seeing you with Milo in London after things had . . . had ended with Gil. You seemed so frightfully happy, so very much in love. And I would have sworn he adored you."

I shrugged, scooping up a handful of small, round pebbles and then let them fall, one by one, through my fingers. "Perhaps he did, for a time. Such things don't last."

"Don't they?"

"No, I'm afraid not. You see, what men like Milo love most are themselves. Marriage was a diversion, and now the amusement has run its course." I dropped the rest of the pebbles, brushing the last few clinging grains from my hands. How much of what I was saying was the truth, I wasn't sure, but the words served my purpose. I had come not to contemplate my marriage but to cause Emmeline to contemplate hers.

Of course, I didn't want to overdo it. I smiled. "But we needn't dwell on the melancholy. The day is much too lovely."

"Yes," Emmeline agreed. I couldn't help but notice that there was something in her eyes that hadn't been there before when her gaze wandered back to Rupert.

We chatted lightly for a while after that, and then Rupert walked over.

"What are you ladies gossiping about?" he asked, wiping the water from his face and pulling on his robe.

I stood. "Just a feminine tête-à-tête, Mr. Howe. Nothing to interest you, I'm afraid. But I leave you to your fiancée. I think I shall take a stroll."

"Have tea with us this afternoon, won't you, Amory? On the cliff terrace," Emmeline asked.

I looked up at the terrace high above us. "Of course. I shall see you then."

I left them and began to walk along the shore.

Lionel Blake looked up from his book as I prepared to pass him, and he wished me good morning. His green eyes, accentuated by his surroundings, seemed almost to glow, like a cat's eyes.

I smiled an unenthusiastic greeting at Olive and Veronica as I passed, neither of whom acknowledged me with more than a raised eyebrow or slightly upturned lip. The feeling, then, was mutual.

The next pair my path crossed was Nelson Hamilton and Anne Rodgers. His gaze traveled up and down me like a boat looking for a pleasant spot to land. "Mrs. Ames," he said. "Care for a swim? Anne and I were just about to take a dip."

"Thank you, no. I think I'll just walk a bit."

"Well, perhaps later," he said with a wink.

Wretched man. The more I saw of him, the more I disliked him and pitied his wife.

I passed them all, somehow avoiding Yvonne Roland, and enjoyed a relaxing, solitary walk. I ambled along for a nice stretch, until the beach was cut off by the cliff extending into the water, and then I turned around. By now the sun was high and increasingly warm. I decided to cool myself with a swim. I removed my trousers and jacket and took a bathing cap from my bag. I pulled the cap on, tucking in a few loose strands of hair, and waded into the sea. The water was cold and very refreshing. By the time I had finished sea bathing, it was lunchtime and the beach was deserted.

I mounted the long white stairway back to the hotel. When I at last reached the top, I was thoroughly winded and quite sleepy from my exercise. Still full from breakfast, I decided to forgo lunch and take a brief rest in my room before meeting the others for tea.

A BIT LATER, refreshed from my nap, I changed into a light dress in a pale floral print. I went to Gil's door and knocked, thinking that perhaps he would join us for tea, but there was no answer at his door. I decided to see if perhaps he had already gone down.

When I exited the lift into the lobby, I caught sight of Emmeline. She waved and walked toward me, a slight frown creasing her brow.

"Rupert said he would meet me here twenty minutes ago," she said. "But he hasn't come down. I've rung his room, but he isn't there." She seemed more anxious than the situation warranted. Then again, I could sympathize. In the early days of my marriage, once I had discovered a thing or two about my husband, I had been anxious when he was out of my sight as well.

"Perhaps he's already gone out to the terrace."

"Perhaps, but he distinctly said he would meet me in the lobby."

I refrained, of course, from commenting that men of Rupert

Howe's ilk often did not do as they said they would. It was an uncharitable thought, perhaps, but that didn't make it any less true.

We crossed the lobby and exited to the terrace. Many of the tables were filled with hotel guests enjoying the afternoon sun, but Rupert was not among them.

I spotted Mr. and Mrs. Hamilton at one of the tables, and we approached them.

"Howe?" Mr. Hamilton replied in answer to our inquiry. "Haven't seen the chap all afternoon. Neither has Larissa. Have you, dear?"

"I . . . no," she answered, softly. I clenched my teeth at the way the poor woman was barely given a chance to speak.

Lionel Blake, at a nearby table, confirmed that Rupert had not been seen by anyone currently on the hotel terrace. "I was here before anyone else came out for tea, and I have not seen Mr. Howe."

"Well," Emmeline said, "he may have gone down to the cliff terrace. He may have misunderstood and thought we would meet him there."

"We can probably see from here," I said, pointing to an overlook that allowed a sweeping view of the sea, and looked down upon the cliff terrace below.

We walked to the overlook, which had a waist-high stone wall that served as a barrier between the overlook and a very steep drop. The wind was strong this afternoon, and I doubted there would be anyone having tea on the cliff terrace. Backed against the rocks of the cliffs as it was, the area would be buffeted by the strong breezes that were rolling in off the sea.

Emmeline put her hand atop the wall and leaned, catching herself when the top stone wobbled beneath her hand. "Goodness. That could be a hazard."

An ill feeling swept over me at that moment. Emmeline had backed slightly away from the wall. She had not looked over the barrier, but I had leaned over far enough to see the cliff terrace and the crumpled form that lay below.

Rupert.

THE NEXT HOUR passed in a blur. I had taken Emmeline away from the overlook, and some of the hotel staff had rushed down to the cliff terrace. There was nothing to be done; Rupert Howe was dead. Emmeline, quite naturally, had gone to pieces, and a doctor had been called to see to her.

I went to the hotel's sitting room to be alone until the authorities wished to hear my account of the accident, what little I knew of it. Rupert had, I supposed, leaned too far over the edge. A stone had probably given way, and he had tumbled down . . .

The sitting room, decorated in calming shades of yellow, white, and green, did little to ease my troubled nerves. I was more than a little shaken by the experience. I had not particularly liked the man, but to see his body lying at the base of a cliff was not something I would have wished upon him in the worst of circumstances.

The news spread quickly, but I was mercifully left alone until Gil found me in the sitting room. "Amory, are you all right?" He reached out as if to embrace me, then seemed to think better of it and took my hand instead. I was surprised how much comfort I derived immediately from the simple warmth of his grip.

I drew in a breath. "It was awful, Gil," I said, surprised by the steadiness of my voice when my insides were still trembling. "Quite the most terrible thing I've ever seen."

"Let me order you a drink."

I shook my head. "No. No, thank you. I'll be all right."

He sat down beside me on the sofa, his hand still holding mine. "Emmeline's resting now. I've just come from there. The doctor's given her something. Poor darling. She's taken this very hard."

"She loved him very much," I answered softly. I couldn't imagine what she must be feeling. I barely knew the man, and I still felt very shaken by it all.

"She's better off," Gil said, almost under his breath.

I hadn't time to reply before my name was spoken from the doorway.

"Mrs. Ames?" A gentleman in a gray suit and hat entered the room. He was around fifty, of average height and build, with an air of confidence about him that was immediately noticeable, the sort of unassuming person to whom one's eyes were unaccountably drawn.

I stood. "Yes."

"I'm Detective Inspector Jones, CID."

"CID?" I repeated, surprised. What on earth would the Criminal Investigation Department be doing here? To the best of my knowledge, they had never been much concerned with accidents.

"Yes," he answered, then turned to Gil. "And you are, sir?"

"Gilmore Trent. My sister, Emmeline, was engaged to Mr. Howe."

"Allow me to express my sympathies."

"Thank you."

"And now, I wonder, Mr. Trent, if you would mind my speaking to Mrs. Ames alone?" he asked, perfect politeness doing little to mask rather obvious authority.

This seemed to rub Gil the wrong way. "Is that really necessary, Inspector? Amory . . . Mrs. Ames has had a bad shock."

The inspector's brown eyes flickered across my face in a searching glance and then returned to Gil. "She looks like she'll hold up, Mr. Trent."

I saw Gil's mouth draw into a hard line, but I patted his hand. "It's all right, Gil. Let me speak to the inspector, and I'll come and find you. I could use a good strong cup of tea."

"Very well."

The inspector offered him what was not a very warm smile. "I should like to speak to you later, Mr. Trent."

"If you wish," Gil answered.

He left the room without further comment, and I turned to the inspector. "Now, what may I do for you?"

He indicated the seat from which I had arisen. "Sit down, won't you?"

I took a seat on the pale green sofa, and he sat in a chair opposite as he removed his hat, exposing dark hair that was turning silver, and pulled a notebook and a pencil from his coat pocket. "If you don't mind, please tell me exactly what happened this afternoon."

I related the events that had led to the discovery of Rupert's body, from Emmeline's expecting to see him in the lobby to my viewing his body from above. He let my story flow on, uninterrupted, as he jotted down notes.

"There was a loose stone on the wall," I concluded. "I wonder if he might have lost his balance. It's all so terrible."

He looked up from his notebook, his eyes very mild and steady. "It's more terrible than you think, Mrs. Ames. It appears that Mr. Howe was murdered."

"Murdered?" The word was an unexpected jolt to my system. A feeling of denial swept through me, and something more . . . fear. I sucked in a breath, trying to steady myself. I could sense the inspector's calm gaze on my face. I had the feeling that he was gauging something in my reaction.

"I don't understand, Inspector," I said at last. "I . . . it seemed to me that he fell." Even as I spoke, I realized that I did not sound completely convinced, even to myself. Had there been something, in the back of my mind, that had made me wonder if it might not be an accident?

"Did you see his body? Up close, I mean."

"No. I . . ."

"Did you know Mr. Howe?"

"Not well, no."

"And your impression of him?"

"Honestly?" I met the inspector's gaze. "I didn't care for him. Of course, I'm sorry that he's dead."

Inspector Jones inclined his head. "Honesty is always appreciated in my line of work. What was it about Mr. Howe that you found . . . disagreeable?"

"Just that he did not seem a very nice sort of man," I answered. "Nothing substantial. I thought he and Emmeline were ill suited. I . . . I suppose it was none of my business."

"Can you think of anyone who would have reason to hurt him?"

"Certainly not."

I realized that he was watching me very intently. There was something unnerving about the man, a quiet intensity. He was, I imagined, very accomplished at instilling a sense of unease in the guilty. I felt vaguely on edge myself.

His next question, phrased in the same almost uninterested tone, caught me by surprise.

"You are registered here under your own name. Your husband did not come with you?"

This I hadn't expected. "I don't see what that has to do with Mr. Howe's death," I answered, somewhat more tersely than was probably proper when being interviewed by a detective inspector with the CID.

His eyes met mine, and he was obviously unperturbed by my irritation. "I'm just trying to form an accurate picture of things, Mrs. Ames. Little flecks of paint make up the whole picture."

I sighed. "No, Inspector. My husband is not here. In fact, since you have no doubt already ascertained as much, I came at the invitation of Mr. Trent."

"I had, in fact, already ascertained that detail." He seemed to me to be a very quick worker, this inspector. I wondered what else he might have learned. I did not have to wait long to find out.

"You're staying in separate rooms, however."

"Certainly," I replied, less than civilly. There was, as far as I could see, no call for such intrusive and insinuating questions. "There is nothing untoward occurring between us."

"And yet you don't wear a wedding ring?"

I stiffened. "I've taken my rings off. I was sea bathing this afternoon." These were both true, though unrelated, statements. I had been sea bathing, but that was not why I had removed my rings. I had not worn them to the Brightwell, though they were tucked away in my jewelry case upstairs. It hadn't felt quite right to leave them at home.

"I see. But you and Mr. Trent are close friends."

"We've known each other for years, yes."

"And Mr. Howe? Were he and Mr. Trent close?"

I wondered, a bit uneasily, where these questions about Gil were leading. "I only just met Mr. Howe," I answered carefully. "I didn't have much chance to observe them together."

"Indeed." Something in his expression made me wonder if he knew I was being purposefully evasive. "And were you with Mr. Trent this afternoon?"

"I . . . yes. That is, we parted ways after breakfast and intended to take tea together."

"But you didn't see him on the terrace when you and Miss Trent were searching for Mr. Howe."

I hesitated for a fraction of a moment. "No, I didn't."

He scribbled something in the notebook and then flipped it closed. "I think that will be all for now, Mrs. Ames. I imagine you'll be around if I should wish to speak with you again?"

"Of course." I stood, and he followed suit, placing his hat back on his head.

"I'm only too happy to do all that I can," I told him, wondering if I might possibly end up regretting my words.

He nodded and began to walk away, but I had to know. "Inspector?"

He turned.

"You're quite certain that it was murder?"

He hesitated for just a moment, as if determining how much information to share with me, and then spoke carefully. "Yes, Mrs. Ames. For one thing, someone made certain no one would go down to the terrace. A 'closed for repair' sign was placed where the steps veered off the landing. If it hadn't been for you, the body might not have been discovered until sometime later."

"There could be any number of reasons for that sign. An oversight, perhaps?"

He shook his head. "None of the staff knew anything about it."

"But that, in itself, does not rule out an accident."

"Correct. But you see, Mr. Howe fell straight to the terrace, landing on the stone floor and hitting the back of his head. The medical examiner seems to think his neck was broken, killing him almost immediately. There are no marks on his body to indicate that he hit the cliff at any point on the way down."

Such dreadful information failed to enlighten me. "I still don't see how that indicates he didn't just slip and fall."

"Because, if he fell, nothing accounts for the blow he received here"—two fingers touched his left temple—"from what appears to be a blunt instrument."

My lips parted, but nothing came from between them.

He tipped his hat. "Good day, Mrs. Ames. I trust we shall meet again."

A HEAVINESS HAD fallen over our party because of the tragedy among us, but, like the steady, resilient, upper-class we were, we all dressed and met for dinner. I wore a gown of dark gray silk with caplet sleeves. None of my more brightly colored gowns seemed appropriate somehow. We were all in attendance except Emmeline, who was still in her room. I had looked in on her earlier, but she had been asleep. Whatever the doctor had given her, it had put her clean out. I wondered if it was really the best thing for her. As dreadful as the truth was, perhaps it would be better for her to face it at once rather than in a lingering lethargy.

I sat beside Gil at the dinner table. He was quiet, his features solemn, but the calm steadiness I had always admired in him was still there, and I felt calmer myself because of it.

Olive Henderson looked as though she could have used a dose of something a bit stronger than the water she was sipping. Her face was colorless, and I noticed her trembling hands each time she raised her glass to her lips. Rupert had hinted at something between them; perhaps she had loved him as well. Lionel Blake, who sat beside her, seemed solicitous, speaking softly and even earning a smile once or twice. I hoped that it would do her good.

The meal was subdued, and, of course, none of our party danced. Watching other couples move about the floor, strangers untouched by our misfortune, I found it hard to believe that we had all been so carefree only the night before. The sensation caused by Rupert's death had not been too heavy a blow upon the other Brightwell guests, and I assumed they had been fed an official line about an unfortunate accident. They had no doubt tut-tutted sympathetically and then went about their holidays relatively undisturbed.

The press was being kept away by a policeman left on the premises, and I hoped that rumors of a murder investigation would be kept quiet. I was not at all confident such a story could be concealed for long; I knew perfectly well how relentless the press could be.

For my part, I was still recovering from my own very trying day. The general ghastliness of Rupert's death aside, I was still shocked by the inspector's revelation. I had sat alone in my room all afternoon, a thousand questions swirling in my head. It seemed simply impossible that anyone would have wanted to murder Rupert Howe. People don't kill one another while on holiday, I told myself stupidly. But apparently, they did.

I glanced around the table, trying to fathom the possibility that one of us might have done it. I didn't even know if any among my own party was aware of the inspector's suspicion that Rupert's death had been murder. I hadn't been asked to keep the information to myself, but for some reason I had not wanted to discuss it with anyone, not just now. I hadn't even mentioned it to Gil, and then I had felt guilty for withholding it from him. What was more, I couldn't help but feel as though I had failed in some illogical way. Gil had asked me here to help him, and things had turned out more horribly than any of us could have imagined.

Talking of Gil, I couldn't seem to dismiss my uneasiness at the direction of the inspector's questions concerning Gil's relationship with Rupert. The two of them had certainly not been friends, and I suspected that fact wasn't much of a secret. Had the inspector picked up on it, or was he merely fishing for information?

If I was honest with myself, I had to admit that the conversation I had overheard between Gil and Rupert the night before was very much on my mind. The plain fact of it was that they had argued, and now Rupert was dead. I could not for one moment suspect Gil of something so horrible as murdering Rupert Howe. Despite the time that had passed, I knew him too well for that. And yet the conversation nagged at me, and a vague sense of uneasiness hovered at the back of my thoughts.

My head began to throb, and I pressed my aching eyes with my fingers.

"Are you all right, Amory?" Gil whispered, his hand touching my arm beneath the table. "You don't look well."

"I don't feel well," I admitted. "The shock, I suppose. It's been a horrid day."

"Shall I escort you to your room?"

I shook my head. "I don't think I could sleep. Not yet. And I don't want to be alone at the moment." It was true. My mind was tired of attempting to process my constantly churning thoughts; what I needed at the moment was the soothing comfort of familiar company.

"Shall we go for a walk on the terrace, then?"

"Yes," I said. "I could use the air."

We excused ourselves from the table and exited out one pair of the French doors that lined the wall of the dining room.

We were on the terrace that ran along the east side of the hotel. The night air was cool, and there was no one in sight. There was no view of the sea from this side unless one walked to the back of the terrace, and the moon had gone behind a cloud. Gil and I stepped out of the rectangle of light made by the doors, and we were alone, bathed in dark blue dimness.

I breathed deeply of the salty air and let the sound of the waves hitting the rocks wash over me. I found that there was something infinitely soothing about the sound of the sea, as though for just a moment everything was all right.

"I'm sorry you're unwell," Gil said, leaning against the balustrade beside me. Even in the dimness, I could see he was studying me closely.

I touched his arm. "I'm fine, Gil. Really. It's just so wretched that something like this had to happen. I feel dreadfully for Emmeline."

He was looking down at my hand on his arm. "I'm sorry you had to go through this, Amory." The backs of his fingers moved to brush the top of my wrist. "But I will confess that I am glad you're here."

There was a noticeable change in the air as his fingers caressed my hand. I looked up at him, unable to take my eyes from his. "Are you, Gil?" I asked softly.

He nodded and reached up to brush a stray hair back behind my ear, his hand remaining on my cheek. "Very glad."

He was very close to me now, looking down into my eyes. In the space of an instant, I knew he was going to kiss me, and I was still wondering if I would let him as he leaned closer.

His mouth was inches from mine. "Gil . . ."

"Ah. Here you are." The smooth, dry voice spoke from behind us as the moon appeared as if on cue from behind the clouds.

Gil dropped his hand from my face, and I turned, already knowing who had spoken.

"Milo." I was gratified to find that my tone was completely calm, displaying none of the surprise I felt. "What on earth are you doing here?"

MY HUSBAND SMILED at me, his white teeth glinting in the moon-light. "Weren't expecting me, I see."

"I never know when to expect you," I answered lightly. Remembering my manners, and relishing the slight dig at my errant spouse, I gestured to the man who had been about to kiss me. "You remember Gil Trent, I suppose."

"Very well," Milo answered amiably. "How are you, Trent?"

"I'm very well," Gil replied, somewhat curtly. I could feel the tension in him from where he stood, slightly behind me. It was obvious that he did not care for the intrusion, and I knew he was probably embarrassed. I didn't imagine that kissing married women was much in his line.

"Yes." Milo took a cigarette from the silver case he kept in his pocket and put it in his mouth, lighting it. "You seem to be getting along all right."

"You haven't answered me, Milo," I put in, before Gil could make some sort of remark. Men could be such idiots at moments like this.

His eyes moved back to me, flickering silvery in the darkness. "I'm sorry, darling. I seem to have forgotten the question."

"What are you doing here?"

"I received word that there had been a death in your party." He blew out a stream of smoke. "I'm glad to see you haven't allowed it to upset you too much."

"Now, see here, Ames," Gil said, moving slightly forward. I put my hand on his arm.

"It's really been quite an ordeal," I said. "Emmeline, Gil's sister, you remember, she was engaged to the young man."

"My condolences." He sounded as sincere as Milo ever sounded, but then one could never be sure just what he was really thinking.

"Yes, well, I think I'll just go check on Emmeline," Gil said. Without another word or a backward glance at me, he walked past Milo and into the hotel.

Milo and I were alone. We stood for a moment, looking at one another. His expression was as maddeningly impassive as ever. He just stood there, placidly smoking his cigarette as though we were enjoying a quiet evening in our cozy parlor.

"Who told you there had been a death here?" I asked at last.

"These things get around." He dropped his cigarette and ground it out with his toe. "I was concerned for you at once, of course."

"And so you rushed to my aid?" I made no attempt to hide the skepticism in my voice. This business was all very odd, his concern definitely suspect.

"Naturally. Shall we go inside, dearest?"

"Not yet." I moved to him. "I want to know why you're really here. News of Mr. Howe's death could not have appeared in the papers in time for you to make it here this evening."

He made a gesture of assent. "Very well. I read in the evening paper that there had been an accident here at the Brightwell this afternoon, but that wasn't my sole reason for coming."

"No. I thought not."

"I had come to have a word with you about this other business. I assumed that if you chose to carry on with Trent, you would at least be discreet."

I was surprised by his admission, but I made no attempt to deny his accusation. Denial would serve no purpose. "You have always cared so little for discretion, Milo. I don't see why I should be any different."

"The difference between us, darling, has always been that you care for your reputation." He reached into the pocket of his dinner jacket and pulled out what appeared to be the folded page of a newspaper. "This appeared in the paper this morning."

I took the slip of paper and moved into the patch of light from the dining room doors.

It comes as a surprise to few, no doubt, that a certain lady has had more than her share. The wife of a well-known rogue, lately returned from Monte Carlo, seems to have left for the seaside in the company of the man she jilted to marry said rogue. Do we dare predict divorce proceedings followed by wedding bells?

I thrust the paper back at him. "How perfectly disgusting."

"My sentiments exactly."

"I wonder how they found out that I was coming to the seaside. I only left yesterday."

Milo's eyes moved over the article again and then looked up at me, his brows raised. "Am I really a rogue?"

"This is nothing to laugh about, Milo."

"Who's laughing, my dear? Do you expect I am amused to find you and Trent making the most of the moonlight?" His eyes slid over me in a way that would have been positively indecent were he not my husband, and may have been indecent in any case. "Although, I can't say I blame him. You're looking very beautiful tonight, Amory."

I tried not to think about how long it had been since he had looked at me with that wicked gleam in his eyes.

"Really, Milo." I sighed. "I am in no mood for your charm this evening. Did you come all the way down here to confront me with a gossip column? After all the ghastly things they print about you, I'm surprised one little article should so inspire your interest in my affairs."

"Affairs? Are there more than one?" he asked dryly. "Is poor Trent being duped as well?"

"This is ridiculous," I said. "I've had a very trying day. I'm going in. Good night."

"How did the chap die?" His voice stopped me. There seemed to be something underlying the almost-uninterested tone.

I turned. "He went missing before tea. Emmeline and I went in search of him...I saw him from the overlook. He was sprawled on the cliff terrace." I stepped toward him and lowered my voice, though I wasn't sure why. I was not even sure why I suddenly felt the need to confide in him. "It looked like an accident to me, but the inspector that was here today says it was definitely murder."

Milo registered a marginal amount of surprise, indicated by the slight raising of one dark brow. "Murder, was it?" The corner of his mouth tipped up in what was half of a sardonic smile. "Well. It appears, my dear, that this jaunt to the seaside may prove to be more than you bargained for."

I HAD THOUGHT, after the events of the day, that I would have difficulty falling asleep. But the old adage about the head hitting the pillow was never more apropos, and I awoke as the morning sunlight filtered into my room with no memory of having fallen asleep.

I bathed and dressed in one of my more somber ensembles, a tailored, belted dress made of emerald green silk, and went down to breakfast.

Only a smattering of our party was present in the breakfast room. Mr. and Mrs. Hamilton and Mr. and Mrs. Rodgers sat together, talking in subdued voices. Lionel Blake was with them, though I noticed he did not seem to be participating in the conversation.

Gil was not in there, and I assumed he was with Emmeline. I was worried about her, especially now that it appeared Rupert's death had been more than an accident. The next few months, the next few days especially, were going to be very hard on her.

Milo, of course, was nowhere to be seen. He was not what one would deem an early riser by any stretch of the imagination, and I had little doubt he was still enjoying the comforts of his bed. His room was on the same floor as mine, by chance or design I didn't know.

I sat at a table alone but near enough to the others to avoid appearing uninterested in their company. Unlike the morning before, I was afraid I could not summon the appetite for a lavish breakfast. I took some toast and tea and a bit of fruit.

A moment after I had begun to pick at my food, Anne Rodgers leaned over to me from a nearby table, her hand on my arm. "Have you seen Emmeline?"

"No. Have you?"

She shook her head, platinum hair bouncing. "Gil said she was much too distraught. The doctor had given her something rather strong, I believe."

"Perhaps we will be able to see her today."

"It's the most terrible thing," she continued. "I can't believe poor Rupert is gone. We were all so fond of him."

"Well, not all of us," Mr. Hamilton said with a smirk. "I'll wager Trent wasn't crying into his pillow last night."

"Nelson," Mrs. Hamilton said softly, "what a terrible thing to say."

"That doesn't make it any less true," he replied, but he let the subject drop. If he had any specific knowledge of bad blood between Rupert and Gil, he was not in the mood to share it at present.

"This all could have been avoided if they had put up a suitable railing," Mr. Rodgers intoned. "The legal implications of such a hazard likely have never occurred to the hotel. If Emmeline, after a suitable period of mourning, of course, would care for me to look into the . . ."

"Oh, Edward," Anne Rodgers said, waving her fork at him. "Not now."

He frowned at his wife's gentle reprimand but didn't finish his sentence.

Nelson Hamilton guffawed as he took an overlarge bite of egg. "Always on the lookout for a bit of business, eh, Ned?"

Larissa Hamilton had watched the exchange with the same look of vague alarm that I had come to realize was her natural expression. "I'm sure that's not what he meant, Nelson," she said softly.

"Not a bad idea, though," Hamilton continued, as if his wife had not spoken. "Negligence, pure and simple."

They were not aware, then, that it was murder. I wondered why Inspector Jones would have revealed the fact to me and not to the others. Under the circumstances, I thought it best to keep the information to myself for the time being.

I wondered who else knew about the bad feelings between Gil and Rupert. When the news was made public that Rupert had been murdered, people would be quick to point the finger at anyone besides themselves who might have had a reason to do him harm, and Gil's dislike for Rupert might be construed as such. Of course, dislike for someone was not necessarily a motive for murder. Yet the fact remained that Rupert was dead, killed by a blow to the head from someone with whom he had presumably been arguing above the cliff terrace.

I still did not believe, even for a moment, that it might have been Gil. And after all, if Gil had been angry enough to strike Rupert, he could very well have done it that night when they had been alone on the terrace outside my window. No, I could not make myself consider that the overheard conversation was especially significant. That did nothing to ease my worry about what others might say, however.

A thought came to me suddenly. Perhaps if I could establish Rupert's movements before his death, I could remove Gil from the scene completely. Perhaps it would rid me of my growing uneasiness.

"None of you saw Rupert walking about on the terrace yesterday afternoon, I suppose?" I asked casually, pushing my fruit around my plate with my fork.

"I hadn't seen him since we were on the beach," Anne Rodgers said. "Edward and I were napping. Weren't we, dear?" She smiled luminously at her husband, and I rather thought he flushed.

"As I said yesterday, I hadn't seen him either," Mr. Hamilton said, a bit defensively, I thought.

"I saw him in the lobby after we came up from the beach," Mrs. Hamilton said suddenly. She glanced at her husband as though worried he might cut her off and then continued. "He said something about having a meeting with someone later in the afternoon."

That was curious. I remembered distinctly that yesterday afternoon she had agreed with her husband that they hadn't seen Rupert.

"I . . . I only just remembered," she said, as though reading my thoughts.

I wondered. It seemed more likely that Mr. Hamilton had encouraged her silence.

"I took it to mean his tea engagement with Emmeline," she went on, "but perhaps . . ."

"I'm sure it was nothing," Mr. Hamilton said abruptly.

"Yes, I'm sure you're right," she echoed, but her eyes met mine, and I saw the question in them. I would have to speak with her about it later, when her husband wasn't present.

"I understand your husband arrived last night." The crisp voice of Veronica Carter broke into the conversation. I turned to see her approaching my table, regarding me with those cold blue eyes of hers.

"Yes," I answered indifferently. "Quite unexpectedly."

A rather vicious smile played on her trifle-too-red lips, and I fancied I saw her eyes glint just a bit. "How inconvenient."

As much as I abhorred indelicate language, at the moment I would have been able to think of several appropriate names for the woman.

"Your husband?" Anne Rodgers asked. "I thought . . ." She paused, and an awkward silence descended.

"And will you be going home now, after this accident?" It was Lionel Blake who broke in with a fresh question, thankfully obliterating the necessity of an explanation of the current state of my marriage. He had been silent throughout my conversation with the others, but I had noticed he had been listening with apparent interest.

"I'm not sure," I answered. "What about all of you?"

It was my turn to be met with an awkward silence.

"We're not sure either," Anne Rodgers said at last. "It sounds frightfully coldhearted, but we may finish out our holiday."

"The rooms are paid for," Mr. Rodgers said, taking a bit of his kippers.

"I think it's dreadful," Larissa Hamilton said softly. "I wish we could go home today . . . now."

"Nonsense, Larissa." Her husband spoke, I thought, a touch louder than was strictly necessary, given their proximity. "Rupert would want us to finish out our stay, life of the party, he was. No good packing up and heading home."

"I expect Emmeline will go back with . . . with the body, when everything is cleared up here," Anne Rodgers went on. "The funeral won't be for several days yet, and we can attend when we go back to London."

"Life goes on, eh?" Hamilton said, almost defiantly.

It seemed that there was nothing further to say, so I rose from the table. "If you'll all excuse me, I think I'd better go take some aspirin. I have a headache."

It crossed my mind as I left the room that I greatly hoped my friends would be just a bit more distressed were I to meet with an untimely end.

A SHORT WHILE later, I tapped softly on the door to Emmeline's room, and I heard the low murmur of voices before the door opened. Gil looked out at me. "Hello, Amory." His tone was noticeably aloof.

"Hello, Gil," I answered, as though I hadn't noticed the lack of warmth in his greeting. "How is Emmeline?"

His eyes darted back into the room. "Not very well."

"Let her come in, Gil," Emmeline's voice behind him sounded very weak and faint. Gil pulled open the door to allow me to enter.

I stepped into the dark room. The curtains were drawn against the cheerful sun, and Emmeline sat on the sofa, a blanket draped over her. Her face was wan, and her eyes were swollen and red from crying.

I moved to her and sat down beside her on the sofa, taking her soft, cold hand while Gil seated himself in a nearby chair. "Emmeline, I'm so sorry," I said. "I know there's nothing you can hear now that will make you feel any better, but I truly am sorry."

Her eyes immediately filled with tears. "I don't know what I shall do," she whispered. "I...I...don't know how I'll get on without him..."

I squeezed her hand in mine. "You mustn't think about that now. Concentrate on getting your strength back. One day at a time, dear. That's all you can do."

She shook her head. "Even one day seems too much without Rupert. I loved him so..." Her words trailed off into sobs that shook her slight frame.

I did my best to comfort her as she cried. Eventually, the weeping subsided and she fell into an exhausted sleep.

I stood and pulled the blanket over her. "Poor dear," I said softly.

I moved toward the door, and Gil walked with me. I stopped halfway across the room and turned to him, almost without thinking about what I was going to do. "Gil...I need to tell you something."

"Yes? What is it?" he asked, his tone flat. It seemed to me that he had tensed ever so slightly, as though preparing himself for something he didn't want to hear.

"It's about Rupert. That Detective Inspector Jones...well, he says that Rupert was murdered."

I watched Gil's face as I said the words. His features remained perfectly smooth, but he blinked twice, very rapidly, as if he could not quite conceal his surprise.

"He told you that?" he asked.

"Yes."

"Is he certain?"

"It seems so."

"What else did he say?"

He asked the questions calmly, but I sensed urgency beneath them. I began to wonder if perhaps I should not have said anything.

"He only said that he'd been hit on the head before he fell."

Gil blinked again, almost a flinch. "Did he say who he suspected?"

I hesitated. He hadn't, not in so many words. The inspector had asked me questions about Gil, but mentioning it might cause Gil undue alarm. "I think it's rather early for him to have determined that."

Gil let out a short breath. "He can't know anything for sure," he said, almost to himself.

I frowned. This wasn't exactly what I had expected. I had thought Gil would be shocked, perhaps a bit skeptical, as I had been. Instead, it seemed almost as though I had confirmed some private belief of his. Either that . . . or he knew something.

"You mustn't say anything to Emmeline about this," he told me, glancing over his shoulder at his sister's sleeping form. "She's far too distraught for any more bad news."

"She'll have to know eventually, Gil," I said gently.

"Yes, I suppose you're right . . ." His voice trailed off, and his gaze wandered, as though he were lost in thought.

"I asked at breakfast if anyone had seen anything. Perhaps if I talk to everyone . . ."

His gaze came sharply to mine. "Don't," he said. "Don't start asking questions."

"But I only . . ."

"No good can come of it, Amory. Trust me."

I was surprised by the vehemence of his reaction. "Gil, is there . . . do you know something about this?"

He recovered his composure and smiled a very forced smile.

"Of course not." He almost managed to make his voice sound normal, unconcerned. "I only meant that the investigation is bound to be unpleasant, and I would hate for you to be involved in it."

I suspected there was more to it than that, much more, but it was very apparent that Gil was in no mood to confide in me at present.

"Perhaps you're right," I answered, hoping to let the subject drop.

Gil looked immensely relieved, and I felt much more uneasy. Was there something that he was refusing to tell me?

I turned toward the door again, but his hand caught my arm. "Amory, wait. I . . . I have to ask. What is Milo doing here? What are his intentions?"

"One never knows with Milo," I answered.

There was a sudden intensity in Gil's expression as he looked down at me. "I don't like his being here, not now."

"I can't very well send him packing, can I?" I retorted. Something in his manner was irritating to me. It wasn't as though I summoned Milo here. His presence had been as unexpected—and unwelcomed—to me as it had been to Gil.

His hand dropped from my arm. "I'm sorry. I know it isn't your fault. I just . . ." The dark brown flecks in his eyes stood out, as they did when he was troubled. In that moment, I felt a rush of affection for him, and sensation of guilt over all that I had put him through. It wasn't Milo that had hurt Gil; it was me. And for that, I felt rather shabby.

"You don't have to explain, Gil," I said gently. "We're all on edge at the moment. And I know how you feel about Milo."

He offered a smile that seemed forced. "He is your husband, after all. I really have no right to . . . feel the way I do."

Our eyes met and caught for just a moment. He was very close, and I could smell the heady scent of his aftershave. I thought he might try to kiss me again, but instead he reached behind me, his arm brushing mine, and pulled the door open, the click of the latch loud in the heavy silence of the room.

"You had better go," he said in a low voice.

I nodded. "We'll talk later, Gil. I think there are things we will both want to say, once things have settled down a bit."

"Yes."

I left Emmeline's room and took the lift down to the lobby. I wasn't certain where I was going. I only knew I didn't intend to return to my room to sit idly thinking. My mind was much too full for quiet solitude at the moment. The murder, Milo, Gil—everything seemed to be tumbling about in a disorderly jumble in my head.

Gil's behavior was puzzling, to say the least. It was disturbingly obvious from his reaction to my news that he knew, or at least suspected, more than he let on. His determination that I not get involved only strengthened my resolve to help in some way. Gil was worried about something, and if he wouldn't confide in me, perhaps I could put the pieces together on my own.

There was so much to think about. What I needed was a steady sea breeze in my face and the roar of the waves in my ears. A brisk walk along the shore would serve me nicely.

The lift opened, and I stepped, preoccupied, into the lobby, nearly walking directly into the arms of Detective Inspector Jones. I stepped back, a trifle quickly, and hoped he would not be of the impression that I had leapt away in order to avoid contact. Such an idea was not one I cared to cultivate with the police.

"Mrs. Ames," he said, politely enough, "just the person I wanted to see."

"How frightfully popular you are, Amory," Milo drawled from behind me.

I turned to him, less than enthusiastic that he should choose this moment to descend upon the scene. "Hello, Milo."

"Hello, darling." He dropped a kiss on my cheek and then paused, leaning in close for just a moment, his mouth very near my throat.

"You smell of aftershave," he noted in a low voice.

"Do I? How very odd," I answered, my attention turning back to the inspector. "Inspector Jones, this is my husband, Milo Ames. Milo, Detective Inspector Jones of the CID."

"Mr. Ames." The inspector extended a hand, which Milo shook.

"Always pleased to make a friendly acquaintance with the law," Milo said. "One hears so many things about the police these days." The way in which Milo said this could, perhaps, be construed as less than complimentary.

"And I have heard of you," Inspector Jones replied unperturbedly. "Mrs. Ames mentioned that you weren't expected, I believe."

Amusement turned up the corner of Milo's mouth. "I certainly wasn't."

"I suppose you wish to speak with me alone," I interjected.

"I had thought to ask you for a private interview, if you would be so kind"—he glanced at Milo with the same sort of perfunctorily requesting gaze he had given Gil the first time he had interviewed me—"and if your husband has no objection."

Milo gave an elegant shrug. "I am becoming accustomed to having her spirited away."

"Indeed . . . However . . ." He paused, his expression blank. "I see no reason why your husband should not be party to our conversation. Perhaps we should all step into the sitting room."

I had no idea why he would wish to include Milo in our conversation, but I had no strong objection. In fact, if anyone was disinclined to participate in the interview, it was my husband. Murder would be of very little interest to Milo.

Nevertheless, he followed the inspector and me to the sitting room. The inspector motioned with his hand for me to precede him, followed by Milo, and then he entered and shut the door behind us.

I took a seat on the green sofa, and Milo sank easily into a white chair, a vaguely indifferent look on his face. As for myself, I was beginning to dislike this room intensely. It had come to represent, in my mind, all the charms of an interrogation room, not that I was actually acquainted with such places.

The inspector remained standing. "There are just a few things I wanted to ask you, Mrs. Ames," he said, pulling out his notebook. He flipped it open, and I could make out bold but neatly printed notes.

"The medical examiner has concluded that Mr. Howe was killed sometime between noon and four o'clock. Had you seen him at all yesterday afternoon?"

I shook my head. "That last I saw him was at the beach in the morning."

"At what time?"

"Ten, or perhaps half past."

"Was anything of interest said then?"

I thought back. "No, nothing of consequence. Rupert was swimming. I stopped to speak to Emmeline, he came up, we chatted briefly, and I moved on."

"What about at dinner Saturday night?"

"He was there. We spoke very little, danced once."

"And he seemed . . . untroubled?"

"Very. He seemed quite pleased with himself."

"In what way?" The questions were shorter now, his tone more expectant. I was not entirely sure I cared for it.

"In the way of a man who has everything he wants and feels that he unquestionably deserves it," I replied.

He paused for just a moment, looking up at me over his notebook with his calm brown eyes. Was it a glint of approval I saw there?

"What made you look down to the cliff terrace?"

"Emmeline told me that we were to take tea there. She thought perhaps he had gone down to wait for us rather than meeting in the lobby as they had discussed."

"And when you discovered the body, he was lying facing upward?"

"I only saw him from the top of the cliff," I replied. "I don't really recall seeing his face, just his body lying there."

"Yet you were quite certain it was he." He flipped to another page in his notebook, his eyes scanning the notes written there. "The hotel manager said that you told him that Rupert Howe had fallen off the cliff."

"You're rather good at this, Inspector," Milo interposed dryly.

The inspector's gaze flickered to my husband, and for once I was glad of Milo's maddening insouciance.

"Next thing, you'll have her confessing, though I'm quite sure if she were to bash in anyone's head, it would be mine. Am I right, darling?"

"Milo, really . . ."

"I am merely ascertaining the facts," Inspector Jones said calmly. "It is my opinion that Mrs. Ames would have neither sufficient motive nor force of will to kill Mr. Howe."

"How very kind," I replied crisply.

"Nevertheless, I should like to know how you knew it was he at the base of the cliff."

I cast my mind back, forcing myself to remember what I had been doing my best to forget. I had looked over the edge... "Now that you ask, I am not at all certain why I was so sure. I was expecting to see him, I suppose."

"Perfectly logical." He turned to Milo. "And you arrived when, Mr. Ames?"

"Oh, is it my turn now?" Milo smiled. "I arrived last night, around nine."

"You came directly from London?"

"No. From our country house in Kent."

"On what train?"

"I don't recall. One of the afternoon trains. I'm sure my ticket stub is about somewhere, if you should require it."

The inspector jotted another note. "Very good."

He turned back to me. "Just one more thing. You can think of no one with motive to do harm to Mr. Howe?" he asked. It seemed to me there was something expectant in his gaze, as though he were ready for a specific answer.

"No, I..." The memory of the conversation I had overheard between Rupert and Gil once again made an unexpected and unwelcome appearance in my mind. I had convinced myself that it was nothing... yet... no, I decided, I needn't mention it, not until my own mind was settled about the matter. To do so would be disloyal to Gil. I only hoped no one else had overheard it. "I am quite sure I don't know why any of our party would wish to do harm to Mr. Howe."

"The hotel is nearly at capacity," Milo noted, once again relieving me of the piercing official stare. "I'm sure that must give you any number of suspects, a much larger field than in the mystery novels."

A tight smile showed itself on the inspector's mouth. "It's very unlikely, I should say, that a complete stranger would care to—how did you put it?—bash in Rupert Howe's head. There has been no connection made between any of the other persons staying at the Brightwell. It is highly probable, then, that it is someone of his own acquaintance."

"You're certain this was no accident?" I asked, knowing the question was a futile one. Whatever else Inspector Jones might be, he was certainly competent.

"I'm afraid there's no question. He was definitely hit by a blunt instrument. The medical examiner is certain the wound could not have been caused by the fall. There will be an inquest tomorrow. You will give evidence?"

"I have little evidence to give, Inspector," I answered. "However, I would be happy to relate my experience."

He nodded. "Very good. Until tomorrow, then."

"Yes." I stood. "If that is all, I think I might go out and take in some fresh air."

"Going for a walk?" the inspector asked. "With all that's oc-curred, perhaps it would be best if Mr. Ames accompanied you."

"He needn't bother," I said with a glance at Milo. "I'm sure it's much too early for him to be getting any sort of exercise."

"Nonsense," Milo replied, not moving a muscle. "I am perfectly capable of physical exertion in the cause of chivalry."

"I doubt I shall need your gallant protection, but you may come if you wish." I turned toward the door, and Milo rose languidly from his seat.

"A pleasure to meet you, Inspector," Milo said. "Our acquaintance has been most enlightening."

"Indeed, it has, Mr. Ames," Inspector Jones replied. "Indeed, it has. I hope you enjoy the rest of your stay."

"Well, it's not exactly the Côte d'Azur, is it?" Milo answered. "But I daresay I'll find some way to amuse myself."

"Yes, I don't doubt it." The inspector's thoughtful gaze moved from Milo to me and then back again. "Well, good day, Mr. Ames. Mrs. Ames."

"Pleasant chap," Milo observed, as Inspector Jones walked off, no doubt in search of other victims to interrogate. There was something distinctly unnerving about the man, but I suspected that was a useful characteristic in his line of work.

"A very efficient policeman, I should think," I replied. And a clever one, unless I missed my guess. There was something Inspector Jones was getting at, something he suspected and was trying to confirm. For some reason, the thought was discomforting.

My thoughts went back to the conversation between Gil and Rupert. If one imagined hard enough, one might be able to see some sort of vague threat on Gil's part, and it worried me more than a little. Not that I believed for a moment that Gil was capable of murder. It was just that if I had overheard the conversation, others might have, and they might not interpret Gil's words as innocently as I had.

I wondered if that was what had worried him when we had spoken earlier in the day, but somehow I thought it was more than that. I wished, not for the first time since coming to the Brightwell, that Gil would take me into his confidence. Then again, I had long ago forfeited my rights on that score.

That didn't mean, of course, that there was nothing I could do. Perhaps I should continue to talk to the others, to see if any of them had an inkling of what might have happened. Even if they had seen nothing, they might have their own suspicions—or hidden motives.

". . . I shall have to change my clothes," Milo was saying.

I turned to him. "I beg your pardon?"

"Before we go traipsing about on the beach, I shall have to put on some other clothes." He was wearing a blue suit that fit him to perfection, but that was neither here nor there.

"We're not going to the beach," I answered.

"No?"

"No. I've changed my mind."

"Very well. Am I dismissed?" Something very subtle in his posture gave me the impression that he was ready to be gone, that there was something innate in him like a tide, ready to sweep him away from me. A calm sea with restless, swirling currents.

I almost laughed at my absurd philosophizing. If Milo could have heard my thoughts, he would no doubt have had something very droll to say about them.

"Yes, you may go," I said loftily, in keeping with his general lack of gravity. I headed toward the back of the hotel, ready to get out into the fresh air of the terrace.

"Amory."

I turned.

"Before I go, may I offer you one piece of sound, husbandly advice?"

"And what is that?" I asked, wondering if he could possibly have any sort of counsel that could prove useful to me, for some reason hoping that he did.

He stepped closer. Then a look of amusement flickered across his eyes, and, even before he spoke, I knew that he was not serious.

"That scent on your neck is not at all becoming, I'm afraid. Your usual gardenia is much more suited to you."

OUTSIDE, I WAS met by a blast of warm, salty air that I was sure would carry away any lingering traces of Gil's aftershave. I stood there for a moment, drinking in the sight of the sea that stretched into the distance and trying to ignore the sense of dissatisfaction I felt after my encounter with Milo.

The terrace was nearly empty, as it had been the morning before, with most of the hotel guests on the beach. Once again, Larissa Hamilton sat alone, a cup of tea before her, gazing out almost fearfully at the sea. As she was by herself, I thought it would be a good time to ask what Rupert had said to her about some sort of meeting on the terrace.

"Hello, Mrs. Hamilton," I said.

She dragged her eyes away from the water to look at me. "Hello."

I indicated the empty seat across from her. "Might I sit down?"

I did not imagine the briefest hesitation before she nodded. "Of course."

As I sank into the chair, she glanced around, and it occurred to me that she might be worried her husband would see us. The fact that he was an intolerable boor was more than obvious. I wondered if the public boor might also be a private brute.

"The sea is very beautiful today," I observed, glancing out at the water. Strange how the sea provided a sense of serenity, even in such circumstances.

Larissa Hamilton did not share my sentiments.

"If I am honest," she answered, "I must say I don't much care for it." She smiled faintly, but the barest hint of warmth entered into her eyes. "I grew up near the forests and hill lands of Derbyshire," she said. "Flat, open places feel foreign to me."

I wondered why, then, she sat on the terrace for hours, staring out at the endless expanse of sea.

"I once visited Derbyshire as a young girl," I said. "What I remember most is green, vibrant green every way one looked."

She smiled then, the first genuine smile I had seen from her. "It's beautiful. No place is so dear to my heart." She glanced back toward the water, the smile fading from her lips. "So very unlike my home, this place. I've hated the sea, ever since . . . ever since I was a child."

"Well, it feels so good to get a moment's peace out here," I said, "after everything that has happened."

"Yes, it's all been so dreadful."

"Did you know Rupert Howe well?" I asked.

She shook her head. "No. He was a friend of friends; you understand. My husband and I were thrown into his company quite often, but I . . . we were not close." Her eyes drifted back out toward the water. "I'm very sorry for Emmeline."

"How did they meet, do you know?"

"I believe Emmeline said they met at a play in London. I don't remember the details—some story about his rescuing her from a man who had set his sights on her. She would have done better, I think, to have avoided Rupert." She looked suddenly rueful. "I suppose it's not nice for me to say such things."

"You didn't think much of him, then?"

"It isn't kind to speak against the dead," she answered, and I recognized that the topic was closed, for the time being, in any event.

"Have you talked to the inspector who has been wandering about?" I asked, switching subjects.

She blinked, but her gaze remained on the sea. "Yes, he asked me a few questions about the accident."

"Did you tell him what you told me earlier, about Rupert saying he was to meet someone?"

"Yes, I told him," she said, and when her gaze met mine, I saw something unexpected: determination. Despite her meek appearance, there was an underlying strength to her that I had not seen until now. "Nelson hates terribly to get involved in things. He'd rather we just go on as if nothing happened . . . but I didn't think it right not to tell the inspector."

"No," I answered, "I think it was best that you did." I understood very well what she meant. I, too, was finding it difficult to go on as normal after all that had happened.

"He seemed to think it of little consequence."

I plunged ahead. "What was it that Rupert said?"

"He told me that he had an engagement on the terrace for that afternoon. He only said it in passing. I'm sure he meant tea with Emmeline."

"Perhaps."

"At least, I feel quite sure that I took it at the time that he meant

Emmeline. I think he may even have said as much. I do wish I could remember . . ."

I weighed my options for just a moment. It would be best for me to tell her the truth. I could get her honest reaction, before she had time to hide her initial response to the news.

I leaned forward, hoping to convey a conspiratorial air. "The inspector says that he is certain that it was not an accident. In fact, he believes it was murder."

She turned her eyes back to me, and there was some emotion in them that I didn't know how to read. Was it fear? "Murder? Surely not."

"That's what I said, but he seems to be quite sure."

"It seems a stupid way to kill someone," she said, almost absently.

"But effective, nonetheless." I noticed that she had not wondered who should like to kill Rupert; I wondered whom she suspected. There was one way to find out.

"Who could have done it, do you think?" I asked.

"I couldn't venture to guess," she said carefully, but there was something in her tone that made me feel a bit more prodding would result in her confidence.

"But one always has suspicions, doesn't one?"

She seemed to be considering what to say next. When she spoke, it was with great hesitation. That streak of strength I had seen moments ago seemed to have faded back into wariness. "I . . . I had wondered if perhaps it might not have been an accident . . . Not a real accident, I mean . . . but the result of a quarrel . . ."

"Yes?" I urged her on.

She looked as if she would finally force out the words, but we were interrupted by her husband's voice. "Larissa," he called gruffly from the doorway.

She started and stood hastily. "Coming, dear."

As he turned, she placed her hand on my arm and leaned in. Her hand was cold; I could feel it through my sleeve. Her voice was so faint, it was nearly torn away by the wind. "I don't know who it might have been, Mrs. Ames. But I am not surprised it was murder," she whispered. "Not surprised at all."

WITH THAT INTERVIEW behind me—or postponed, if I had anything to say about it—I weighed my options. I wondered whom it would be best to speak with next. I still was not certain what part I was intending to play in all of this. My innate practicality and a sense of decorum honed by years at stern boarding schools told me to heed Gil's advice and leave the matter to the police. However, my instincts told me that there was more trouble on the horizon and that it might be judicious to take the offensive. Besides, there could be no harm in eliciting the impressions and opinions of the other guests. If nothing else, I might learn something of interest to tell that detective inspector when next he came prowling about the premises.

Lionel Blake spared me the trouble of deciding whom to speak with next, as he was the first person I encountered upon reentering the hotel.

"I'm going to the village, Mrs. Ames," he said, after we had exchanged pleasantries. "Is there anything I can pick up for you?"

I didn't hesitate, knowing this was the perfect opportunity to put my investigative inclinations to work. "Might I come with you?"

He smiled. "Of course. I would be delighted to have your company."

"I'll just run up and get my handbag."

I made my way to my room and gathered up a handbag and a light jacket. There were clouds gathering in the distance, and I wouldn't be surprised to see rain before the day's end.

I was a bit afraid of encountering any members of the press as we left the hotel grounds, but it seemed the reporters had been dissuaded by the police and the lack of any further dramatic developments. We were undisturbed as we made our way to the hotel car.

As we found ourselves driving slowly down the hill toward the village, I took a moment to observe Lionel Blake. He had the quality—rare, I thought, for an actor—of being as good-looking close-up as he was from a distance. His was an easy sort of handsomeness, self-assured but lacking arrogance. In fact, he seemed to distinctly lack the sort of bluster and bravado I had come to associate with gentlemen of the theatrical profession. I realized, of course, that my assumptions were based on clichés, but I had known a fair share of actors, and many of them demonstrated decidedly stereotypical qualities.

"It's nice to get away from the hotel for a bit," I said at last, breaking into the comfortable silence. "Especially with this dreadful business of Rupert's death." It was not exactly a subtle approach, but I felt it was entirely within context.

"Yes," he answered. "Poor Rupert. It was rather a shock to all of us, I think, to have something like that happen."

"You were very good friends, weren't you?" I asked. "It must be very hard for you."

"We were friends, yes," he answered. "Though I wouldn't say that we were close. Rupert was a hard man to get to know."

"How so?"

He hesitated. "I think the best way to describe it is that one could never be certain if he liked one or not. There was always the front of friendliness, but it could have been genuine or an act." He smiled, a bit sadly I thought. "I don't mean to speak against the dead."

It was surprising how often people prefaced their disparaging comments about Rupert Howe with those words.

"You haven't," I answered. "I don't mean to pry. I was just curious. It's strange how when something like this happens, it makes you want to understand about the person, to get to know him . . . now that it is too late."

"Morbid curiosity, I suppose."

"Yes, I suppose. I feel so sorry for Emmeline. She's terribly upset."

"I hope she will recover shortly. She is young; love will come for her again."

It was a practical statement and probably true, but I was a bit surprised by the cool way in which he dismissed her love for Rupert.

"Some would say that one loves only once," I said mildly.

He looked at me, and I sensed skepticism in his gaze. "Some people love many times," he said, and I knew precisely what he was driving at.

"You mean Rupert? There were women, I understand," I said carefully.

He shrugged noncommittally. "One hears things."

I had heard, of course, about Olive Henderson and suspected it was common knowledge. Had there been others? He seemed disinclined to elaborate, and I could think of no conceivable way to ask such an indecorous question, so I shifted my focus.

"You were on the veranda when Emmeline and I came looking for Rupert, and you said you hadn't seen him. How long had you been sitting there?"

He looked at me then, with his strange green eyes. "You are beginning to sound like that police inspector."

I laughed. "Oh, dear."

He smiled, but said nothing further.

The car stopped at the edge of the village, and Lionel got out and opened my door. "What time shall we drive back?" he asked me.

That fact that he had failed to answer my question was not lost on me. While he gave every appearance of amiability, I thought it odd that he should neglect to reply to the most innocent of inquiries. There was something evasive in his manner that roused my suspicions.

"I will be ready whenever you are," I answered. "I really have no special reason for coming to the village. I just wanted to get away from the hotel for a while."

"Would you care to accompany me, then?" he asked.

"I would love to." I followed him around the car to the road. "Where are we going?"

"There's a little theater up this way," he said, and pointed at a street that ran off from the main thoroughfare. "Someone mentioned that it might be the ideal place to put on a small production."

We started walking toward the side street he had indicated. The village was rather large, owing much of its success to the holiday trade. We passed a few of the more traditional enterprises: butcher, post office, apothecary, as well as businesses that appealed to seaside visitors. There were several people milling about, and the village had an air of busy leisure.

"What sort of production are you planning?" I asked.

"My friend, the backer, was considering taking our play on tour. He thought a seaside venue might be just right, and I told him I would look into it. I heard from a chap at the hotel that the local theater building might be just the thing."

We had crossed the main street and had begun to wander up the street that he had indicated. We walked at a comfortable pace. It was a pleasant day, despite the clouds gathering in the distance, with a breeze off the sea. There were few people about on this road, and the noise from the village faded as we followed the path winding its way toward an edifice a good distance from the town.

We stopped as it came into view. The building, far from impressive, looked as if it had been a factory. In fact, it looked as though it was one still. It was large, square, and unappealing and had a few windows, darkened with wooden shutters. The grass surrounding it seemed long overdue for a trimming.

"Is that it?"

"Yes. Rather awkwardly situated, isn't it? This fellow told me that it was some sort of factory during the war. A local philanthropist took it upon himself to have it renovated as a favor to the village. Doesn't look as though they much appreciated it."

Lionel Blake walked to the door and rattled the handle. "Locked."

"Surely there's a caretaker about somewhere." I looked around for a nearby cottage or building, but there was nothing nearer than the village proper.

"Yes, I suppose." He stepped back from the door, still surveying the building. "I shall have to find out the proper channel of enquiry."

"If we ask at the village, I'm sure they will tell us."

"Well, it seems there is no need for us to linger." He walked back toward me and indicated the path. "Shall we?"

We began our return to the village, and I thought it was not my imagination that Lionel Blake seemed preoccupied.

"Do you think you will recommend it to your backer?" I asked nonchalantly.

"It depends, I suppose, on a number of things," he replied absently.

"It's not a very good location. I don't see that it would be a terribly good investment."

He stopped walking abruptly and turned to face me. "To be honest, he's in something of a bad way financially. He was counting on a good venue . . . quite desperately in need of it, in fact. It was his way of thinking that a cheap but well-placed venue might get him out of the mess he's in. Of course, I would prefer it if you not mention this to anyone."

"Of course."

We continued back to the village and reached the car just as a light rain began to fall.

"I was afraid it might rain," I said as Lionel slid into the car and pulled the door shut behind him.

"Yes, I'm afraid we may be in for a spell of bad weather," he remarked, looking out of the window. "I hope it clears up quickly. I don't relish the idea of being stuck inside that hotel for days with only the Hamiltons and the Rodgerses for company."

"Yes," I sighed. "That does present a rather unappealing prospect."

BACK AT THE hotel, I wanted nothing more than to return to my room for a few moments of peace before dinner.

I was somewhat put out that my afternoon of inquiries had yielded so very little. Charming companion though Lionel Blake may be, there had been very little in his conversation that could have any bearing upon Rupert Howe's murder. Surely someone must know something. At least dinner would be another chance to insert casual questions into the conversation.

I walked into the hotel and spotted Mr. and Mrs. Rodgers sitting together in the lobby. He was reading *The Times* and she was thumbing through an issue of *Vogue*. Despite the time we had spent together, I still could not help being struck by the contrast between them. They seemed such an unlikely pair, but I sensed solidarity in their relationship, as though they were really very devoted to one another. Perhaps opposites really do attract.

I had gleaned so little from Mr. Blake. I wondered if perhaps Mr. or Mrs. Rodgers might have a bit more information to offer. I walked to where they sat. "Good afternoon," I said.

They both looked up, and he began to rise from his seat. "Don't get up, please," I said quickly. "I didn't wish to disturb you. I only came by to say hello."

"Looks like rain," Mr. Rodgers said, by way of polite conversation, before picking up his newspaper again. Mrs. Rodgers seemed a bit more inclined to chat.

"You've just come back?" she asked, and I could tell she was curious where I might have been. Though they had been well mannered enough to conceal it for the most part, I knew my somewhat unorthodox relationship with Gil and Milo was the cause for much speculation among the members of our party.

"Yes. I took a ride with Mr. Blake to the village, just to get out for a bit."

"Lionel's such a dear. And so handsome, isn't he?" she said. I noticed her husband did not look particularly concerned by her comment. In fact, his attention did not shift from his newspaper.

"Yes. He's very nice," I said.

"So many handsome men are here this weekend," she went on. I sensed that this latest comment was for her husband's benefit. Her way of teasing him, perhaps. I suddenly had the impression that, though Mrs. Rodgers enjoyed calling attention to her appearance for the benefit of assorted handsome gentlemen, she was very much in love with her husband.

"I . . . hadn't really thought about it," I answered.

She laughed. "I suppose you're accustomed to looking at that husband of yours, but he's a feast for the eyes for the rest of us."

"Really, Anne," Mr. Rodgers said, folding his paper and looking sternly at his wife. "I think that's not at all a polite thing to say."

"I only meant it as a compliment," she said innocently, but I detected a note of triumph in the fact that she had finally roused him from his reading.

"It's all right," I smiled. I turned my attention to Mr. Rodgers, hoping to shift the conversation in a more meaningful direction. "Anything interesting in *The Times*?"

"The usual things, I suppose. Talk of that American flyer, Amelia Earhart, the rising unemployment rates, and an abundance of politics and death. I had thought we'd escaped the last of those things, at least, coming down here. It seems I was wrong."

"Yes," I said. "Poor Mr. Howe. Were you very close to him?" It was by no means the smoothest transition of topic, but they did not seem to notice.

"I wouldn't say so," he answered flatly.

"We've really come to accompany Nelson and Larissa," Mrs. Rodgers said. "We've known the Hamiltons for several years now, since just after they were married."

"So you've not been long acquainted with the Trents or Mr. Howe?"

"No, though we knew them casually, of course. Gil is a dear, and Emmeline is such a sweet thing. She seems a fairly quiet girl, but she was so . . . so very vibrant with Rupert." She hesitated before pressing on. "Rupert was very charming and handsome, and I suppose she couldn't help but fall in love with him. You can imagine how it was."

"Yes." I could imagine it very well.

"Rupert always seemed very pleasant," she continued. "I had nothing to say against him."

She said it as though I expected she would have.

"I'm very sorry for Emmeline," I said.

Mrs. Rodgers hesitated ever so slightly. "Yes. I imagine she's heartbroken."

"She's very young," I said, picking up Mr. Blake's line for the sake of moving the conversation along. "I expect, eventually, she will find love again, and it will help all of this fade. Love has a strange way of making one forget the past."

Mr. Rodgers looked up at me then, his gaze suddenly shrewd. "I think you're quite right about that, Mrs. Ames."

The movement was so subtle, I almost didn't notice it. Mrs. Rodgers's hand slid from her lap and brushed her husband's leg, ever so slightly. If it was a cue, he took it at once. He lifted his paper back up and began reading it.

"I'm sure we all wish Emmeline well," Mrs. Rodgers said with a bright smile, and I sensed that it was the end of the conversation.

"Well, I suppose I had better go up and prepare for dinner," I said, not wanting to outstay my welcome. "I shall see you both then?"

"Certainly. It's been lovely chatting with you, Mrs. Ames."

I left them and crossed the lobby toward the lift, wondering what that exchange had been about. There had been something behind Mr. Rodgers's comment, but whatever it had been, his wife had not wanted him to elaborate. Curious. It seemed that every way I turned people were concealing things.

I entered the lift, and, as the doors closed, I cherished the moment of peaceful silence. Truth be told, I did not feel at all like dressing and spending the evening with these insipid people. I could hold up under the strain as well as anyone, I supposed, but the murder had shaken me more than I cared to admit.

I had always prided myself on my independence, but at that moment what I longed for was someone with whom I could talk and share my troubles. It was in moments like these that I felt the hollowness of my marriage the keenest. In those whirlwind days of my courtship, I had failed to take into account the fact that storms of life called for stronger stuff than the easy flow of smooth endearments and witty banter.

As was my habit with morose contemplation, I pushed the thoughts away for another time. I turned my thoughts from what I lacked to what I had, for I was not friendless by any means. A letter to my cousin Laurel, my closest friend and confidant, was long overdue, but at the moment I lacked the stamina that the task required.

The lift opened, and I stepped out onto the landing just as Veronica Carter approached. We exchanged cool pleasantries. I have never ceased to be amazed at the intuitive dislike that can arise with little or no provocation between two women. Perhaps I am of biased opinion, but there was something distinctly unpleasant about Miss Carter. It seemed to me that she carried about with her an icy disdain that radiated from her jaded gaze and smug little mouth. Aside from these unfortunate traits, she was admittedly very pretty.

I expect that in the time I was summing her up, she was doing the same to me. I had obviously impressed her even less than she had me. "You look all done in, Mrs. Ames," she commented with false sympathy. "I expect finding Rupert as you did gave you quite a turn."

"It was terribly shocking," I said.

"It's too bad, really, for his company was very enjoyable. I'm afraid I shall miss him."

"You were close?"

"Not as close as I should have liked," she said, and I wondered if she meant it the way it sounded. "I knew him before he met Emmeline and found him charming, but we were never much in one another's company."

"Oh," I said casually, "then you've known him longer than Emmeline?"

She sighed, as though my question was immensely trying, but answered it anyway. "No, Emmeline and I were at school together, Olive too. That's why we decided to come down here when we heard that the Trents and Rupert were coming."

"I see. I was curious how everyone knew one another."

She livened a bit at the chance to gossip, though she spoke with the same general lack of enthusiasm that I had come to expect from her. "I suppose the Trents had some business dealings with the Hamiltons and Mr. Hamilton attached himself to them. Rather a social climber, I'd say. I don't have anything to do with them. I think he's too horrid for words."

So we did have something in common, after all.

"I believe Mr. Rodgers is some friend of Mr. Hamilton's, so he tagged along as well."

That fit with what Mr. and Mrs. Rodgers had told me.

"And we picked Lionel up someplace quite some months ago," she went on. "He's become quite a pet. We invited him along when we knew we were all coming down. It sounded like rather a lark, our holiday. Of course, we couldn't have known all this"—she waved her hand in a sweeping and disdainful gesture—"would take place."

"It's been especially hard on Emmeline," I said.

"Yes. I went to look in on her earlier, but Gil has her practically under lock and key."

"I believe the doctor has given her a sedative."

I was certain that it was apathy I saw lurking in her china-blue eyes. "Oh? Well, perhaps it will do her good. Though things are so dull around here, I feel as though I'd had one. I've barely needed my sleeping tablets these past few days." Then her eyes glinted with amusement. "At least until your charming husband arrived. I had forgotten how excessively amusing he is."

"Yes, he's a darling, isn't he?"

Her smile faded as I once again failed to be baited. "In any event," she went on, "Rupert's death has ruined the entire week. I wish I had never come."

How very careless of him to spoil your fun, I was tempted to say.

"I don't know what he might have been doing before he fell. No doubt he slipped and went over," she replied, absently examining her bloodred fingernails.

I decided to try my little experiment of surprise enlightenment once more. "Oh, didn't you hear?" I asked casually. "The inspector says it was murder."

She looked up at me, and, for the briefest of instants, I was sure

I saw something other than that perpetual boredom in her expression. Was it surprise . . . or had it been fear? Then the cool mask slipped back into place.

It was nearly the same reaction I had received from Mrs. Hamilton on the terrace, a flash of alarm that they both had quickly concealed. Could it be that both of these women knew something about which they were hesitant to speak?

"Murder? I don't see how it could have been. Who would want to murder Rupert?"

"I imagine Detective Inspector Jones would give a great deal to know just that."

"Well, this has all been fascinating," she said lightly, touching her glossy red hair, "but I'm afraid I must go to my room and dress for dinner."

"Of course."

She left me then and entered the lift. I had reached the door to my own room before I began to wonder what she had been doing on this floor if her room was elsewhere.

DINNER PASSED MUCH as usual, despite the addition of Milo to our party. He sat at my table, playing the dutiful husband, but we had very little to say to one another. Veronica Carter seated herself across from him and engaged him in conversation whenever possible. No doubt he was amusing her excessively. Gil did not come down to dinner, and I found myself worrying over him as well as Emmeline.

Mr. Hamilton seemed to be doing his best to amuse me. "You look smashing tonight, Mrs. Ames," he said, his eyes moving over me in a disconcerting way. My bias-cut gown of ivory satin was not at all revealing, but I felt rather as though he were looking straight through it.

"Thank you," I answered with all the politeness I could muster.

"I've half a mind to steal you away from that husband of yours," he said in a false whisper. Larissa Hamilton looked about as amused as I felt.

"I hope Mr. Ames isn't the jealous type," he went on, in what seemed to be a progressively louder voice. He seemed to enjoy calling attention to himself.

"Not at all," Milo said, as he cut into his fillet. He looked up at Mr. Hamilton and smiled. "I married Amory for her money. And she married me for mine."

Mr. Hamilton laughed heartily. "From what I've heard, neither of you were disappointed! That's the way to go about it." He indicated his wife beside him with his fork. "Larissa here married me for my money, but she'd never admit it."

"Nelson!" she whispered as her face flushed bright red. "I didn't . . ."

"Of course, she was a looker then," he went on, oblivious to, or more likely uncaring of, his wife's distress. "Well worth the price."

I felt my jaw tighten at his completely inappropriate remarks, and poor Larissa Hamilton seemed on the verge of tears.

"What line of work are you in, Mr. Hamilton?" Milo asked, smoothly diverting the conversation. It was good of him to do so. I knew perfectly well that he had about as much interest in Nelson Hamilton's line of work as I had in Veronica Carter's dental history.

"Well, I'm a self-made man," he began. Pleased to ramble on about himself, he let drop the subject of his marriage, and Larissa Hamilton's flush gradually faded into her usual pallor.

Everyone was relieved, I think, by the change in topic. Mrs. Rodgers had been trying without much success to conceal a disapproving frown throughout the conversation, and she turned then to Mrs. Hamilton and began speaking animatedly. I still could not quite tell what the relationship between the two women was. Though Mrs. Rodgers said they had known each other for many years, their interactions thus far had not seemed to be those of very close friends. Nevertheless, they seemed at ease in one another's company. I found myself hoping that Mrs. Hamilton might have a true friend in Mrs. Rodgers; she could certainly benefit from one.

"Perhaps you'd like to come up to my room for a drink after dinner, Larissa," Anne Rodgers said. She reached out and squeezed her husband's arm. "Edward has some tedious legal briefs to read, and I'm feeling like company tonight. I've some new magazines we might read."

"I should like that," Mrs. Hamilton replied, and I noted with approval that she did not first ask her husband. "That is, if Mr. Rodgers doesn't mind."

"Edward doesn't mind. Do you, darling?"

"Certainly not," Mr. Rodgers said, and I noticed that his normally dry tone was friendlier than usual. It seemed as though he were acting on his wife's unspoken instructions to be kind to Mrs. Hamilton. "We should both be glad of your company. Anne gets cross with me when I ignore her, and I find it difficult to concentrate when she prattles on at me."

Anne Rodgers laughed, and Mrs. Hamilton smiled, that spark of warmth coming back into her eyes. The mood at the table seemed to have lightened considerably, despite the fact that Mr. Hamilton was still going on to Milo about some very astute business decisions on his part, his voice growing louder to drown out our conversation.

I was glad when the meal was over so I could escape to the hotel sitting room. It was unoccupied, as I had hoped it would be. Most of the guests, I had noticed, stayed in the dining room dancing long after dinner had ended.

The soft, cool colors of the room in the warm glow of the lamplight were soothing after the brightness and noise of dinner. I moved to the writing desk that sat against one wall. I pulled open the top drawer and found a neat stack of crisp ivory paper bearing the hotel's name, along with a pile of envelopes.

I sat at the desk chair and pulled out a sheet of paper. I had been meaning to write my cousin Laurel, and now was as good a time as any. I could confide in her, and perhaps the organization of my thoughts on paper would be beneficial to me as well.

I was feeling overwhelmed by everything that had happened in the past few days. I had accepted Gil's invitation to the Brightwell somewhat rashly and with little forethought, and now it was time to acknowledge that I may have gotten in over my head. It had never been my nature to give in easily, however. Perhaps that was why I had endured my obviously failing marriage for as long as I had . . .

Who had murdered Rupert Howe? The question repeated itself over and over in my mind. I had learned little so far, except that the murdered man had not been very highly regarded by his friends and acquaintances. The carefully neutral answers of nearly everyone with whom I had discussed Rupert had spoken loudly. No one had liked him, not really.

It seemed only poor Emmeline had been blind to his faults. I felt very sorry for her. No matter what I or anyone else had thought of Rupert, she had loved him, and now he was gone. Despite Lionel Blake's prognosis, it was going to take her time to recover from this tragedy.

My thoughts shifted to Gil. He knew more than he was saying, of that I was sure. But what? I suspected he would be horrified to learn that it had been his adamancy that I not ask questions that had provoked my determination to do just that.

That was not to say that I acted without misgivings. If I was honest with myself, I was forced to acknowledge that I was venturing into territory in which I had no business. Rupert Howe's murder, however unfortunate, was really none of my concern. Detective Inspector Jones seemed extremely competent. Nevertheless, his leading questions regarding Gil's whereabouts at the time of the murder had alarmed me. There was always the chance he might come to the wrong conclusion, and that was a risk I was unwilling to take. If there was some way I could help clear suspicion from Gil, then I would do it.

Of course, my motive posed its own problems. It was all very well to tell myself that I wanted to aid Gil, to be certain that he didn't get swept up in the murder of his sister's fiancé, but I had not confronted the reason I wanted to do so. What was Gil to me? A friend or something more? Even now, when I attempted to sort out my uncertain feelings toward him, I could come to no other conclusion than that I still wondered what might have been. Five years was a long time and much had changed, and yet some things still felt so very much the same . . .

With a sigh, I set pen to paper and began my letter.

Dear Laurel,

I promised to write to you, thinking my seaside excursion would produce very little that would prove to be newsworthy. How wrong I was. This trip has been more than I had bargained for. I am sure you have heard of the death of Rupert Howe, Emmeline Trent's fiancé. This terrible news has been exacerbated by the fact that his death was nothing less than murder. It was I who discovered the body, and tomorrow I must attend the inquest. Knowing how you love a mystery, I am sure you will be envious. Do not be. Murder is not nearly as romantic in real life.

As if matters needed to be further complicated, Milo has arrived, swooping down upon us unannounced. I have no idea of his purpose for coming here, but I am certain no good can come of it. He and Gil already appear very cool to one another, and in the midst of an investigation does not seem the proper time to contemplate the state of our marriage.

A hurried set of steps alerted me to someone's approach.

"Oh, excuse me."

I looked up to see Olive Henderson standing in the doorway. I had seen little of her the past two days, and I had been surprised at dinner to see how wan she was. She looked even more distressed now, her face ghastly pale, save for her red-rimmed eyes.

"I didn't mean to disturb you," she said softly. Her eyes looked almost pleading, as if she longed for a confidant as much as I did. I was surprised she would choose me; she had never seemed very fond of my company before.

"You aren't disturbing me at all," I answered, folding my letter, to be finished later. "I would be glad of the company, in fact."

She entered the room and sank into the sofa, her white hands clenched in her lap. "Things are perfectly ghastly here, aren't they?" she said, almost to herself.

"It has been a rough couple of days."

Without further provocation, she burst into tears. "I'm so dreadfully unhappy," she said, sobbing into a handkerchief that had appeared from nowhere.

Having grown up in a reserved, emotionally distant family and subsequently being married to Milo, flagrant shows of emotion were foreign to me and, truthfully, somewhat uncomfortable. I moved to sit beside her on the sofa and did my best to affect a soothing manner.

"I'm sorry you're distressed. Is there anything I can do?"

She shook her head. "No. You wouldn't . . ." She looked up at me suddenly, her gaze intense. "Have you ever been truly, madly in love?"

I hesitated only a moment. "I thought so once."

"Then perhaps you know how it feels to lose someone . . ."

Steps sounded outside the door, and I looked up to see Gil standing there. Olive stiffened beside me and dabbed her face rather aggressively with her handkerchief.

"I'm sorry to interrupt," Gil said. "Shall I come back?"

"No," Olive said, rising. "I was just leaving."

Without a backward glance at either of us, she left the room. I couldn't help but feel that her sudden and unexpected confidence had been surprising. I should have thought I would be the last person to whom she would unburden her heart, but perhaps there had been no one else.

It seemed obvious she was referring to Rupert. He had spoken of their past relationship with decided flippancy; obviously, Olive's feelings had been much stronger. Had she loved him that desperately? If so, things could not have rested easily between them, not with his being engaged to Emmeline. I recalled her apparent sadness that first night at dinner. Might it have turned to anger? It was certainly something to consider.

Gil regarded me with raised brows. "She seemed upset."

"I believe she was." I didn't elaborate. There would be plenty of time to think things over alone in my room tonight. A bit of familiar company would be soothing just now. I indicated the sofa beside me. "Care to sit?"

He sat, leaned back, then sat forward again, turning to look at me. "I owe you an apology, Amory."

"Nonsense."

"Yes, I was terse with you today, and there was no call for it. I asked for your help, and you were nothing but kind. And then, because things didn't go as planned, I acted badly. I'm sorry." He looked so forlorn, I fought the urge to embrace him.

"Think nothing of it. We're all tense at the moment."

"It isn't just that. Your husband . . . dash it all, Amory." He sighed. "I think you should know that I . . ."

"Gil," I stopped him with my hand on his, longing to hear what he had to say but not wanting him to go on. "I don't think now is the best time."

He looked at me, his brown eyes serious yet warm and golden in the yellow light. "You're probably right, but there may not be another time."

"There's plenty of time," I said. I didn't want to encourage him, to give him any sort of false hope. But at the moment I was so unsure of everything, and Gil was the closest thing to security I had ever known. I hadn't known that when I threw it all away, but I realized it now and was hesitant to completely relinquish it, whatever my feelings for Milo might be. "When all this is over, Gil, we will talk. But I also think you should know that I . . ."

It was his turn to squeeze my hand. "Don't tell me now, Amory," he said with a tired smile. "Let's wait until this is all over."

11

THE FOLLOWING MORNING, the day of the inquest, was suitably gloomy. The rain splattered against my window as I rose and dressed. I had tea and toast in my room, for I was in no mood for company. The thought of encountering Nelson Hamilton was especially unbearable.

The inquest itself was remarkably brief, such a cold, formal way to account for the ending of a man's life.

It was held at the local inn, attracting a small crowd of locals curious about the mysterious death at the Brightwell and a handful of reporters, eager for some hint of scandal. Few from our party were there. Most of them had nothing to contribute, and the rain seemed to have dissuaded those with only a casual interest in attending.

Emmeline, her face white, sat in one of the hard wooden chairs until it was her turn to speak. She gave her halting account of the events that had led up to our gruesome discovery, and it was obvious that only the very greatest of efforts was keeping her from hys-

teria. When she had finished, Gil helped her to her seat. Grief and
fatigue had left her weak and ill, and I was very sorry for her that
her dreams of happiness had vanished in an instant.

When it was my turn to speak, I gave a statement regarding my
role in the discovery of Rupert Howe's body. There was precious
little to tell, and I was brief.

The coroner reiterated what I had learned from Inspector Jones.
Rupert had been hit on the head with a blunt instrument before
being tossed over the railing. The blow itself had not had sufficient
force to kill and might have been administered by either a man or a
woman.

Inspector Jones gave his evidence, but I learned from him few
details that I did not already know. No one reported having seen
Rupert exit the hotel. No one could be certain when he fell.

The verdict came quickly and confirmed what we all already
knew: murder by person or persons unknown.

"MRS. AMES, MIGHT I have a word with you?" Inspector Jones approached me outside as I moved toward the hotel car. The rain beat
a steady drumming on our umbrellas as we stood huddled in a
rather forlorn little group.

I turned to Gil, who had just settled Emmeline inside. "Will
you wait a moment, Gil?"

His eyes flickered to the inspector and back to me. "Of course."

"If you'd like, Mrs. Ames, I can give you a ride back to the hotel. I had intended to pay a visit there this afternoon in any case."

I turned to Gil. "You had better take Emmeline back. I'll be
along soon."

He hesitated only briefly, then nodded. "Very well."

The car pulled away, and the inspector indicated his car, which was parked at a short distance. "Shall we?"

We walked toward it. The grass was sodden, and I could feel the dampness seeping into my shoes. They were entirely inappropriate for the weather, but in packing for this trip I had brought very little to wear in the rain and even less to wear to an inquest.

"I admired your recounting of events," Inspector Jones said as we walked. "You were clear and concise in relating your information. You'd make a very credible witness."

"Witness to what, exactly?" I inquired. His tone indicated that there was more to what he was saying than his words suggested. There was something very clever, in a devious sort of way, about Inspector Jones.

"I am speaking in generalities," he said. "A policeman values a witness who knows how to recount events without embellishment or excessive emotion. Pure, simple truth is always admirable."

I stopped and turned to face him. "You are quite right. And I would appreciate the same directness now, Inspector. Whatever it is that you have to ask or say to me, perhaps it would be best if you came out with it."

The barest of smiles touched his lips. "Very well, Mrs. Ames. But perhaps we should get out of the rain."

We walked to his car, and he opened the door for me before going around and sliding in behind the steering wheel. He inserted the key but didn't turn it. Hands on the wheel, he turned to look at me.

"You would like me to be blunt, so I shall be. I think there is something you are concealing from me."

I was somewhat surprised by this accusation, but I fancy that I was able to hide it. "Oh? And why do you think that?"

"Come now, Mrs. Ames," he said. "When one has been at this job as long as I have, one begins to develop a sense about these things. Twice I asked you if you knew of anyone who would have reason to harm Rupert Howe. There was something you hesitated over. I would like to know what it is."

"It was nothing of consequence."

"Why don't you let me be the judge of that?"

I hesitated. I truly believed Gil was innocent, but the inspector might not feel the same way. If I told him that I had heard Gil arguing with Rupert Howe the night before his murder, it could go very badly for Gil. But perhaps the truth was the wisest course of action. Inspector Jones appeared to be very thorough and conscientious in his methods, and I doubted my information would form his opinion of the case one way or the other. This was my chance to rid myself of the nagging sensation that I was doing something wrong in concealing information. Furthermore, if I told Inspector Jones all I knew, perhaps he could begin to focus his attention in a direction more likely to bring results.

I spoke quickly, as though in doing so I could minimize the damage. "The night before Mr. Howe's murder, I happened to . . . overhear an argument between him and Gil . . . Mr. Trent. As I said, it was nothing of consequence."

"What sort of argument?"

"Gil wanted Mr. Howe to end his engagement to Emmeline. Gil wasn't happy about the match. He had told me as much. It wasn't a secret."

"What did you hear?" I was wary of the calm, casual way he asked the questions. His ever-present notebook was nowhere to be seen, but I hadn't the slightest doubt he was jotting neat little notes somewhere in his mind.

"Did Mr. Trent threaten Mr. Howe?"

"Gil wouldn't . . ."

"Did he threaten Mr. Howe?" There was a smooth persistence to his questioning that I found unnerving.

I thought back. Had Gil threatened Rupert? Not in so many words. "No. He told him that men like Mr. Howe always have their price. I didn't overhear the entire conversation. I had fallen asleep and awoke to catch just a bit of it." This was not the unvarnished truth, but it was not a lie.

"I'm sure it was nothing," I concluded.

"There must have been some reason you chose to conceal it until now."

"I didn't want you to draw the wrong conclusions. Gil and Mr. Howe weren't overly fond of one another, but there was nothing violent about their argument. Besides, if they'd argued outside my window, it seems unlikely Gil would have waited until the next afternoon to do harm to Mr. Howe."

He didn't reply to this bit of logic.

The rain drumming against the window was the only sound for a long moment. Then he asked, "Where exactly does the relationship between you and Mr. Trent stand?"

I stiffened ever so slightly. "That's a rather personal question, isn't it, Inspector?"

"Perhaps. But that makes it no less relevant."

Despite the situation, I smiled. "You're very good at your job, aren't you?"

He returned the smile. "I like to think so."

I sighed. "Gil and I were once engaged to be married."

If he was surprised, he didn't show it. Then again, perhaps he already knew.

"Who ended it?"

"I did. I . . . met my husband."

"I see. And the current state of affairs?" His choice of words was not lost on me.

"Gil asked me to come to the seaside with him on the pretext that I had left Milo. I don't know if my husband's name is familiar to you, Inspector, but he has something of an unsavory reputation." His brief nod conveyed that he was well aware of Milo's exploits. I went on. "Gil thought I might lead by example. He felt Emmeline might be able to see the error of her ways having been witness to my own misfortune. In hindsight, it was all quite ridiculous and completely hopeless."

"And your husband was amenable to this scheme?"

"My husband had very little to do with it."

"Apparently, he is unaware of that fact," Inspector Jones commented wryly.

"Milo very seldom makes informed decisions. There's no telling why he is here."

"Isn't there?"

I ignored the insinuation. Milo was not inclined to jealousy. He had admitted as much last evening. The most likely explanation for his arrival at the Brightwell Hotel was that he had found our empty home dull and knew arriving unannounced would create a stir.

"In any event," I continued, "Gil would never have hurt Rupert Howe. That is the reason I hesitated to tell you anything about the discussion I overheard. I feared it would cause you to suspect him unduly."

"I seldom suspect people unduly, Mrs. Ames."

I was not quite sure what to make of this statement, but the opportunity to ask dissipated as he turned the key and started the engine, easing the car down the wet road toward the Brightwell Hotel.

BACK AT THE hotel, the inspector and I parted ways. I was not sure what his business at the Brightwell was, and he did not see fit to confide in me. Quite possibly, I was still holding rank on his list of suspects, though I couldn't conceive of what my motive for killing Rupert Howe might be.

I was still not certain I had done the right thing by telling him about the conversation I had overheard between Gil and Rupert. Like any good British subject, I was brought up to tell the truth and respect the law, but I did not feel that my silence had violated either of these principles. Knowing Gil as I did, the argument seemed irrelevant. I hoped Inspector Jones would come to view it similarly.

It suddenly occurred to me that the next best course of action would be to alert Gil to what I had done. It was only fair that I should give him warning, in the event that Inspector Jones should wish to question him. I only hoped he wouldn't be too angry with me.

I checked first at his room and got no answer. A soft tap on Emmeline's door also went unanswered. A check of the dining room was also unsuccessful. I tried the sitting room next.

Anne Rodgers and Lionel Blake sat on the sofa.

"Oh, Mrs. Ames," said Mrs. Rodgers as I entered, "you must come hear Lionel read these poems and sonnets. Really, he's too talented! He does accents so well; you should hear his Robert Burns!"

"I would love to," I said, "but first I need to locate Gil. Has anyone seen him?"

Mrs. Rodgers shook her head. "Lionel and I have been here reading since lunch."

"How was the inquest?" Lionel Blake asked, setting the book of poems aside.

"Well . . ." I paused, as if hesitant to reveal the news. "I'm afraid they've discovered that it was murder."

"Murder!" Anne Rodgers practically shrieked. "Oh, no. Who-ever did it?"

"A very good question," Lionel answered dryly. "What have the police to say, Mrs. Ames?"

"I don't really know," I replied, "except that I am sure we are all suspects."

As I had hoped, this alarmed Anne Rodgers into effusive speech. "I don't know why I should be a suspect," she protested. "I barely knew Rupert. Oh, well, we were friendly enough, but not the kind of friendly where you want to murder the person. Just wait until I tell my Edward about this. I'm sure he knows a good barrister if any of us is accused. If anyone did it, I expect I could guess. Perhaps Emmeline finally got tired of his making eyes at other women. And Olive Hen-derson never did get over it when he chose Emmeline." She halted then, as though aware she had said too much. "Not that I think Em-meline or Olive would kill anyone," she added, somewhat belatedly.

"Of course not," Lionel Blake said with a cynical smile. "None of us would kill anyone."

STILL HOPING TO find Gil, I walked past the breakfast room and saw Mrs. Hamilton sitting alone at a table near the windows. I thought it would be an ideal time to speak with her; I was so sel-dom able to catch her away from her husband's prying gaze.

"The verdict of the inquest was murder," I told her when we had exchanged greetings.

She nodded, and I could detect no hint of surprise in her expression.

"You said the other day that you were not surprised Mr. Howe's death was a murder. Why did you say that?"

She frowned. "Did I say that?"

I suddenly had the feeling she was being purposefully evasive. I took a chance on directness. "What is it that you aren't saying, Mrs. Hamilton?"

She didn't meet my eyes as she spoke. Instead, she gazed out of the rain-specked windows at the sea. "I shouldn't have said that. I didn't mean it. I only meant that there were so many people who might have had cause to . . . to quarrel with Rupert."

"Yes, you mentioned a quarrel. Do you mean someone specifically?"

She looked at me then, and I saw again that flash of determination in her gaze, as though she had come to the private conclusion to move forward. "I only know I heard some rather nasty rumors about . . . well, women. And then I saw them, Rupert and Olive—I mean, together—talking on the beach as they followed Emmeline, who had gone up to change. They all walked past me on the terrace. I was reading, and I don't think they noticed me, you see. I might have thought nothing of their chatting together, but I'm fairly certain I heard Olive say that she wanted to meet Rupert later, that she wanted to talk to him about something."

This was certainly news. Had Rupert and Olive been carrying on their affair, then?

"What did Rupert say?"

"He said he would see if he could get away . . . but he seemed somewhat reluctant. I don't think he much cared for her anymore.

When he mentioned a meeting later, I... well, I thought he just meant tea with Emmeline."

It was a flimsy excuse for having concealed the truth, but I suspected Mrs. Hamilton was desperate not to cause any trouble. And this information had the potential to do just that. Could it have been Olive that quarreled with Rupert on the terrace that day? Or had it been someone else?

"Who else was on the terrace when this conversation occurred, Mrs. Hamilton?"

She hesitated for a fraction of a moment before replying. "Mr. Trent had come out and was talking with Emmeline. I thought I saw them turn around and look at Olive and Rupert, but the sea is very loud, you know. They may have been too far away to overhear them."

Somehow, I didn't think so. The sea was not as loud as Mrs. Hamilton made it out to be.

"Why didn't you say something before? Did you tell this to the inspector?"

She shook her head. "I was sure it was nothing. I may have misheard, and I didn't want there to be any difficulty. Oh, dear. What a mess all of this is."

I couldn't agree more.

"Thank you for telling me, Mrs. Hamilton," I said, almost wishing that she hadn't.

"I didn't know if I should," she said with a shaky smile. "But I feel better now that I have."

I felt much worse, myself. This bit of information was certainly not in Gil's favor. If he had overheard Rupert planning an assignation with Olive, it would certainly have increased his dislike for

Rupert. Inwardly, I sighed. Rather than clearing up, things seemed to be getting murkier.

UNABLE TO LOCATE Gil anywhere in the hotel, I returned to my room. The rain showed no sign of letting up. Indeed, it seemed to have increased in fervency since my arrival back at the hotel. There was something slightly claustrophobic about the atmosphere. The rain pounding against the windows, leaving us, for all intents and purposes, caged in with a murderer.

Wearily, I lay on the bed, hoping to nap before dinner. My thoughts, however, would give me no such reprieve. Over and over, the events that had occurred since my arrival played in my head. Who would have reason to kill Rupert?

Gil as good as threatened him, my traitorous mind reminded me. For the first time, I fleetingly allowed for the possibility. Might Gil have done it? Though I had denied a threat to the inspector, Gil's words to Rupert that night below my window had held a warning. It just wasn't possible. Was it? No. No, I could not believe that Gil would resort to murder, no matter how desperate the circumstances.

It must be someone else. My mind played over the other members of our party, but I could think of no conceivable motive for anyone to have killed him. Mr. Hamilton seemed the type that would kill someone who crossed him, but a negative opinion of his character did not a motive for murder make.

Anne Rodgers had reminded me that Olive was involved with Rupert before he met Emmeline, and she had said that Olive wanted to meet with him on the day he died. Perhaps he had spurned her advances once again. Was she hurt enough to kill him? It was possible, I supposed. But there had been real sorrow in her eyes; I was sure of it. I didn't believe she could have killed him.

Then who could have done it? It was all such a muddle.

Without provocation, my thoughts turned to Milo. What, I wondered, were his intentions now that he was here? I had not seen him yet today, and I could only imagine what he was up to. His arrival had only complicated matters, and it seemed apparent that he was intent on making a nuisance of himself for the foreseeable future, a role I suspected he would enjoy.

I sighed. More weary than when I had lain down, I rose to bathe and dress for dinner.

12

MR. HAMILTON WAS the first to greet me as I took my seat for dinner. "Mrs. Ames, what's all this business about Rupert being murdered?" he thundered at me. I wasn't sure if he was angry or merely put out that he had not been given advance notice of this information.

"That was the verdict of the inquest," I replied as calmly as I could.

"Nonsense," Mr. Rodgers said, before forking a large bite of quail into his mouth. "Rupert fell. It was all negligence on the hotel's part." I wondered if he was being purposely obtuse or if he really regarded everything in terms of inane legal ramblings.

"The police are quite sure."

Mr. Rodgers didn't look convinced.

"I don't like this," Mr. Hamilton blustered. "I don't like it at all."

Larissa Hamilton was very pale as she watched her husband. When she looked up to see my eyes on her, she offered a small smile before quickly looking away.

Olive Henderson had not come down to dinner, so I assumed she was feeling poorly. I wondered if she might possibly be troubled by a guilty conscience.

I glanced around the dining room. Gil was not here either. The slightest trickle of fear began to seep down my spine. I hoped he was all right.

Milo sank into the seat beside me. "Looking for someone, darling?"

"Have you seen Gil?"

"No, I'm afraid I haven't."

"What do you think about this murder business?" Hamilton inquired of him.

"All very unfortunate," Milo replied as he placed his napkin in his lap. I hadn't seen Milo since my return from the inquest, and I wondered who had told him about the official verdict. Of course, I assumed the whole hotel would be talking about it soon enough. Since coming to dinner, I had already noticed the curious glances of people at nearby tables.

"But supposing it is true. Who could have done it?" Rodgers interjected. "I see no reason why anyone would kill Rupert."

Hamilton snickered. "Only the husbands of half the women in London."

"Nelson," Larissa Hamilton whispered. "Please."

I wondered if Nelson Hamilton was privy to the information his wife had shared with me today.

He ignored her. "Something of a ladies' man, old Rupert was. He was fond of Emmeline, but we've been acquainted for years and it was always very apparent that he enjoyed the company of the women."

"I think you may be misjudging him," I said. I, of course,

suspected that this was indeed the case, but I thought that present-ing myself as sympathetic would perhaps be useful to my cause. More flies with honey, so the saying went. I was not entirely sure that this applied to murderers, but it didn't seem that it could do any harm.

"He was always very pleasant," put in Anne Rodgers. "And he seemed to me to be a true gentleman."

"You're a woman, Anne," Mr. Hamilton said, with what seemed to be more than a touch of familiarity in his tone. "Of course you'd be charmed by him. Women don't see through that sort of charm. They're all susceptible to it. Aren't they, Ames?"

Milo looked up from his plate, an impeccably guileless look on his face. "I'm afraid I'm not really in a position to know."

"You're much too modest." This comment came from Veronica Carter. She had sauntered into the room in a lovely gown of scarlet silk.

"Of all my attributes, my modesty is the one of which I am most proud," Milo replied.

She gave a tinkling laugh. "How clever you are."

I resisted the impulse to roll my eyes, but only just.

"We were just discussing this business of Rupert's murder," Mr. Rodgers said. "Have you any theories on that matter?"

"So it is murder, is it?" she asked, sinking in a sort of sensuous melt into the chair the waiter had pulled out for her. She seemed to have been in doubt of the truth of my statement until now. "I'm very much surprised that any of us would have the stomach for such a thing."

"Doesn't take much stomach to shove someone off a ledge." This bit of wisdom came from Mr. Hamilton. He was proving to be more insufferable than usual this evening.

"One of us?" Anne Rodgers said. "Surely none of us would have killed Rupert."

"Theoretically," said Mr. Rodgers, "such a thing would be hard to prove. Despite what the police say, how can they possibly know for certain that Rupert was pushed? An accident still seems to be the most plausible solution by far."

"There's truth in that," said Mr. Hamilton, looking at me almost defiantly. I had the feeling that he held me personally responsible for the fact that Rupert's death had been declared a murder.

"Yes, but he was hit on the head before he fell." A brief silence greeted my announcement.

"Hit on the head with what?" Mr. Hamilton demanded.

"I'm afraid I don't know."

He snorted his disgust. "The entire thing's ludicrous."

I happened to glance then at Larissa Hamilton. She looked far from amused. I could only imagine how it must be to be married to a bore like Nelson Hamilton. In comparison, Milo was a model husband.

"It's all very upsetting, but I suppose that is no reason we should discuss it at dinner. Let's talk about something a bit more pleasant, shall we?" I asked.

The conversation shifted then to mundane topics, but there was no escaping the underlying tension that hung heavily in the air. Veronica Carter did her best to attract all of Milo's attention, and she seemed to be succeeding. More troubling than this, however, was my worry about Gil. It wasn't like him to disappear without notice. I had once again knocked on the door to Emmeline's room before dinner, but there had been no answer. If he was there, he was not taking visitors.

The meal was finished at last, and I was only too happy to see it end. I wanted nothing more than to escape to my room and enjoy the rest of the evening in solitude. If only Gil would turn up . . .

"I wonder what has become of Gil," I said to Milo as we rose from the table. "I haven't seen him all day. I do hope he is all right."

If I expected sympathy or concern from Milo, I was to be disappointed. He looked at me, something of a hard smile playing at the corners of his mouth. "He has survived the last five years without you, Amory. I think he will manage."

WE DISPERSED AFTER dinner. I watched Milo follow Veronica Carter out of the dining room, ostensibly for a game of cards. Though I was well accustomed to his neglect, it grated on me that her blatant flaunting of her assets should prove successful.

Repressing whatever feelings of jealousy I might have, I went once again to Gil's room, but there was no answer to my knock. I considered calling Inspector Jones, but I really had nothing to report. Gil probably just wanted to spend some time alone. If he hadn't surfaced by morning, I would contact the inspector, but I tried to convince myself that such a step would be needless.

Mentally exhausted, I retired to my room. I threw my gown over the back of a chair, and my stockings over its arm. Then I took a soothing bath in gardenia scent before I pulled on my scarlet-colored nightgown.

I had just begun to brush my hair when a knock sounded at my door. Hoping it would be Gil, I set down my brush and hurriedly pulled on a silk flower-printed robe.

I cracked the door, expecting to greet Gil, and found Milo, still in evening attire.

"What are you doing here?" I asked, somewhat rudely.

He leaned against the door frame, hands in his pockets. "Amory, my darling, aren't you going to ask me in?"

Under the circumstances, I felt it ridiculous to leave my husband standing in the corridor. I pulled back the door, and he entered, flashing me one of his smiles as he did so. I was instantly suspicious.

"You look extremely fetching," he said. "I don't believe I've seen that negligee before." He leaned closer. "And you smell positively enticing."

I shut the door and crossed my arms, hoping the gesture did not appear as defensive as it felt. "To what do I owe the pleasure? Is your own room not to your satisfaction?"

He gave my room a casual, cursory inspection before turning to me. "Veronica Carter is there at the moment. I thought it best not to disturb her."

Despite myself, I tensed. What possible reason could he have for coming to flaunt his newest liaison? I resisted the urge to order him from the room. There was no need for a scene. My anger would mean very little to him.

My tone, when I spoke, was cool and, I hoped, uninterested. "Oh? I take it she is expecting you back soon?"

"I haven't the faintest idea what she is expecting."

I smiled coldly, my eyes narrowed. "Come now, Milo. Surely you don't mean to imply that you don't know her purpose there. She is certainly responding to your invitation."

"Nonsense. We played cards and then parted ways. I had a drink and was coming down the corridor when I saw her enter into my room. Really, darling, I'm surprised at you. A woman secretes herself in my bedchamber, and I come running directly to you. I should think you would be impressed by my steadfast loyalty and devotion."

"You must have done something to give her the impression that she would be welcome."

He smiled, almost grimly. "Women, I have learned, tend to believe what they wish to believe."

I would not give him the satisfaction of acknowledging that I had often seen this to be true.

"She indicated that you were acquainted with her in Monte Carlo," I went on.

"She was there, though she was wasting her dubious charms on me." He sighed. "Give me the least bit of credit, Amory. What would I want with a nasty bit of goods like Veronica Carter?"

The argument, to some odd extent, was sound. "I admit I thought your taste would be somewhat better."

"Of course." He smiled. "I married you, after all."

My anger was not to be offset by his charm. "You were speaking to her a great deal at dinner."

"And you were speaking with that blowhard Hamilton. However, I didn't notice you inviting him into your boudoir." He glanced around, brow raised. "He isn't here, is he?"

I sighed, almost managing to contain my smile. "Really, you *are* ridiculous."

He smiled. For a moment, there was something of the old familiarity between us.

"Do you want a drink?" I asked.

"Thank you, no." He settled himself into one of the white armchairs, pulling at his necktie. "It's dashed inconvenient to have that woman clogging up my room."

"Perhaps it would be more effective for you to ask her to leave."

"I thought coming here might be more efficient. It speaks volumes, but discreetly."

"Poor, dear Milo. You just aren't used to saying no to women."

He picked up one of my stockings from the arm of the chair and toyed idly with it. "I suppose I shall have to stay here all night."

"Oh, you want to stay here, do you?"

"Of course, there may be scandal," he answered, sotto voce. "Whatever will people say? Imagine, a man spending the night with his own wife."

There was no point in ignoring the obvious. "It is rather unusual, as we haven't shared a room in some time."

His eyes met mine, and he seemed as though he was about to reply when there was a light tap on the door.

Milo's brow quirked. "Expecting someone?"

"Certainly not."

In actuality, I was irritated to be interrupted when we were on the brink of this particular discussion.

I pulled open the door, and Gil rushed in before I could say anything. "Amory, I need to speak with you."

At the sight of Milo lounging in my chair, long legs extended, arms folded on his chest, one of my silk stockings dangling from his hand, Gil stopped short. "Ames," he said.

Milo smiled pleasantly. "Trent. Fancy meeting you here."

"I've just dropped by to speak to Amory."

"So I see. Well, don't let me stop you." He waved a hand in a magnanimous gesture. "By all means, speak with her."

"I . . . had rather thought to speak with her alone."

"I expect you did."

"I have been looking for you all day, Gil," I said, before they could begin to trade barbs. "I was beginning to be afraid that something dreadful had happened to you. Wherever have you been?"

"That's what I need to speak to you about." He cast a glance at

Milo, then looked back to me, lowering his voice. "It's rather urgent."

"We are all ears," Milo said.

Gil's jaw tightened, and his reply was directed at me. "I'd rather speak to you alone, Amory. If you don't mind."

I turned to my husband. "Milo, perhaps you would give us a moment," I said. Whatever Gil had to say would not take long, and if he would feel easier in telling it without Milo, then so be it.

"Really," Milo replied, "I'm not certain I should leave. In fact, I might, under other circumstances, be inclined to ask what exactly a gentleman is doing coming to your room so late at night."

"I might ask you the same thing," Gil replied, turning to face Milo. His posture was tense, and there was a decidedly unpleasant look on his face. Though a gentleman in every respect, I was not entirely certain that Gil would be above landing a blow in a tense situation.

Milo appeared unperturbed by the threat of imminent fisticuffs. "I have every right to be here. She is my wife, after all."

"How nice of you to remember at last," Gil retorted.

"Please," I interjected. "It's been a very trying week, and I would appreciate as little additional turmoil as possible."

Gil looked at me and had the good grace to look at least marginally ashamed. "I'm sorry, Amory. I'm afraid I'm on edge myself."

"It's all right, Gil. There isn't any need for quarreling," I went on.

"None at all, my dear." Milo's tone was light and his face remained impassive, but his eyes were uncharacteristically cold. "Except for I believe the general practice is to be affronted at attempts on one's wife."

Gil was, I think, about to reply to this, but my glance stopped him.

It was at this inopportune moment that another knock sounded at the door.

"You should charge for admission, Amory," Milo drawled from his seat. "You may be able to offset the expenditures of this little holiday."

"Oh, do shut up, Milo."

I crossed to the door and opened it to find Inspector Jones looking placidly back at me. Without my invitation, he stepped into the doorway, hovering somewhere between the hallway and my room proper. "I'm sorry to disturb you, Mrs. Ames, but . . ." His eyes caught sight of my guests.

"Mr. Ames, Mr. Trent." There was an irritatingly interested note in his voice. He stepped fully into the room, and I shut the door behind him.

"Inspector Jones," Milo smiled, "I'm glad you could join us. The party was just beginning to get dull."

"Throwing a party, are you, Mrs. Ames?" He glanced from me to my husband to Gil and back to me. "A rather exclusive one, it appears."

"An accidental gathering," I assured him. "Milo came here because Miss Carter is in his room and he doesn't wish to disturb her."

I ignored the low, derisive laugh that came from Gil.

Inspector Jones looked at Milo, and his gaze came back to me, vaguely expectant.

"A gross misunderstanding," Milo said, as though the phrase would explain the entire situation. Then again, I was not certain it merited explanation. Our bedrooms were not exactly the business of Inspector Jones.

The inspector's brows rose ever so slightly at Milo's reply, though his expression did not change. I was certain he would begin to think we were all mad. "I see. Mr. Ames arrived because Miss Carter is in his room. And"—he turned to Gil—"who is in Mr. Trent's room?"

Gil frowned irritably. "There is no one in my room, Inspector. I needed to speak to Amory."

"Alone," supplied Milo.

"As intriguing as all of this may be," said Inspector Jones. "I came here for a particular reason. I came to enquire, in fact, if you knew of the whereabouts of Mr. Trent." He turned to Gil. "And here you are."

"Yes, here I am. What is it that you wished to see me about, Inspector?"

"You were apparently gone from the hotel for a good deal of time today, Mr. Trent. I couldn't locate you, and no one seemed to know where you had gone. Would you mind telling me where you were?"

Gil stiffened ever so slightly and hesitated for only a moment before he spoke. "At the risk of appearing to be rude or uncooperative, I must say that I don't particularly see that that is any of your business."

I was surprised by this answer. It seemed to me Gil could have no conceivable reason for concealing such information, especially at a time like this.

"Is that any way to speak to a policeman?" Milo asked.

Gil turned to Milo. "I should be careful, Ames, if I were you. I am very close to losing my temper."

"I think you'd better be careful about making threats, Mr. Trent," said Inspector Jones. "It puts you in rather a bad light."

There was something in the inspector's tone that made me uneasy. Gil must have sensed it, too, for he was composed in an instant. "What exactly does that mean, Inspector?"

"It means, Mr. Trent, that I am arresting you for the murder of Rupert Howe."

13

I GASPED, COMPLETELY stunned by this latest and completely unforeseen development. "You can't possibly mean it, Inspector."

He regarded me coolly. "I'm afraid I never jest about such matters, Mrs. Ames. I am perfectly in earnest."

"But this is absurd," said Gil, finding his voice after the moment of surprise. "Why on earth would I kill Rupert Howe?"

"To prevent him from forming an undesirable attachment to your sister. Mrs. Ames heard you threaten him while standing outside her window," he said, nodding in the direction of the windows that faced out to the sea. "The night before he was murdered. You warned him to leave your sister alone."

I was both angry and upset at this betrayal of my confidence. "I said no such thing!" I exclaimed. "You have mistaken what I told you, Inspector."

"Mrs. Ames, I realize this is uncomfortable. No doubt you are also angry that I have taken into account the information you gave me. However, you did tell me that the two of them were having a heated discussion outside your window."

I turned to Gil. "I didn't mean for this to cause trouble, Gil. I was trying to find you today, to let you know that I had spoken to the inspector." I turned back to Inspector Jones, my voice cold. "I had thought you would be inclined to interpret that information in a reasonable manner."

"It is very reasonable, Mrs. Ames," he said, unfazed by my anger. "Unfortunate as it may be."

Gil took my hand and squeezed it. "It's all right, Amory. I'm sure this will all get straightened out in time."

I turned back to the inspector. "You haven't any evidence against him, not really."

"I'm afraid that's incorrect," he said calmly. "Mr. Trent was seen on the terrace in the company of Mr. Howe not long before the time Mr. Howe was believed to have been killed."

This was another piece of news that caught me completely off guard.

"By whom?" I demanded.

"That is something I would rather not disclose at this time."

"This is outrageous!" I said.

"I understand how you might think so," Inspector Jones answered in that irritatingly calm way of his. "But I am inclined to see it somewhat differently."

"You can't possibly . . ."

"Never mind, Amory," Gil said, gently interrupting my protest. "We'll sort it out. I'm ready, Inspector. We may as well go."

"I don't believe you did it for a moment, Gil," I said, clutching his arm. "I'll do whatever is necessary to clear this matter up. Don't worry."

He smiled. "I know you will, Amory. It will all be all right."

"I apologize for the inconvenience, Mrs. Ames," said the inspector. "I realize my intrusion may have been inopportune."

"I shall be taking this matter up with your superiors, Inspector," I said.

The man actually smiled at me, an amused little smile that I found to be highly annoying. "I'm sorry you feel that way, Mrs. Ames, but you must do what you feel is necessary." He nodded slightly in Milo's direction. "Good evening, Mr. Ames."

"Inspector," he returned. He sounded almost bored, as if this whole thing had been a scene in a play that he didn't find particularly interesting.

Inspector Jones and Gil reached the door, and Gil offered me one last feeble smile before they left. The look in his eyes clutched at my heart. He was worried, despite his assurances to me. Murder was no small charge. Determination welled within me. I certainly wouldn't let him be hanged for a crime that he didn't commit. I would find out who killed Rupert Howe if it was the last thing I did.

"An unpleasant business," Milo said from behind me. He had remained quiet throughout the climactic scene, and for that I was grateful. If he had uttered one of his little bon mots, I may have lost my temper.

I turned to face him. "This is madness. Absolute, utter rubbish."

He rose from his seat. "Let me get you a drink."

"I don't want a drink, thank you."

I paced toward the sofa and then back toward the door. This was terrible. "I should never have told the inspector what I heard. If I'd have thought for a moment that Inspector Jones would misconstrue what I was saying, I would never have spoken with him. Gil didn't kill Mr. Howe. It's utterly preposterous." Despite my shock, the irony of the situation was not lost on me. I had been terribly afraid that someone might implicate Gil, and I had managed to do it myself. How dreadfully stupid I had been.

"You're as pale as death, Amory," he said, pressing the glass into my hand. "But perhaps that is the wrong expression to use at present."

"I don't want it," I said, pushing the drink he had given me back toward him.

"It's only soda water," he replied. "I haven't forgotten your aversion to stronger beverages."

"Thank you, then." I took a sip. Strong beverage or not, the cool crispness of it seemed to help clear my head, which had begun to throb. I pressed my fingertips to my temple.

"And why don't you take these." There was a bottle of aspirin lying on the table, and he picked it up, opened it, and handed me two of the tablets.

"I do have quite a headache." I took the pills and then set the water down before moving to the sofa. I felt suddenly overwhelmed by the events of the evening.

"Gil didn't kill Rupert Howe," I said again. My eyes met Milo's. "You know he didn't."

"I don't know that for certain and neither do you."

"I've known him for years, Milo. Much longer than I've known even you. I *know* him. He wouldn't kill anyone."

"You'd be surprised by what you don't know about the people closest to you," he replied, settling onto the sofa beside me.

"That's nonsense."

"Take me, for example. How much do you know about me, really?"

I looked at him. It was an odd question, but I considered it.

"Not as much as I should, I suppose," I said at last. That wasn't the half of it, but now was not the time to engage in that particular discussion.

"Precisely."

"But I know that you wouldn't kill anyone."

He raised a brow. "Do you?"

"Would you?" I challenged.

He contemplated. "I might. If the occasion called for it."

"Don't be absurd," I said. "In any event, we're not talking about you; we're talking about Gil. Something must be done."

"Well, there will be plenty of time to fret over it tomorrow," he said. "How's your head?"

"It seems to be a bit better, thank you." I reclined against the sofa pillows. For some unaccountable reason, I felt much more relaxed than I had a few moments before.

"Shall I turn down your covers?"

"I can manage. You should probably go to your room," I said with a yawn. "I assume Miss Carter's given up on you by now." Despite my distress, I was suddenly so very sleepy that I could barely keep my eyes open.

"I think I'll wait around a bit longer," Milo said.

I was too tired to argue. "Suit yourself," I said and closed my eyes.

I AWOKE TO the sound of the sea and the warmth of sunlight shining through my window. I lay perfectly still with my eyes closed, enjoying the feeling of being deliciously relaxed and refreshed, as though I had slept for years. When did I fall asleep? What had gone on the night before?

It came back to me in a rush. Gil had been arrested. My eyes opened.

I was vaguely startled to see Milo lying in the bed next to me, his dark hair contrasting with the soft pastel of the pillow, the covers pulled up to his chest. He was wearing his undershirt and, I assumed, the rest of his underclothes. I wore my nightgown, minus negligee. How had we ended up in bed together? Clothed or no, I should have remembered going to bed with him. And then I realized what had happened.

I sat up. My head swarmed momentarily, but the sudden rise of anger quickly cleared it.

"Milo," I shook his shoulder. "Milo!"

He turned his head on the pillow, not opening his eyes. "Hmmm?"

I shook him again, more aggressively. "Wake up."

He opened one eye. "What is it, darling?"

"What did you give me last night?"

He sighed. "What?"

"What did you give me?"

"Soda water."

"No, those pills. What were they?"

"Oh, those." His long black lashes fluttered open, and he looked up at me. "Aspirin. What's the matter with you?"

A fresh wave of anger pulsed through me at the attempted deception. "They were not aspirin. They were sleeping tablets."

He frowned. "Why do you keep sleeping tablets in your aspirin bottle?"

I grabbed the blankets and pulled them off of him. "Get up and get out of here."

"I wondered why you fell asleep so quickly." He folded his

hands behind his head and regarded me with a sleepy smile. "I normally don't have that effect."

I was not at all amused. "You're sure you didn't give me sleeping tablets?"

"I did no such thing." He favored me with a semi-serious expression. "Why would I want to put you to sleep?" Then a wicked grin flashed across his face. "If you're worried, I can assure you nothing untoward occurred. I was the perfect gentleman all evening."

"Don't be ridiculous, Milo. What are you doing in my bed?"

"Sleeping . . . or trying to. It's awfully early."

"For heaven's sake." I tossed aside the portion of the blanket covering me and stood up. The sudden movement sent a wave of dizziness through me, and I clutched the bed for support. For a moment, I was afraid I was going to topple to the floor.

Milo propped himself up on his elbow and regarded me. "Really, Amory, perhaps you better lie down. I think you're overwrought. This murder business has been rough on you."

"I tell you there was something in those pills. I feel as though I'm wading through molasses, Milo. That isn't a common aftereffect of aspirin."

He sat up. "Can I get you something?"

"I'll get some coffee in a bit," I said, sitting down on the edge of the bed. "I'm all right. I . . . I just need a moment."

"Let me ring for coffee." He got up and went to the telephone and called for coffee to be brought to my room.

I made my way into the bathroom. I turned on the sink and washed my face in cool water. I felt strange and not at all well. A glance in the mirror showed that I was also very pale. It was all quite disconcerting.

I returned to the bedroom. Milo had pulled on his trousers and was buttoning his dress shirt. He pulled his cigarette case from his pocket. "Smoke? It may clear your head."

I shook my head as a wave of nausea passed over me. "I feel as though I may be sick."

"Can I do something?"

"Thank you, no. I'm sure it will pass."

"At least sit down," he said.

He came to me and took my arm, leading me over to a chair. Then he sat across from me and watched me as he smoked. "You do look terribly pallid, darling."

"I'll be all right," I replied. "It's just so very odd. I don't know what's come over me."

"Perhaps you're pregnant," he suggested casually.

Our eyes met. It was not a very subtle way of inquiring just how much had been going on between Gil and me while Milo had been away.

I regarded him with raised brow. "Not unless there has been some change in procedure of which I haven't been informed."

Was it my imagination, or did something very like relief cross his eyes? "Well, one can never be certain."

"Sometimes one can."

We looked at one another, neither of us willing to address the elephant in the room. What a farce this marriage was.

We were spared any further awkwardness by a timely knock at the door.

"It's the coffee," I picked up my negligee and pulled it over my nightgown. "As you said, it will be just the thing."

He rose from his chair and went to open the door. The maid came in with a tray, setting it on the table. If she noticed Milo's dishabille, the fact that he was in my room wearing last night's clothes, she gave no sign of it. "Your tea, sir."

"I rang for coffee," Milo said.

"I'm sorry, sir," the maid replied. "Things are all askew at the moment. Everyone is in a flutter. You see, one of the guests tried to commit suicide this morning."

14

"ATTEMPTED SUICIDE? WHO?" My heart began to pound as I feared the worst. "Not Gil...Mr. Trent?"

I felt Milo's eyes on me even as the color drained from my face. The thought that Gil might have harmed himself while in police custody made me feel weak with fear. Would he have done such a rash thing? I didn't think so, but I was beginning to believe there was much about Gil I didn't know. I was not the same as I had been five years ago; neither was he.

"No, madam," the maid answered. "It was a woman, that Miss Henderson."

"Olive Henderson?" I sat down on the sofa. "Why would she do such a thing?" I cast my mind back to the conversation we had had in the sitting room. She had been very unhappy, that was true. But I shouldn't have taken her for the kind of girl to take such drastic action.

The maid shook her head knowingly. "Some women are like that, madam. One never knows what they will do next."

"Yes, I suppose," I commented absently. It just didn't make sense.

The maid would have been happy to go on telling tales, whether or not she knew any further details, but Milo adeptly ushered her to the door and rewarded her handsomely for her gossip.

As the door closed behind her, he turned to me. "I suppose you'll have to settle for tea."

"That will be lovely, thank you."

He poured me a cup and brought it to me, dropping into the seat across.

I took it absently, still lost in thought. "Thank you. Why would Olive Henderson try to kill herself? Surely not for love of Rupert?"

He shrugged. "I assume the story will come out. You know these people can't go any length of time without sharing whatever it is they know."

"It's all so very strange." I took a few sips of the tea as a fresh determination settled within me. "We shall have to go down to breakfast, Milo. I need information."

"Amory, you're not well. You should lie down, not traipse about the hotel embroiling yourself in matters that do not concern you."

I had felt vaguely that way until Gil's arrest, but things were different now. Gil had been wrongfully accused, and I could not stand by and do nothing while a killer went free. Until last night, I had been driven by my own curiosity and a vague sense of unease, but Gil's arrest had raised the stakes considerably. My fears had come to pass, thanks at least in part to my own foolishness, and there was nothing to do now but devote myself completely to the cause of justice, as it were. I had waded into this investigation thus far; now it was time to dive in—headfirst.

"Nonsense." I felt revived by the hot, strong tea and the newfound zeal for my cause. I set my cup and saucer down on the table and stood. "This may have something to do with the murder. We should investigate."

"We?"

I looked down at him, surprised myself that I had included him in my plans. He could prove useful, perhaps, but I suspected his potential usefulness was not what had fueled my impulsive invitation. However, now was not the time to contemplate my personal motives for enlisting the aid of my wayward husband. Instead, I forged ahead.

"Aren't you at all interested in solving a murder?" I asked him.

"In clearing Trent, you mean?" he replied easily. "I'm not sure that I am."

"He's innocent. I'm certain of it."

"I don't particularly care."

"Nonsense, Milo. I know you want to help me."

I didn't, of course, know any such thing. Milo was not generally inclined to be cooperative when it didn't suit him. Nevertheless, he rose, albeit somewhat reluctantly, from his seat.

"Amory darling, I . . ."

I patted his arm, effectively cutting off any sort of protest. "Go put on something appropriate and we'll go down to breakfast. And for goodness's sake, don't let anyone see you skulking out of my room in your evening clothes."

IT OCCURRED TO me as Milo left my room that our party was diminishing day by day. First Rupert's death, then Gil's arrest, and now Olive Henderson's suicide attempt. It was an alarming prospect.

Yet another reason why I should do what I could to investigate.

I bathed and put on a smart dress of navy chiffon with white polka dots over a navy underdress. Though I still felt a bit under the weather, my reflection revealed that, though a bit wan, I looked rested. I still couldn't fathom what might have put me into such a deep sleep. I was fairly certain that the tablets had not been aspirin. In fact, it felt as though I had been given a strong sedative.

I picked up the bottle and opened it, pouring a few of the round, white tablets into my hand. I studied them closely, and I was soon convinced that I was right. They were very similar to aspirin tablets, but I was fairly certain that they were not, in fact, aspirin. How had they come to be in my bottle? Perhaps it wasn't even my bottle. Had I somehow acquired someone else's tablets by mistake? I tried without success to think how such a thing might have happened. It didn't seem at all likely.

The alternative, however, was much less appealing. If it wasn't a mistake, then someone had deliberately tried to drug me. I could think of no reason why Milo should have done such a thing or why anyone else would have. It was very odd. Another piece of the puzzle that I could not seem to explain.

I dropped the pills back into the bottle and slipped it into my handbag. Perhaps I could find some way to have them examined. Apparently, they had been harmless enough, but it was chilling to think the bottle could easily have contained something much less anodyne than sleeping tablets.

If they had been giving some such medicine to Emmeline, it was no wonder she had been unable to see anyone. Thinking of Emmeline, the thought suddenly occurred to me that she was no doubt in a state this morning. If, that is, she had heard of Gil's arrest. If she hadn't, it would probably be best that I break it to her gently. I needed to see her immediately.

When Milo tapped on the door of my room, I was ready for him.

"I've forgotten Emmeline," I said as I stepped into the hallway, trying not to notice how very handsome he looked, cleanly shaved and wearing a light-gray suit. "The poor dear probably has no idea what's become of Gil. I'm going to speak with her."

"Before breakfast? First, you have me up at this absurdly early hour, and now you want to deprive me of sustenance."

"No, dearest," I told him. "You shall have your breakfast. It will be your duty to spy upon our fellow travelers."

"Really, darling..." He was protesting, but I was certain I saw amusement in his eyes. I suspected that the idea of inserting ourselves into a murder investigation appealed to his reckless streak. Though it was entirely possible he would be more of a hindrance than a help, I thought we just might yield results if we collaborated. Together, we were quite a capable pair.

Though I didn't like to admit it, I suspected that this was at least part of the reason I had drafted him into service; it would be nice to feel like partners in some endeavor, however fleeting it might be.

"Come now," I said. "You know you will enjoy it, and you may as well make yourself useful."

"Very well. I'm sure I shall be able to provoke Mr. Hamilton into making some sort of revealing statement." He grinned. "Shall I take notes?"

He was going to enjoy this, perhaps too much.

"Just see what you can find out," I said, walking toward the lift.

"And after breakfast, your room or mine?"

"Mine. Veronica Carter may still be hanging about yours."

"I didn't invite her to my room, you know."

I turned, wondering if I could trust the sincerity in his expression. "Let's not talk about it now, though I'd like very much for us to finish this conversation at some point."

"Yes, Amory. I should like that, too."

MILO DISPATCHED TO the breakfast room, I went to see Emmeline. She opened the door to her room almost immediately when I knocked.

"Oh, Amory," she said. An aura of distress hung about her like a cloud. Her face was pale and taut, and she was visibly trembling. The poor thing looked as though a slight breeze could topple her.

I entered the room, shutting the door behind me, and took her arm, leading her to the sofa. "Do sit down, dear. You look all in."

"Amory," she clutched my arm with frigid fingers. "Have you heard about Gil?"

"Yes, I've heard. It will be all right."

"The inspector came by last night to tell me . . . Gil didn't kill Rupert. He would never . . ."

"I know, dear."

"How could anyone believe that he could do such a thing?" Though I was no medical expert, I thought she seemed on the edge of nervous collapse.

"Has the doctor been here this morning, Emmeline?"

"I . . . think so, yes." She rubbed a hand across her face. "I . . . I'm so tired, Amory."

The poor thing was extremely distraught. She seemed as though she might break down completely at any moment, and I found the prospect a bit alarming.

"Have you eaten, Emmeline?" I asked.

"No. I'm not hungry."

"That will never do," I said. "You've got to keep your strength up."

I moved to the telephone and ordered a light breakfast. It was only a matter of minutes before the food was brought up, a little tray with some porridge, toast with butter and jam, and a dish of fruit.

"Now, dear, you must eat some of this," I said.

"I couldn't."

"You must keep your strength up. For Gil's sake. He may need you."

She wavered, then nodded. "Yes, you're right, Amory."

I supervised while she took tiny bites of each of the dishes in turn. It was not a hearty breakfast by any means, but at least it was nourishing. Emmeline looked as though she had lost a good deal of weight in just the last few days.

I wondered if she had heard about Olive Henderson, but I felt that this was not, perhaps, the best time to bring it up.

"Why do they think he did it?" she asked.

I hesitated. There was really no need to conceal the truth. "They think he didn't want you to marry Rupert."

"Oh, I know he didn't," she said, to my surprise. "Gil never liked Rupert, not from the start. The day they met, there was a noticeable coolness between them, as though Gil had already made up his mind about Rupert . . ."

"Did you . . ." I hesitated, not wanting to upset her. "Did you ask him what he had against Rupert?"

Had Emmeline paused before she spoke? Her eyes darted away for a moment before coming back to mine. "I suppose it was just in Gil's nature to be protective of me." It was a careful answer, and I realized that despite her distress she was still very much on her guard.

I was beginning to find it immensely frustrating to be met with such chariness at every turn.

"There must have been some reason." I pressed. "Gil isn't the type of man to take an instant dislike to anyone without reason."

"I...I don't know," she answered, and, to my horror, her eyes began to fill with tears. "I only know that I was the only one who really understood Rupert, and now he's gone..."

"I'm sorry, Emmeline. I didn't mean to upset you," I said. This was very distressing. Perhaps I should have sent Milo to speak with Emmeline. He would have handled the situation with much more finesse, I was sure.

"I don't mean to cry. Everything is just so terrible." She swiped at her tears. "But you must know that Gil's innocent. He never would have killed Rupert just because he didn't like him...He didn't kill him. He didn't."

"I know," I said, rising from my seat. "And rest assured, Emmeline, I'm going to find out who did."

WALKING AWAY FROM Emmeline's room, I realized that I had made quite a commitment. Finding Rupert's killer would be difficult, and there was every possibility that it could be dangerous. Nevertheless, I remained undaunted. I did not believe for a moment that Gil was guilty of this crime, and I did not intend that he should hang for it.

Milo was waiting in my room when I arrived, lounging on my sofa and thumbing disinterestedly through the novel I had been reading.

"Well," I said without preamble, "did you learn anything?"

He tossed the book aside. "It seems Olive Henderson went at

her wrists with a razor blade. I had a tray sent up for you." He indicated the silver tray that sat on the table. I lifted the lid. It was cold porridge, which I abhorred, but I thought it sweet of him to think of me.

"Her wrists? How ghastly." I sat down on the chair opposite him, the rapid pace of the morning beginning to catch up with me. I was still somewhat drowsy, though the heavy lethargy seemed to have worn off.

"I thought it rather theatrical myself."

"How terribly insensitive of you," I remarked. "After all, the girl might have died."

"Well, she didn't. Eat your porridge, Amory. You look as though you need nourishment."

"I'm not hungry, thank you. She'll live then?"

"Yes, she did a poor job of it, it seems."

"What do you mean?

"Either she had reservations about actually seeing it through or she's weak as a kitten. The wounds weren't deep enough to do serious harm. They probably won't even require stitching."

I was actually quite impressed. "Milo, how in the world did you manage to discover all of this?"

He smiled. "A truly competent investigator never reveals his sources."

"Oh, so you're an investigator now, are you?"

"I thought I might as well try my hand at it," he said, sitting back in the sofa, that familiar gleam in his eyes indicating one of his rare bouts of enthusiasm. It had been a long time since I had seen him look that way. I felt an unwarranted bit of satisfaction, as though I was somehow responsible for capturing his interest.

"Anything more?" I asked.

"Not much. Miss Henderson was the sole topic of conversation this morning; no one was talking of anything else."

"Well, I must say you did well," I told him.

He smiled. "This is shaping up to be more amusing than Monte Carlo. And what of you? Did you learn anything from Emmeline?"

I sighed. "She's nearly gone to pieces. I'm not sure how much longer she shall be able to hold it all together. She seems to be in a constant state of near hysteria. Of course, she's been through so much. Were our situations reversed, I'm sure I should not be in a much better state."

"Nonsense," Milo said. "You'd bear up."

I wasn't sure if it was a compliment or a criticism, so I replied with a light tone. "Do you think so?"

He tossed me a grin. "Naturally. If I were to be murdered, I would leave you with heaps of money and free to do as you please."

I stood and turned toward the door. "You needn't be murdered for that," I replied, looking back over my shoulder. "I could just as easy accomplish it with a divorce."

"Touché, my love," he said.

MY FIRST COURSE of action after parting ways with Milo was to visit the police station to see Inspector Jones. I didn't feel he had dealt fairly with Gil, or with me for that matter, and I intended to see what I could do about it.

Milo's objective would be to gain whatever information possible from the rest of the guests. His usual lack of interest in what people had to say could prove invaluable in this situation. I hoped people would be willing to speak to him, thinking it of little consequence. There was always the possibility that someone might give away a telling bit of information without meaning to.

Inspector Jones was occupied when I arrived, but the helpful sergeant gave him my message, and it was only a few moments before I was ushered into his office. The space was well kept and orderly, as I would have expected his office to be. There were few personal items to be seen, save a photograph of the inspector with a pretty dark-haired woman I thought might be his wife. He sat behind a desk covered in neat stacks of paper. Everything about the place bespoke quiet efficiency.

He rose when I entered. "Mrs. Ames," he said. Though he didn't smile exactly, there was a pleasant expression on his face, as though he were not altogether displeased to see me. I had the feeling that he was amused by me, which I found grating, and the begrudging sense of admiration I had felt for his competence had been shaken by Gil's arrest. Nevertheless, he was obviously an intelligent man, and I hoped that he would come to see reason.

The heat of anger with him had faded since last night. Nevertheless, I was still disinclined to be friendly. "I think you know why I've come, Inspector," I said coolly, seating myself in the hard wooden chair he had indicated.

"You feel that I abused my position when you spoke in confidence to me," he said without preamble. "That's understandable, and I'm sorry you feel that way. Nevertheless, if Mr. Trent is guilty of murder, it is my duty to see that he is arrested and charged for it." There was something in his calm logic that diffused my indignation. I couldn't very well fault the man for carrying out his duty, however misguided he might be.

"Very well. I can accept that," I replied. "But you've made a very grave mistake. Gil Trent no more killed Rupert Howe than you did."

He regarded me for a long moment before speaking. "May I be frank with you, Mrs. Ames?"

"I wish you would be, Inspector."

He chose his words carefully. "I think, perhaps, that you are letting your, shall we say, affection for Mr. Trent influence your judgment."

I considered this possibility for only a moment before dismissing it. "I know Gil, Inspector," I replied. "He didn't do it."

"Were you there when Rupert Howe was killed?"

"No."

"Then you cannot tell me with any certainty that you know what did or did not happen on the cliff that day."

I realized then that anything I could say was only vain repetition of last night's sentiments, but I could think of no other way to convince him of my sincere belief in Gil's innocence.

"I am not just some meddling fool, Inspector."

He met my gaze. "I don't believe for a moment that you are, Mrs. Ames. Far from it. But consider it from my position. If you had reason to believe a man was guilty, would you take the word of a woman who had, if you'll pardon my saying so, rather a vested interest in the outcome of this investigation?"

I wondered if he assumed there was more between Gil and me than I had let on. "There is nothing between Gil and myself but an old friendship," I said.

"Whether it is an old friendship or something more is really none of my concern," he replied smoothly. "The fact of that matter is that I did not arrest Mr. Trent solely on the information you related to me. There are other factors to be considered."

I remembered then what he had said in my room the night before. "Who told you they had seen him on the terrace with Rupert that afternoon?"

He smiled placidly. "As I said last night, I'm not at liberty to divulge that information at present."

He really was the most infuriating man.

I was not going to concede so easily. "Supposing someone did see him on the terrace. That doesn't mean he killed Rupert."

"That, in itself, is not sufficient, no. When combined with a good motive, supplied by you, and backed by an apparently long history of bad blood between the two men, it puts things in a different light."

"But wasn't his arrest rather premature? Did you even speak with the other members of our party? They all seemed startled to learn it was murder."

Inspector Jones reached to the corner of his desk and held up a file, thick with paper. "My dossier on the guests of the Brightwell, Mrs. Ames. Thorough histories, including those of you and your husband. Very interesting reading."

I didn't know what inference he was attempting to make, so I ignored it. "Then you must know there are others with motive."

He looked at me speculatively for a moment. "I'd be interested to know what it is you think you know, Mrs. Ames."

I mentally chided myself for revealing my hand once again. He really was much too perceptive, this inspector.

"I've heard things," I replied evasively.

"Yes, I expect you have," he said, leaning back in his seat. "Anything in particular?"

As if I should be inclined to take him into my confidence now. "I doubt rumors would be useful to you, Inspector."

"Perhaps not. Then again, many a murderer has been caught with useful information gleaned from rumors."

"Then you agree that Gil is not the only one who could have done it," I said, pouncing upon his admission.

"Certainly . . . which is why I've instructed all the members of your party not to leave the hotel just yet."

This bit of news came as a surprise to me. I hadn't heard that the guests had been told not to leave. "Then you're not convinced it was Gil?"

"I arrested Mr. Trent because he appears to be guilty. I would be remiss in my duties if I did otherwise. I cannot ignore the evidence. But rest assured, Mrs. Ames. I have not closed the book on this investigation just yet."

Was he trying to tell me something? I couldn't be certain. He was so exasperatingly hard to read, almost as bad as Milo. One thing I did know: he wasn't going to give me any more information at present.

"Is Mr. Trent all right?" I asked.

"He is being very well cared for."

"May I speak with him?"

"I'm afraid that won't be possible just now. Perhaps if you'd come back tomorrow?"

I rose, knowing there was no point in detaining him further. "I shall be here in the morning."

He smiled. "I am sure you will, Mrs. Ames."

I WAS WEARY and disappointed as I returned to the Brightwell. If I had expected to swoop in and discover a murderer within a few hours, I had greatly overestimated my abilities. I had hoped to glean something from Inspector Jones, but he was determined to play his cards close to his chest. I would have to see what I could learn on my own.

The lobby was fairly empty, for it was a beautiful day and most of the guests were taking advantage of the beach after the day of rain. I knew that Rupert's death had elicited great curiosity at the Brightwell, but thus far people had been content to watch and whisper from afar.

I stopped at the desk, where I was given a letter from Laurel. I put it in my pocket, looking forward to reading it. Laurel always had a way of lifting my spirits, and I was sorely in need of a bit of encouragement at the moment.

I was walking toward the lift when I caught the sound of conversation and laughter coming from a table in the corner. Almost immediately, I recognized the speaker was Milo. Curious to see whom he had engaged in conversation, and hoping it would prove to be in connection with our investigation, I walked to where I could have a vantage point without being seen.

I was more than surprised to discover that the laughter belonged to Larissa Hamilton. She and Milo were seated where I could see them in profile. It was the first time I had ever seen Mrs. Hamilton look completely at ease. Her posture was relaxed as she sat across from my husband, a smile lighting her face, making her look prettier than I had ever seen her.

Milo leaned toward her and said something, and the soft peal of laughter broke out again.

If I had not heard it and not known Milo, I wouldn't have believed it. She was positively aglow. It seemed my faith in Milo's charms was justified.

I moved away before either of them could spot me.

I had just turned back toward the lift when I saw Mr. Rodgers enter the hotel sitting room. Now seemed as good a moment as ever to do a bit of investigating of my own. I might not possess Milo's charisma, but I felt fairly confident that I could learn something . . . if, that is, there was something to be learned.

I entered the room on the pretext of finishing the letter I had begun writing to Laurel.

"Oh, Mr. Rodgers," I said, feigning pleasant surprise upon encountering him. "How are you?"

"Well, thank you," he replied. "Though I have some rather urgent business to attend to."

I expected that was a hint that he wished to be left alone, but I pretended not to notice.

"It's a shame it must interfere with your holiday," I said, taking a seat at the writing table.

"Yes, well . . ." His voice trailed off as he began to read over the paper in his hand.

This was not working as well as I had hoped. He seemed to have very little interest in conversation. I decided perhaps a direct approach would fare best. "What do you think of this murder business?"

He looked up at me. "I think it's highly unlikely that Gil Trent had anything to do with it," he said. "I've wired Sir Andrew Heath, one of the best barristers in London."

"Gil will be grateful you've selected someone for him," I said.

"Gil asked me to send for Sir Andrew," Mr. Rodgers replied, his eyes back on the document before him.

This bit of news caught me by surprise. "Gil asked you . . . when?"

"Yesterday morning."

"Before he was arrested?"

"Yes," he looked up at me again, very little interest in his tone or expression. "He must have guessed that that inspector suspected him. He asked me right after breakfast if I knew of a good barrister. I suggested Sir Andrew at once."

I was silent while I digested this latest bit of information. Why would Gil have requested the advice of a barrister before he knew he was going to be arrested? It just didn't make sense. It must have been something to do with what Gil had been trying to tell me last night. I would need to see him as soon as possible. Perhaps he could tell me what was going on.

Mr. Rodgers and I lapsed into silence. He seemed disinclined to continue our conversation, and I felt that any further attempts on my part might be perceived as intrusive. I began a second letter to Laurel without opening the one she had sent me. I knew she would be intrigued by the latest developments. I had just finished writing it when Veronica Carter entered the sitting room.

She acknowledged me with a nod, not the least bit self-conscious that she had tried to seduce my husband only the night before. Under the circumstances, I found my feelings were barely civil. I returned her nod because I was bred to be polite.

She glanced at Mr. Rodgers, but he did not look up from his papers. I was rather surprised when she came and sat in the chair beside the writing desk. She said nothing for a moment, and I wondered what this was leading up to.

She looked a bit less haughty than usual, as though she had deflated somehow, and I felt an unwanted twinge of sympathy for her.

At last, she seemed to have formed the words she was seeking. "It's dreadful about Olive, isn't it?" she said. Though her features were perfectly composed, there seemed to be genuine sadness in her eyes, and the usual cool confidence of her voice had faded into a sort of soft uncertainty.

"Yes," I agreed. "I was sorry to hear about that. I understand she should be all right, which is good news."

"I went to the hospital. They wouldn't let me see her." I was surprised that she should have gone out of her way to visit Olive, but perhaps I was judging her harshly.

"I can't understand why she would do such a thing," she went on, almost as though she was speaking to herself.

"Perhaps . . . because of Rupert?" I suggested.

Her gaze came up to me, somewhat sharply, I thought. "No, it couldn't be. Olive didn't care for Rupert," she said.

I wondered how well Veronica really knew her friend. Olive had seemed quite upset when I had spoken to her in the sitting room. Perhaps she had loved Rupert more than anyone was aware. Or perhaps she had another reason . . .

"I understood that they cared for one another before Rupert met Emmeline."

"Oh, perhaps a little flirtation, but nothing serious. But Rupert was like that. Even in Monte Carlo, he . . ." She stopped, as though aware she might be saying too much, but then finished airily. "He was always something of a flirt."

Rupert had been in Monte Carlo as well? Milo had never mentioned that to me.

"And now he's gone, and Olive . . . It's dreadful here now, isn't it?" she said. "I would leave at once, if that awful inspector hadn't insisted we remain."

"It will be over soon enough," I said.

"Yes, I suppose it will." She stood then, and the indifferent mask had slipped back into place, but not before I realized that perhaps we were not so very different, after all. For the first time, I realized that Veronica Carter was much like me: a young woman from an affluent family, facing a difficult situation without the benefit of anyone on whom she could completely rely.

———

BY THE TIME I left the sitting room, Milo and Mrs. Hamilton were no longer anywhere to be seen. I wanted to know if he had learned anything from Mrs. Hamilton, but there would be time for that later. I simply didn't feel up to Milo at the moment.

I returned to my room, contemplating the events of the morning. The inspector's criticism had done little to shake my confidence in Gil's innocence, but this newest development regarding the barrister was difficult to explain away. Perhaps Mr. Rodgers was correct. Perhaps Gil had been aware that suspicion was likely to shift in his direction and had chosen to be prepared.

And then there had been something in the inspector's manner that had puzzled me. He seemed as though he knew more than he was saying. I could not rid myself of the feeling that he had meant to tell me something, though I couldn't begin to imagine what it was. I hoped that he would prove to be my ally in this; if he was not set on Gil's guilt, perhaps he could find who had really killed Rupert Howe.

I opened the door to my room, still lost in thought. Then I stopped. Something was amiss, out of place. It took me only a moment to realize what it was. It was not that something was missing but that something had been added. A glance into the bathroom confirmed my suspicions. Stepping to the wardrobe and flinging it open, I felt a surge of indignation.

Milo had had all of his things moved into my room.

16

I CHECKED IN on Emmeline before I went downstairs and found that she was eating a quiet dinner in her room. Her color had improved, and she seemed in slightly better spirits. "I don't know how I shall make it without . . . without Rupert, but I couldn't bear it if something should happen to Gil," she said. "I feel so much better knowing you're doing what you can to help him."

I only hoped it would be enough. I felt the great weight of her confidence upon my shoulders.

"Emmeline," I ventured after a moment, "can you think of any reason anyone might have killed Rupert?" I had been hesitant to ask her anything concerning his death, but who was in a better position to know?

She paused and, to my relief, appeared to calmly consider it. "I've thought and thought about it, but I just don't know why anyone would . . . would do such a thing. He got along with everyone, except perhaps Olive. They had been . . . close at one point."

"You knew about that?" I asked, surprised.

"Yes, it was common knowledge, though Rupert said there was really nothing to it. And I don't think for a moment that Olive would have done anything so dreadful."

I thought of what Mrs. Hamilton had told me and decided to press ahead with my questions. "But didn't Olive say she wanted to meet with Rupert that night? I was given to understand they were talking as you all came up from the beach. Perhaps they met and quarreled."

Emmeline frowned and shook her head. "No, I don't think she said any such thing. We all walked up at the same time and perhaps Olive and Rupert fell into step together, but they usually tried to avoid one another. I'm certain they cared nothing for each other. You see, she . . ." She hesitated a moment, as if about to say something, and then shook her head again. "Well . . . they just didn't care for one another. They certainly wouldn't have wanted to meet."

I kept my opinion on this to myself. I was relieved she didn't ask where I had acquired my information. I knew how uneasy Mrs. Hamilton had been in relating the story. Perhaps she was right in doubting herself. She may have misheard, or perhaps she had been correct in her assessment that the noise from the sea had been too loud for Emmeline to overhear the conversation.

Still, I could not convince myself to dismiss it.

I WAS EARLY for dinner. Edward and Anne Rodgers were already at the table when I arrived.

Mr. Rodgers still appeared preoccupied, but Anne Rodgers and I chatted about mundane things for a few moments. I had the impression that she was chatting on to fill the silence. We discussed neither the murder nor Olive, and I found I didn't have the will to bring either topic up at the moment.

The rest of the guests trickled in to the dining room, and soon our usual group was all in attendance. It was somewhat strange how we all marched on, as one by one our members dropped away to one unfortunate fate or another.

"You're looking lovely this evening," Milo said, sliding into the seat beside me, eyeing my sleeveless, fitted gown of sapphire-colored satin. "I've always fancied you in blue."

"You're looking rather lovely yourself," I replied. "I see your dinner clothes were not among the things you had transferred to my room."

"Ah, so you noticed."

"I did."

Larissa and Nelson Hamilton arrived at our table, and Milo rose with the other gentlemen until Larissa was seated. He spoke to her, and her face lit up. She said something too quiet for me to hear, and Milo laughed. They seemed to have developed quite the camaraderie over the course of the afternoon.

Taking his seat again, he turned to me and said in a low voice, "I thought, perhaps, since we are partners in this endeavor, we might make your room our headquarters, so to speak."

I placed my napkin in my lap. "Does that necessitate your sleeping there?"

"Don't you want me to sleep there, Amory?" he asked. He was speaking so close to my ear that I couldn't see his face. I couldn't be sure if the low caressing tone was meant in earnest or if he was merely teasing me.

"What do you think about them keeping us here against our will, Ames?" For once I was grateful for Mr. Hamilton's intrusiveness.

This was not a conversation I wished to have with Milo at the dinner table.

"Are we here against our will, Mr. Hamilton?" Milo asked, picking up his wineglass. "I thought we were here on holiday."

"They sent a policeman round to inform us that we aren't to leave, didn't they? I'd say that's being held against my will!"

"In any event, it's usually best to cooperate with the police," Mr. Rodgers put in.

"Well, I don't like it!"

"It isn't as though they've locked us up, Nelson," Mrs. Hamilton said quietly.

"Nonsense, Larissa. You don't know a thing about it. They've caught their man. Why should we be forced to remain here?"

"You can't mean you think Gil is guilty of Rupert's death," Mrs. Rodgers protested. "He's much too sweet-tempered to do any such thing."

"One can never tell," Mr. Hamilton said.

"I shouldn't think Gil capable of any such thing," I said mildly. "I have no doubt everything will be straightened out directly." Though I longed to speak heartily in his defense, I thought perhaps I could best serve my aims by maintaining the pretense of confidence in the police. To protest too loudly might draw attention to the fact that I was somehow involved in the case. It would be better for me to say as little as possible, though I hated not being able to speak more heatedly of my indignation at Gil's wrongful imprisonment.

I looked up and found Milo was watching me with a sardonic gleam in his eyes, a thinly veiled smile of mocking hovering on his mouth. He knew perfectly well what I was feeling, and he was relishing my discomfort.

"I'm sure Mrs. Ames is right," Anne Rodgers concluded. "It was probably an accident...or...or some stranger..." Her voice trailed off, and I knew what she was thinking. If, in fact, it wasn't Gil, it was most likely that it was another one of us.

"Did they say what the weapon was?"

"A blunt instrument," I replied, recalling what I had heard at the inquest. "Not too thick and probably with a smooth edge. I don't believe the police have found it."

"This is horrid dinner conversation," Anne Rodgers said suddenly. Of course, she was right.

The conversation eventually turned to trivialities, as though everyone had wearied of such dreary topics. Talk turned to the weather, and most members of the party were making plans for sea bathing in the morning. How quickly they forgot the calamities that had befallen their friends.

Though Mr. Hamilton had protested the need to remain at the Brightwell, I felt that it was more the idea of the thing with which he disagreed. After all, he had told me himself that he intended to finish out his holiday. None of the group seemed much inconvenienced by the inspector's order, and it seemed that, for the most part, life would continue to go on as usual.

The last of the plates was cleared away, and, as the dancing began, the others rose to take coffee and drinks in the sitting room. As they began to take their leave, I remained in my seat. The events of the day and all that I had learned were weighing heavily upon my mind, and I sat for a moment, lost in thought.

Milo turned to me, draping his arm across the back of my chair. "What are you thinking about?"

I turned my attention to him, noticing how very close he was. "Why do you ask?"

"Your eyes go all blue at the edges when you're preoccupied."

"Do they?" I was surprised he had noticed such a thing.

"Yes, and they turn a peculiar silver shade when you're angry. You've lovely eyes, Amory." His tone, though light, lacked its usual quality of artificial affection.

My gaze met his. There it was again. That sudden spark of something between us. I never knew how to take Milo's little bursts of sweetness. It was not that I suspected him of insincerity. It was just that his sincerity was so short-lived I dared not become accustomed to it.

"Thank you," I said, passing lightly over the compliment. "You're right. I was lost in thought. I went to visit Inspector Jones today."

"Ah. And what does the good inspector have to say?" He removed his arm from my chair and sat back, the subtle shift in his posture indicating that we had lost the intimacy of the moment. Though that had been my goal, I found that I felt vaguely disappointed.

"Not much. He's a tight-lipped sort of person. He . . . he wouldn't let me see Gil."

Milo said nothing to this. It was probably the wrong thing to say. For some reason, I seemed to find myself saying all the wrong things as of late.

"I noticed you have formed an acquaintance with Larissa Hamilton," I went on.

"Yes, we had rather a long chat today."

"And what do you make of her?"

"She's not so retiring as people think, not once she's been warmed up."

"Indeed." I could just imagine Milo's flattering attentions, just the kind of thing to warm a neglected woman like Mrs. Hamilton.

"She's quiet because she's unhappy and she hates it here, but that's not all of it. It seems to me there's something she's hiding. She's afraid of something." He was relating these things in an offhanded sort of way, and I sensed that the conversation was losing his interest. His eyes had drifted to the doorway, through which the rest of the party had departed, and his sun-bronzed hand toyed with the napkin on the table.

"Odds are, it's her husband," I said. "Does he harm her, do you think?" Though we were quite alone at the table, I had lowered my voice and found that I was leaning toward Milo in a conspiratorial way. His gaze flickered back to me.

"She wouldn't, of course, have confided in me if he did."

"I think women find it easy to confide in you," I said lightly.

There was no amusement in his eyes as he looked at me. "You don't."

"Mr. and Mrs. Ames," called Lionel Blake suddenly from the doorway. "Would you care for a rubber of bridge? We're two short."

Milo stood and turned to me, a bland, pleasant expression on his features. "Care to, darling?"

"Well, I . . ." There was little use. It was perfectly clear to me that I had lost Milo for the moment. I stood, managing a smile. "I would love to."

I QUITE LIKED to play bridge. I found I enjoyed the mental challenge. Milo, I knew, didn't particularly care for the game, but he was very good when he set his mind to it. As in most things, he was perfectly capable of excelling when he felt so inclined.

I partnered with Lionel Blake, and Milo partnered with Mrs. Hamilton. Mr. Hamilton and Mrs. Rodgers were East and West to Mr. Rodgers's and Miss Carter's North and South.

There was little talk during the game, and nothing of consequence. A Bakelite radio sat on a table in the sitting room, and Mrs. Rodgers turned the dial until she tuned it to BBC, the cheerful strains of an orchestra spilling out into the room. Everyone seemed determined to ignore the fact that there had been a murder, an arrest, and an attempted suicide in the past few days. I couldn't exactly say I blamed them. The mounting stress of it all was beginning to prove trying to my nerves, and I felt constantly on edge, as though waiting for the next calamity to befall us.

The game progressed, but my mind was not in it. I was preoccupied, and I'm afraid I wasn't the best of partners. Lionel Blake and I couldn't seem to make a go of it. Milo, it seemed, was served well by the combination of a competitive streak and genuine skill, honed by years at the roulette wheel and baccarat table. He and Mrs. Hamilton bid rather aggressively and trounced us soundly.

"I'm afraid I was rather a sorry partner this evening," I told Lionel Blake as we tallied our defeat.

"I think you play very well," said Mrs. Hamilton. It was gracious of her, considering she and Milo had just managed a small slam.

After our game dissolved, we took seats about the room and Mr. Blake and Milo fetched us coffee while the others continued their play. Mr. Rodgers and Miss Carter prevailed, much to Mr. Hamilton's obvious dissatisfaction.

He patted his pockets irritably. "Confound it. I haven't any cigarettes. Larissa, give me yours," he snapped.

"I . . . I haven't got them."

"What do you mean, you haven't got them?" He grabbed her handbag and rummaged in it as the rest of us tried not to increase Mrs. Hamilton's mortification by appearing to pay attention. He apparently located her cigarette case and found it empty, for he shoved her bag back at her. "Why bother keeping a cigarette case if you can't remember to put cigarettes in it?" he grumbled.

"I so rarely smoke, Hamilton," she said softly. "I simply forgot."

"Have one of mine," Milo offered.

Larissa smiled her thanks at Milo as Mr. Hamilton proceeded to sit down and smoke sulkily.

I was waiting to see if I could catch a moment alone with Lionel Blake. I was very curious to learn the outcome of his recent expedition. He seemed very at ease, and I wondered if perhaps some of his employer's financial difficulties might have been resolved.

He proposed another round, and Mr. and Mrs. Rodgers agreed, which left them one short.

Veronica Carter declined, excusing herself for the night. She had paid very little attention to Milo this evening, and I assumed that his spending the night in my room had been a clear enough message.

"Mr. or Mrs. Ames?" Lionel asked.

"I think not," Milo replied. "I'm anxious to retire." His eyes met mine, and I was certain I saw a definite challenge in them. Neither of us had forgotten that he was expecting to share my room this evening, but I had not yet decided if I intended to allow it.

"I think I shall also call it a night," I said. "I'm rather tired."

"Mr. or Mrs. Hamilton, then?" Mr. Blake questioned.

Not surprisingly, Mr. Hamilton declined. He had not relished his defeat, and I felt sure he would not give his foes another chance to triumph. "No, I suppose it's time for bed," he said, rising from his seat. "Ready, Larissa?"

"Not just yet, Nelson," she answered. "I think I shall play another rubber with the others."

She didn't look at him as she spoke, as though she were worried that a disapproving glance might change her mind. I dare say she was right. Something like displeasure crossed his face, but it was instantly smoothed away, and he smiled. "Very well, old girl. Suit yourself. Good night all." And with that, he turned and left the room.

"Oh, blast," Lionel Blake said. "My pencil's gone dull. Have you another, Mrs. Ames?"

"In my handbag, I think." I looked around me, suddenly conscious of the fact I had not seen my handbag in some time. "I must have left it in the dining room," I said, rising. "I'll just go get it."

"Shall I fetch it for you, darling?" Milo asked.

"Thank you," I said, "but I'll get it."

I went back to the dining room. They had cleared the tables, so I ventured to the front desk, where the clerk returned it to me.

Turning back toward the sitting room, I stopped as I caught sight of Mr. Hamilton. Something about his manner struck me as strange. He was standing in an open place in the middle of the lobby, and he seemed to sway slightly, as though his body could not quite decide the direction he was going to take. He hadn't spotted me, and I slipped behind a potted palm in a shadowy corner, knowing he was not likely to see me unless I called attention to myself.

I thought for a moment that he was entering the hotel from the terrace, perhaps having taken in a bit of evening air before retiring. However, I quickly saw that he was not approaching the lift. In fact, as I watched, he glanced back toward the sitting room, as if to be sure that no one had observed him. Then he opened the door and slipped out onto the terrace.

Had it not been for the glance over his shoulder, I might have thought nothing of it. As it was, it seemed a very strange and furtive thing to do. Without a further thought, I moved toward the doors leading out to the terrace. If I should encounter him, I would merely say I was getting some air.

There were few guests about at this hour, though the strains of music still floated out from where dancing was going on in the dining room. A couple sat talking in the lobby, but they were engrossed in conversation, and I slipped out onto the terrace unnoticed.

He had exited the terrace on the west side of the building, where we had taken tea the day I first arrived. However, when I glanced around, he was not there. I followed the terrace around to the south side of the building, facing the sea. A gentle, salty breeze rose to meet me, and I could hear the sound of the waves breaking on the beach below.

When I reached the seaward terrace, I discovered that Mr. Hamilton had not stopped to linger in the moonlight. In fact, I didn't see him anywhere. It seemed highly unlikely to me that he should have followed the terrace around to the east side of the building. The only place he could have gone was down the steps toward the cliff terrace or the beach.

I walked to the top of the stairs and looked down. He was indeed making his way, somewhat surreptitiously it seemed to me, down the staircase. In his evening clothes, he was certainly not dressed for sea bathing, and a moonlight excursion seemed highly suspicious.

I decided at once that my only recourse was to follow him.

Gathering the hem of my gown in my hand, I began my descent. Of course, it would be difficult to make my way down the winding stairs toward the beach without being seen, especially as the satin of my gown seemed to fairly gleam in the dim moonlight. If he should catch me lurking behind him, I should have a difficult time explaining. I waited until he had made significant progress before I ventured after him. Luckily for me, the gentle lull of the wind and waves made enough noise to mute my footsteps as I descended.

Mr. Hamilton moved at a steady pace, with definite purpose, it seemed to me. I wondered, for a moment, if the cliff terrace might be his destination. Perhaps there was some reason he should want to visit the scene of the crime.

Truth be told, I had harbored hopes that Mr. Hamilton might be the guilty party. I had never cared for the man, and he seemed the type who would not be opposed to bashing someone in the head. I could think of little motive, however, unless Rupert had attempted to trifle with Mrs. Hamilton. That seemed highly unlikely. I had barely so much as seen Rupert glance Mrs. Hamilton's way.

Mr. Hamilton reached the point where the steps led off to the terrace or toward the beach, and he continued down without a glance toward the terrace. I followed along behind. My shoes were not made for such strenuous activity, and more than once my heel caught between the slats in the wooden steps. When the path gave way to pebbles, I reached down and removed my shoes entirely. The sensation of the stones beneath my stocking feet was not altogether pleasant.

When I finally reached the beach, I could make out Mr. Hamilton walking at a brisk pace away from the path. The moon was not exceptionally bright, but I could still see him quite clearly. He seemed preoccupied, and I could only hope that, if he should choose to glance behind him, I would not be noticeable in the distance.

He stopped at the base of the cliff, just below the cliff terrace. His eyes were on the ground, and he seemed to be making a thorough search, kicking debris this way and that with his feet. He had not brought a light with him, and I could only suppose that he did not want to draw attention to his already highly suspicious behavior. The ground just there was littered with an array of flotsam and jetsam tossed up by the sea. There were rocks, shells, great pieces of driftwood, and an assortment of other things I had not taken the time to catalog.

Suddenly, he reached down and snatched something from the ground, examining it closely in the dim light. From this distance, I couldn't make out what it was, but I saw it glimmer briefly in the moonlight before he shoved it quickly into his pocket.

Then he was walking rapidly back toward the stairs. I turned around and started up as quickly as I could.

I reached the steps and began taking them two at a time. I'm sure I made quite a sight, sprinting up the wooden flight in an evening gown and stocking feet. I knew instinctively that I would not be able to reach the top before he did. There was no way I could escape detection.

A glance over my shoulder showed me that he was making his way up the pebbled path toward the steps. He was watching his feet as he moved over the uneven ground, and I didn't think he had spotted me yet, but it was only a matter of time.

Then I looked up and started as a figure appeared before me. Milo had followed me down and was on the landing. "Amory, what on earth . . ."

There was no time to explain. Mr. Hamilton would be coming up behind me at any moment; we could not make it up without being spotted. There was nothing else to be done.

Dropping my shoes, I flung myself into Milo's arms and kissed him.

17

IF I WORRIED that Milo might have questioned my sudden show of affection, I needn't have. He responded very readily indeed. In the space of a moment, he had embraced me and pressed me against the railing. By the time I became aware of Mr. Hamilton's heavy approaching tread, I was quite sure that it was Milo who was kissing me, and not the other way around. He was doing a rather thorough job of it, and when he finally pulled away at Mr. Hamilton's loud clearing of the throat, I could no longer be certain my shortness of breath was entirely due to my mad dash up the steps.

"Sorry to interrupt," Mr. Hamilton said, a wide smile on his face.

Milo turned his head unhurriedly but didn't bother to step back or remove his arms from around my waist. "We were out taking a moonlight stroll," he said with a smile. "I'm afraid we got carried away."

So he had correctly interpreted my motives. It was gratifying to know that he could, on occasion, prove useful.

"Perfectly understandable," Mr. Hamilton said with a wink. "I was just out getting a little air myself. All the better with a little company, eh? "

His manner was as usual, and I detected no sign of skepticism in his tone or expression. I could only hope that Milo and I had made a good show of it. I assumed we had, as my pulse was still racing. I did my best to summon an embarrassed smile as he wished us good evening and continued up the steps.

Milo turned back to me. He still had his hands on my waist, and I was still pressed very neatly between him and the railing. "I find that this investigating business gets more amusing by the hour," he said in a low voice.

"You can let go of me now, Milo," I whispered, my traitorous heart picking up pace as he leaned closer.

"He may be watching. Perhaps we should resume where we left off."

I was prepared to protest, but he kissed me again before I could rally resistance. It had been some time since we had shared any such amorous moments, and I found that I was not entirely opposed to his attentions now. For just an instant, I allowed myself to remember the heady first days of our whirlwind romance, when I had been so very sure of his love. His kisses had been irresistible then, in the blissful blindness of young love.

Those times were long behind us, however, and, though I could not deny my strong attraction to him, I knew perfectly well that now was not the moment to succumb to passion when there were more important matters to tend to.

I mustered up my resolve and pushed him back ever so slightly, my pulse pounding alarmingly. "That will do, Milo," I said breathlessly.

"I think, my dear, that it won't do at all." The roguish look in his eyes sent a thrill clean through me, and I realized at once we were on dangerous ground.

"Milo . . ."

"Perhaps we should go back to our room," he suggested.

So it was *our* room now, was it? For the briefest of moments, I must admit, I was sorely tempted. He was my husband, after all. Then I strengthened my resolve. He had moved his things into my room without permission; he would not move himself into my bed so easily.

I pushed him back farther and slid from his embrace. "I think that is not a particularly good idea."

"It seems an excellent idea to me," he said with a smile as his eyes lingered on mine. Then he glanced up the stairway. "It shall certainly appear strange to Mr. Hamilton if I return to my room this evening, after such an elaborate display of our devotion to one another."

I hesitated. He had a point, though I hated to admit it.

"Very well," I said at last. "You may stay in my room. I'm sure you will find the sofa to be quite comfortable."

Amusement tilted the corner of his mouth. "That's not exactly what I had in mind."

"No, I'm sure it's not," I said. I stepped closer, braving the risk that he would embrace me again, and lowered my voice. "Mr. Hamilton was searching for something at the base of the cliff. He appears to have located it and shoved it into his pocket."

"Wasn't it a bit foolish to go running after him in the dark? If he's the one who killed Rupert, he'd have no qualms about doing away with you."

"How did you know where I was?" I asked, ignoring his perfectly valid point.

"I came out of the sitting room just as you slipped out onto the balcony. I thought it best to follow you."

"I can take care of myself, thank you very much."

"Yes, I'm sure you could have defended yourself nicely. Perhaps you might have cudgeled him with one of these," he said, scooping up my shoes and holding them out to me.

I took them from him but didn't bother to put them back on. We still had most of the long stairway to climb. "I do appreciate your assistance," I told him grudgingly.

"I assure you, it was my pleasure," he replied.

"What do you suppose it was he was looking for?"

"I haven't the faintest idea."

"You're not being helpful, Milo."

"No?" He leaned against the railing. "Well, I'm afraid I have other things on my mind, darling."

I ignored this comment and the tone in which he said it, despite the unwarranted feeling of anticipation that it evoked in me. "Do you really think he might have killed Rupert? He's a thorough boor and his wife's afraid of him, but that doesn't mean he'd kill someone."

"It's not beyond the realm of possibility, I suppose, though I can't conceive of a good reason."

"No," I sighed, transferring both my shoes to one hand, preparing to grasp the railing with the other. "Neither can I. Well, come, Milo. We may as well go back."

He caught my free hand in his warm one. "Must we?"

"Do you suggest standing out here all night? It seems to be getting rather cold."

"I'll keep you warm," he said, pulling me toward him. He lowered his mouth to mine again, and this kiss was slow and lingering. The cool wind blew around us, and the soft lulling of the waves made for idyllic background music. I could feel my resolve slipping by the second in the comfortable warmth of his embrace, my head beginning to swim. Once again, irrational longing warred with my better judgment. Once again, prudence won the day.

"I think we'd better go back," I whispered at last against his lips.

He pulled back a little and looked down at me in the moonlight, and it was impossible to gauge what he was thinking. Then he released me with a soft sigh. "If you insist."

We trudged up the stairway in a sort of companionable silence. It was strange how in moments such as this things could be so easy between us, and in other moments it was as if a wall had sprung up to separate us.

We reached the balcony and stepped into the pool of light cast by the windows.

"I suppose I should put my shoes on," I said, "though it feels as if I've somehow managed to get a stone in my stocking." Milo offered his arm for support as I bent to slip my shoes on my feet. I straightened and we looked at one another for a moment before I turned toward the door.

Milo reached past me to open it. Then he stopped. "Wait."

He stepped closer, pulling his handkerchief from the pocket of his dinner jacket. "You've smudged your lipstick."

"You've smudged my lipstick," I corrected, noting that he had somehow managed to avoid getting any on his mouth. Another of his many talents, no doubt.

He held my face in his hand and wiped at my mouth before

tucking his handkerchief back into his pocket. His hand was still on my chin as he looked down at me.

I raised a brow, some small part of me hoping he would kiss me again.

Then he dropped his hand from my face and reached for the door. Hand on the knob, he turned to look down at me once again. "One more thing, darling."

"Yes?"

He leaned closer, a smile flashing across his face. "I think it only fair to warn you. I have never slept on a sofa in my life, and I don't intend to start now."

I LET HIM sleep in my bed, but I did not so much as kiss him good night. I decided it would be unreasonable to make him spend the night on the sofa, which was a good deal shorter than he was.

Charitable inclinations aside, however, I felt now would not be the time to begin a seaside affair with my husband. It would only complicate things, especially considering the uncertain state of our marriage. I still wasn't sure of my feelings for Milo, and certainly not of his for me.

He was as attractive to me as he had ever been, but that was not a sound basis for throwing myself into his arms. As long as things were unsettled, it would be better to keep a distance between us physically. Milo had made it perfectly obvious that he had no such qualms, but I felt he had very little say in the matter. As for his husbandly rights, should I choose to use such a vulgar term, I was of the opinion that he would be more entitled to them when he started behaving as a husband.

I will admit, however, that the memory of the kisses we had

shared was on my mind long after I heard the slow, steady sounds of his breathing signal that he was asleep. It seemed ages since I had felt that rush of passion between us, and the knowledge that he still found me desirable came as something of a relief.

Of course, I was not foolish enough to convince myself that the renewal of his interests had nothing to do with the perceived threat Gil posed to our marriage. I sometimes thought that Milo was very like a bad little child who hadn't the least interest in a discarded toy until someone else wanted to play with it. I had the uneasy feeling that it was only a matter of time before his interest would wane.

I turned and studied the sleeping face of my husband in the soft darkness of our room. I had always fancied myself a fairly practical, levelheaded woman, but even after five years of less than blissful marriage, I could not fault myself entirely for having been swept off my feet by him. He was too handsome, too charming, and I had been too young not to be flattered. It would have been to my credit if I had realized before the wedding that good looks and charm were not necessarily the basis for a good husband.

If the folly of youth was my excuse, I sometimes wondered what it was that had made Milo choose to marry me. I was not at all the type of woman to which men of his sort were commonly attracted; a dazzling blonde might have suited him better.

There was so much more that separated us than the little bit of empty bed that lay between us.

As they had been wont to do of late, my thoughts of Milo somehow drifted into thoughts of Gil. I wondered if he too was lying awake at the moment. I hoped he was not too terribly uncomfortable in his prison cell. I still could not believe that Gil had been arrested. What a mess this whole thing was. Tomorrow, I would go to see him. I only hoped he would not be too angry with me. I hadn't meant for anything to come of what I had told the inspector.

I thought of Detective Inspector Jones. That man severely tried my patience. Yet I could not help but feel that there was more to him than met the eye. He was up to something. Of that, I was sure. He had arrested Gil, but he had not said anything about discovering the weapon. As of the inquest, it had still been missing. I would ask him tomorrow just how it was that they could be certain of anything without a weapon.

Thoughts swirled in and out of my head as I edged toward sleep. I was drifting somewhere between wakefulness and a hazy dream when the thought struck me. I sat up, instantly awake.

The weapon.

I looked over at Milo. I felt I needed to share my theory with someone, and he was the closest at hand. "Are you asleep?" I whispered. He didn't stir.

Perhaps it could wait until morning . . . but, no. My mind raced over the possibilities, and I knew it would be impossible for me to rest.

I reached over and switched on the lamp. Milo's eyelids did not so much as quiver.

"Milo?"

The smooth, peaceful lines of his face showed no sign that he was anywhere near wakefulness.

"Milo," I said at last, rather loudly. "Wake up."

He blinked against the light and covered his eyes with his hand. "What on earth . . . what's the matter?"

"I need to talk to you."

"Good heavens, Amory. What time is it?"

I glanced at the clock on my bedside table. "It's just after two," I said. "Are you awake?"

"No, blast it. I'm not."

"Don't be surly, Milo. Listen. I've thought of something. I should have realized it before. I think Mr. Hamilton was looking for the weapon."

He lowered his hand to look at me. "The murder weapon?"

"Yes, he must have been. Perhaps he killed Rupert and then tossed the weapon, whatever it was, over the cliff, where he could retrieve it later."

"Surely your inspector was bright enough to search for it there."

"He's not my inspector, and perhaps it was something that wouldn't have drawn notice, unless one knew what one was looking for."

"Like what, for instance?"

I thought of the pile of debris at the bottom of the cliff, driftwood and stones and bits of shells that the sea had flung upon the shore. "It might have been anything, a loose brick from the wall, perhaps."

"If it was so carefully concealed, why not leave it there?"

"I don't know. Perhaps he was afraid it would be discovered later. Or perhaps he was afraid the tide might wash it out into the open."

I rose from the bed, pulling on my negligee and moving to the little writing desk in the corner. My thoughts were all a jumble, and I knew the best way to organize them would be to write them down. I should have thought of this method before. It always cleared my head to write to Laurel. Once I could organize my thoughts on paper, I could begin to make sense of things. I hoped the same would prove true when trying to solve a murder.

"Darling, can't this wait until morning?"

"It is morning," I said, pulling out a sheet of paper and a fountain pen. "And before you make any complaints, let me remind you that it was your idea to stay in my room, not mine."

Milo sighed. "Yes, well, this wasn't what I had envisioned."

I wrote "Mr. Hamilton" on the piece of paper and drew a line beneath it. "What motive does Mr. Hamilton have?" I asked. "Do you think Rupert may have trifled with Larissa Hamilton?"

Milo sat up, running a hand through his tousled hair, then across the shadow of a beard that was beginning to darken his face. I tried not to notice how very attractive he looked, disheveled from sleep. He was so seldom anything less than immaculately attired that his current rumpled state held a certain sort of appeal. My mind wandered to our earlier kisses, and I forced myself to focus on the task at hand.

"It's possible," he said, "but I shouldn't say likely. I gather Rupert Howe would have preferred a very different sort of woman. Granted, she's pretty enough, but there's that aura of tragedy that hovers over her. She doesn't conceal her unhappiness well. I shouldn't think most men would find it appealing."

"She certainly warmed up under your attentions," I observed.

"She enjoys it when someone is pleasant to her," he said. "From what I've seen, Mr. Hamilton certainly isn't."

"No," I replied. "I can't see why she ever married him."

"You see? You should count your blessings," Milo noted. "You may not have gotten the best of bargains when you married me, but Mr. Hamilton proves it could be much worse."

"A moving argument," I replied dryly. "In any event, I can't see Mr. Hamilton as murdering in a jealous passion. Might he have killed Rupert for some other reason?"

"Perhaps it's something to do with Socialists," he suggested.

"According to the papers, everything has to do with Socialists these days."

"Be serious, Milo." I directed him with a smile.

"Shady business dealing, perhaps?"

"I don't know. Perhaps I can enquire of Emmeline or Gil. They might know if Rupert and Mr. Hamilton had any sort of joint venture."

Milo rose from the bed and put on his dressing gown, moving toward the desk. "From what I've heard of Rupert Howe, he would be likely to get involved in something underhanded, if he thought there was a quick profit to be made from it."

I turned to him, surprised. "Did you know Rupert? Miss Carter mentioned he was in Monte Carlo."

"No. I knew of him, but I didn't know him personally. He didn't quite move in my circles, I'm afraid."

"What a thorough snob you are, Milo."

"It's true, isn't it?" he said with a raised brow. "Money doesn't buy breeding, after all. These people here at the Brightwell aren't exactly of our class."

"They are perfectly nice people."

Milo smiled. "Except for whichever of them is a murderer."

"Yes, excepting that person."

He was right, of course. I had defended them automatically with a charitable politeness that had been instilled in me from an early age, but the plain fact remained that, aside from Gil and Emmeline, none of the guests here were particularly nice people at all. It seemed to me that each of them had their own hidden agendas, their own secrets to keep. However, somewhere amidst the muddle, there were answers. It was only a matter of separating the inconsequential from the significant.

"You may as well continue the list," Milo said, glancing over my shoulder. "Get all the suspects together." He dropped onto the sofa and lay across it, his dark head propped against the arm nearest me.

"All right. Mrs. Hamilton next, then." I hesitated, thinking hard. "Perhaps Rupert paid her unwanted attention. Perhaps it wasn't murder at all. Perhaps she was forced to defend herself from him, and consequently he died and she was too afraid to tell anyone."

"She might have picked up a rock and bashed him with it," Milo conceded. "One can never tell about aggressive bridge players."

"She might have told Mr. Hamilton, and he went searching for the weapon on her behalf."

"Uncharacteristically chivalrous of him, I should say."

"Perhaps. Well, how about Olive Henderson?" I asked. "Rupert insinuated that there had been something between them before he met Emmeline, and Mrs. Hamilton mentioned that they might have had a clandestine meeting. Now, she's slit her wrists. Perhaps it was guilt and not heartbreak."

"Yes, they may have had a lovers' quarrel on the cliff. Perhaps she hit him and he fell over the edge."

My mind went back to my conversation with Olive in the sitting room. She had asked me if I had ever been in love, and I was certain it had been real sorrow in her eyes. Could it have been guilt for killing the man she had once loved? It was possible, but I didn't think it likely. Hers had been the wistful sadness of something lost, not the suffering of remorse. "I have my doubts about Miss Henderson," I said at last. "But it's always possible."

"What of the charming Miss Carter?" Milo asked. "Might she have had a reason to kill Rupert?"

I considered. "Perhaps. It seems that Rupert was inordinately successful where women were concerned. There may have been something between them that none of us were aware of. Perhaps she killed him in a jealous rage."

Milo reached over and retrieved a cigarette from the box on the table. He lit it with a silver lighter from his dressing-gown pocket and smoked contemplatively. "I think it very unlikely that Rupert Howe was having a love affair with every member of this little party," he said at last. "I never met the man, but it seems that his luck could not have extended that far."

"Perhaps you're right," I replied sweetly. "I imagine even you would have difficulty accomplishing such a thing. And you've much more savoir faire than Rupert had."

He blew a stream of smoke into the air. "You flatter me, my dear."

I glanced back at the list. "I'm curious about Lionel Blake," I said. "There's something mysterious about him." I related my visit to the abandoned theater. "He was so secretive about the thing, as though there was some reason he should attempt to hide it.

"Theater people are an odd lot," Milo said dismissively. "It may be nothing. Then again, it may well be that he's the one tied up with the Socialists."

I ignored him. "We'll come back to Mr. Blake. I shall have to ponder over Anne and Edward Rodgers," I said, moving on. "Neither of them seems to have any real motive thus far."

"Rather an odd pair, aren't they?" he commented.

"Yes, that's just what I thought. She's very sociable, and he's so very stiff. I've barely seen him smile since we've been here."

"We may as well ascribe to them the familiar motive. Perhaps she was too sociable with Rupert, and her husband objected."

"I don't know. I have the impression they're really very fond of one another." I glanced over my shoulder at him. "Perhaps you should talk to Mrs. Rodgers. I think she would be more than happy to have a nice, long chat with you."

"I do believe you are using me, Amory," Milo said, turning his head on the arm of the sofa to look up at me.

"Yes, well, you have to be good for something, don't you?"

He laughed. "I should have known better than to match wits with you this early in the morning."

"Or anytime, for that matter," I retorted.

"Might I see your list?" he asked.

I handed it to him.

Milo took the sheet of paper and ran his eyes across it. "I notice you haven't included Trent. Is it really wise to be unwilling to consider the possibility that he might actually have done it?"

"He didn't, Milo. I know it."

"I see. And does your decree of clemency extend to Miss Trent, as well?"

I frowned. "Emmeline?"

Milo sat up and offered me one of his sardonic smiles. "If you go around eliminating everyone you've taken a liking to, you may overlook something important."

I bit back a harsh retort as the truth of his words sank in. Emmeline, by all appearances, was very distraught at Rupert's death. But that didn't mean she was not responsible. It was she who had called attention to the fact that Rupert was missing. Might she have wanted me to be with her to discover the body? Perhaps she had grown tired of Rupert's philandering. Could her paralyzing grief be an act? No, it was impossible. She couldn't be feigning the depth of her sorrow. I had felt her sincerity, seen it in the bleakness of her eyes. She and Gil were both innocent. They had to be.

"I know these people, Milo. I've known them for years. I just can't conceive of the fact that either one of them would kill someone in cold blood."

"Poor darling," he said, shaking his head, "you're not cold-hearted enough to be a detective. You only want the disagreeable people to be guilty, and I'm afraid you'll find that life isn't like that."

I sighed, suddenly very tired. The realization that he might just possibly be right knocked the wind from my sails. I stood from the desk chair and dropped onto the sofa beside him. "What if it is one of them, Milo?"

He looked at me, his gaze searching despite his mild expression. "Would it matter to you so very much?"

"Of course it would."

Milo leaned to grind out his cigarette in the pewter ashtray on the table in front of us. "Are you in love with him, Amory?"

For a moment, I wasn't sure I had heard him right. "I beg your pardon?"

"I think you heard me," he replied easily as he sat back, his blue gaze coming up to mine. "I asked if you are in love with Gil Trent."

"What a question . . ." A rather forced laugh dwindled away into silence, and I could not think of what to say next. The question, coming so unexpectedly, had stunned me. A quick denial sprung to my lips, but I hesitated. What did I feel for Gil? I wasn't sure.

Milo watched me expectantly, waiting for my answer.

"I married you, didn't I?" I said at last, as lightly as I could manage.

The corner of his mouth tipped up. "Yes, well. That's not quite an answer, is it?"

"No," I said softly. "I suppose it's not."

He offered me a smile that revealed absolutely nothing of his feelings. "Your silence speaks most eloquently."

He made a move as though to rise, but I caught his arm. "Please, Milo. Let's not quarrel."

"I haven't the slightest intention of quarreling with you, darling, but it's the middle of the night, and I'm tired."

"It's just that I'm so confused . . . about everything."

"Perfectly understandable."

I recognized the polite, disinterested responses. He was quite done with this conversation, perhaps quite done with me.

My hand dropped from his arm and he rose.

"If you don't mind, I think I shall try to get a bit more sleep before breakfast," he said, turning toward the bed.

I stood, suddenly angry with myself and angry with him. "You're not being fair, Milo."

He turned back to me, brows raised. "Really? I thought I was being more than fair, considering my wife has just told me she's in love with another man."

"I didn't say I loved him."

"You didn't deny it," he replied, as infuriatingly calm as ever. "You couldn't even come up with a convincing lie."

"Now that's something you know all about, isn't it?" I rejoined. "Lies are very convenient when you must keep track of the dozens of women you've been linked to."

"I thought you didn't wish to quarrel."

"I've changed my mind. In fact, I think we're on the verge of a blazing row." My voice, though not raised, fairly shook with anger. I realized suddenly that, throughout the course of our marriage, we had never once shouted at one another. Perhaps that little fact said that we simply didn't care enough.

"I suppose next you'll be hurling things at me, like a fishwife."

In that moment I was sorely tempted to do just that. Perhaps an ashtray to the forehead would relieve him of his thinly veiled amusement.

"Tell me something," he went on. "Have you carried a secret passion for Trent all these years? If so, I wonder why you ever married me to begin with."

"I've forgotten why I married you," I retorted.

It was a cruel thing to say, and I regretted it the moment it escaped my lips. I opened my mouth to apologize but stopped short when I saw the look on Milo's face. His eyes glinted, and a dangerous smile played on his mouth. He had obviously taken my insult as a challenge.

"Have you?"

"I . . ."

I didn't have time to formulate my response before he closed the distance between us, and his arms moved around me and he pulled me against him.

"Shall I remind you?" he asked in a low voice.

"Milo . . ."

Then he kissed me. It was a kiss that made our encounter on the steps pale in comparison. My heart began to race, and I struggled to maintain my indignation of a moment ago.

Finally, I pulled back as much as I could manage. He was holding me quite tightly and made no move to release me. "Milo, I don't think . . ." I began.

"Yes, Amory. For once, don't think."

He kissed me again, and I found it was, indeed, getting increasingly difficult to think clearly. I put my hands against his shoulders to push him away, but I realized suddenly that I didn't want to. My emotions had been reduced to rubble as of late, and I was so very tired of bearing it all alone. I longed for at least the comforting illusion of a link with someone, and perhaps this was the closest I was going to get.

This man, for better or for worse, was my husband, and at this moment I could conjure no good reason why I should not give in to mutual desire. I hesitated for just a moment before letting my arms slide around his neck as I returned his kiss with equal ardor.

18

I SUPPOSE ONE is allowed to forsake her resolve with her own husband. Nevertheless, as diverting as the night had been, something very like regret hung over me as I rose, bathed, dressed, and went down to breakfast.

Milo was still asleep when I left the room, and I was glad of it. I hadn't the inclination to face him now. Our romantic interlude had resolved nothing. In fact, it was very likely it had only worsened matters. The lines that had been drawn between us were hazier now than ever.

Nevertheless, if I was very honest with myself, I was not completely sorry. After all, we had only behaved in the natural way of husbands and wives; there was so little of the typical spousal behavior in our relationship, I was glad we had managed something. In any event, unwise though it might have been, there was nothing to be done about it now.

I was rather late coming down to breakfast, and though the dining room was still scattered with guests, the only person I recognized was Lionel Blake. He sat in a corner of the dining room, a book on the table in front of him. He ate his breakfast in methodical bites, not taking his eyes from the book.

I filled a plate with food from the sideboard and moved toward where he sat.

"Good morning, Mr. Blake," I said, sitting at the table next to his.

He looked up, as though noticing me for the first time, and smiled. "Good morning, Mrs. Ames."

"I don't mean to interrupt your reading."

"Oh, no," he said, closing the book and pushing it aside. I glanced at the title and recognized it as a play. *Die Ratten*, by Gerhart Hauptmann. "I always read when I have nothing better to do, but I do prefer company at mealtimes."

"I expect the others had their breakfast earlier."

"Yes, I've seen most of our party this morning. Rather too much of some of them, in fact."

I raised a brow at this curious statement, but he didn't elaborate. I wonder if he had had a falling out with one of the other gentlemen.

"I'll be glad when we can get this all behind us and go home," he went on. "Back to our normal lives."

Our normal lives. Though I would be glad to leave the Brightwell and its dark connotations behind, I was not certain that I longed to return to the normal state of things. But these were thoughts for another time.

"I've been meaning to ask you," I said casually, stirring some sugar into my coffee, "if you've had any word from your backer."

Was it my imagination or did something very like confusion cross his features before it was quickly erased? He nodded. "Ah . . .

yes, in fact, he's come across a good venue closer to London. He feels quite certain that he will be able to make a good profit. The show goes on, as they say."

"I'm glad it's all worked out for you," I replied. I shifted the conversation to other things as I ate my breakfast. I was beginning to see that Lionel Blake was a hard man to read. He was always friendly, pleasant in a vacant sort of way. I got the sense that he did not reveal his true self easily. Perhaps it was the actor in him that always wished to maintain a part.

An idea came to me suddenly, and I went ahead with it without pause. "What time was it you told the inspector that you saw Gil on the balcony the day Mr. Howe was killed?"

If I had hoped to throw him off his guard into some sort of confession, I was to be disappointed. He met my gaze without blinking. "I told the inspector no such thing."

"Oh," I said, feigning embarrassment. "I'm sorry . . . I must have made the inference . . . You were sitting on the terrace when we were searching for Rupert, so perhaps I assumed that it was you."

"No, it wasn't me." His response was perfectly polite, but I could sense a coolness in his answer. Be it a desire for privacy or something more sinister, he did not care for my prying.

"Good morning! Good morning!" I looked up to see Yvonne Roland sailing into the room. She was wearing a flowing silk gown in an astounding shade of orange. The hazy brightness of the fabric seemed to billow around her as she walked. Looking at her was very like gazing directly into the sun.

Mr. Blake and I greeted her as she moved to the sideboard and began to pile her plate high with sausages.

"So many things happening here lately," she said. "I am reminded of my second . . . no third honeymoon. We were on a Nile cruise and some fellow fell off the boat. I suppose he was eaten by crocodiles . . . and then someone contracted some dreadful disease, and then the weather turned beastly hot, and . . . well, it was one thing after another. I imagine that Gil is rotting away in a dungeon somewhere. And that poor young thing, so in love, cutting herself all to pieces. It's all too much for me. I shall be glad to get back to London."

That said, she took her plate of sausages and sailed out as abruptly as she had come.

I looked at Mr. Blake, and he smiled. "She's like something out of an outlandish comedy," he said.

"A very interesting character, to be sure," I replied. Though she was a strange creature, I couldn't help but like Mrs. Roland. There was something so very alive about her. I expected that vibrancy had translated to allure in her younger days.

"Well, Mrs. Ames," said Mr. Blake, picking up his book and rising, "I have some letter writing to attend to. I'm sure I shall see you later."

"Yes."

He exited, and I picked at the remainder of my breakfast in silence. His denial did not prove he had not spoken to the inspector, but I could not really see any reason for him to hide the fact if he had. In fact, I could think of no good reason why anyone should seek to deny that they had observed Gil on the terrace.

My thoughts were recalled to the present as I heard the rise and fall of Mrs. Roland's exuberant tones in the foyer and the low answering tones of Milo. My husband managed to extricate himself in a surprisingly quick manner, for he appeared in the doorway a moment later. His eyes sought me out and he smiled, and for some reason I felt a nervous flutter in my stomach. I smiled in return, though I'm afraid mine lacked warmth. I felt oddly ill at ease.

I noticed the attention he attracted as he made his way toward the sideboard. I had grown accustomed to the way that women's eyes followed Milo. It was his misfortune, really, that he was so good-looking. If he had not been so attractive, he might have turned out differently, less confident and more considerate. As it was, he took advantage of the fact that he had only to exert a minimum amount of effort to bend people, women especially, to his will. Myself included, apparently.

"Hello, darling," he said, when he was seated at the table with a cup of coffee and plate of food.

"Good morning," I said somewhat stiffly, fiddling with my napkin. I was uncertain how this latest turn of events would affect the uneasy alliance that had developed between us.

Milo, it seemed, felt no such awkwardness.

"It has been a good morning, hasn't it?" he replied with a grin. "Though I was disappointed to awaken and find myself bereft of your charming company."

"We've better things to do than . . . loll about in bed all day," I said in a low voice, hoping to avoid being overheard.

"More worthy, perhaps," he said over his cup, "but certainly not better."

"I've just spoken to Mr. Blake," I said, ignoring him.

"Besides, I wouldn't exactly call it lolling."

"Milo, do pay attention."

"You're making it difficult," he said, setting down his cup and leaning toward me, arms on the table. "When you talk, it only calls attention to your lovely mouth."

"I thought flattery came before seduction," I replied tartly. "Not after."

He sat back in his chair, an exasperated sigh escaping his lips. "Very well. I'm listening. You've spoken with Mr. Blake."

He picked up his fork and began to eat as I talked. "Yes, I tried to get him to admit that it was he who told Inspector Jones that Gil was on the terrace."

"And did he?"

"No. If he did, he wouldn't own up to it."

"Why should it be a great secret, do you think?" Milo asked, echoing my own question, though he didn't sound particularly interested. "There must be some reason the inspector wishes to keep it quiet."

"My thoughts, exactly," I said. "I only wish Inspector Jones would be a bit more cooperative. In fact, I think I shall pay him a visit this morning," I said. I also intended to speak with Gil, but I kept that fact to myself.

"And what assignments have you for me today?" he asked.

"Continue to glean what information you can," I said. "Particularly from the ladies. Perhaps you can discover from Mrs. Hamilton what her husband was doing creeping about on the beach last night. There must be some reason he chose that particular time to investigate."

Milo shrugged. "Perhaps he found a convenient moment and took advantage of it."

"Perhaps, but I can't help feeling that there is something we are overlooking."

Milo listened indulgently to my conjectures as he finished his breakfast. Then we rose from the table and walked together out of the breakfast room and into the lobby. The morning sun shone brightly through the windows, lighting up the walls and giving the room a cheerful countenance. I felt suddenly lighter than I had in days. Perhaps everything would be all right, after all. Perhaps, with Milo's help, I could find who had killed Rupert Howe and see that Gil was set free.

I was about to turn toward the front door when Milo stopped me, hand on my arm. "Oh, Amory . . ."

"Yes?"

"One more thing." His hand slid to my waist. He leaned and gave me a lingering kiss that I couldn't bring myself to break away from, despite the very public place in which we stood.

At last, he released me and gave me a smile. "I'll see you at lunch."

I nodded and watched him enter the lift. Then I sighed. As much as I attempted to steel myself against his charms, I was finding it very difficult to maintain my barriers. Against my better judgment, I found myself enjoying his company and pleased by his attentions. It was not at all wise, but I was the first to admit that wisdom and matters of the heart seldom go hand in hand.

Doing my best to banish such dismal thoughts, I turned to leave the hotel and found myself very surprised indeed to see that Gil was standing in the entryway.

"GIL," I EXCLAIMED. The initial paralysis of surprise wore off quickly, and I hurried toward him.

Though he tried to hide it, his expression indicated that he had seen the exchange between Milo and me. With a heavy sort of certainty, I realized just why Milo had chosen that particular moment to lavish me with affection. I felt a strange mix of anger and sadness that settled into a cold lump in my chest. Milo, ever aware of what he was doing, had timed that triumphant display perfectly.

"They've released you," I said, stating the obvious as I reached Gil's side. I could feel the flush on my cheeks. For some unaccountable reason, I felt as though I had been caught in an indiscretion.

"For the time being." He smiled a very tired smile that didn't warm his eyes. "My barrister is top-notch, it seems." He gave a laugh that was completely devoid of humor. "My barrister. How odd that sounds. I'm to be tried for murder, Amory. It doesn't seem real."

I noticed suddenly that he was pale and had dark circles about his eyes, and he looked older than he had two days ago. I felt a stab of compassion and more than a little guilt. I reached out and took his hand. "It's going to be all right, Gil. I'm so glad you've been released. I tried to come and see you, but Inspector Jones wouldn't let me."

"I'm glad. It wasn't a very nice place. I shouldn't have liked you to visit." His hand dropped from mine.

"Do you want to eat something?" I asked, at a loss for anything more to say. There was little I could say to comfort him, especially now that I could sense a distance between us. In the midst of everything else, neither of us was willing to address the fact that Milo seemed to have come between us once again. Though, in theory, I had done nothing wrong, it must have been a very unwelcome surprise for Gil, fresh from prison, to arrive back and find me wrapped in Milo's arms.

"Thank you, no. I'm very tired. I didn't sleep well. I think I shall go see Emmeline and then rest for a while."

"Of course. She'll be glad to see you. Everything has been so hard on her."

"Yes. I'll see you later then." He started to walk away, and I felt unaccountably miserable as he turned his back to me. I couldn't keep myself from stopping him.

"Gil, wait."

He turned, and I was no longer sure what I wanted to say. This was neither the time nor the place for an intimate discussion. Nevertheless, there was one thing, at least, for which I could attempt to make amends.

"I never meant for Inspector Jones to misconstrue what I had told him," I said. "I should have spoken with you about your conversation with Rupert before I mentioned it; I never thought it would cause you any harm. I'm very sorry."

"Please don't apologize," he said. "You mustn't feel it's your fault that I was arrested."

"But it was my fault, wasn't it," I stated flatly.

He stepped toward me, his expression gentle, and this time it was he who took my hand in his. "It was I who dragged you into this mess. I'm the one who should apologize. I don't know what I was thinking, asking you to . . . Perhaps I wasn't thinking. If I hadn't asked you, you would have been spared all of this."

"No, I was happy to help, and I still am." I squeezed his hand. It was, as ever, warm and dry, his grip firm and reassuring. "I know it will come out all right in the end."

He smiled but did not look assured. "Thank you."

"I'm going to find who did it, Gil. I know you didn't want me to, but I've been asking questions and . . ."

A shadow crossed his eyes, and his grip on my hand tightened. "Please, Amory. I meant it, what I said before. You mustn't do that. You can't put yourself in danger." He glanced around, as though he feared being overheard, but we were speaking quietly, and there was no one within earshot. "I don't want you to involve yourself. Do you understand? Keep back and let the police take care of it."

"I can't stand by and let you take the blame for something you didn't do."

His eyes met mine, and there was an intensity in them that had not been there a moment ago, a spark that warmed the weary coolness of his gaze. "Do you really believe I am innocent?"

"With all my heart."

He smiled, a real smile, and I felt my chest constrict with that familiar affection. "That means a great deal, Amory."

"Did you honestly believe I could think you capable of such a thing?"

"I . . ." His gaze flickered away before returning. "I wasn't sure. It's been a long time, Amory. We've both of us changed."

I knew that he was thinking of how we had been happy and content before Milo had appeared to alter both our lives. "Things are different, yes," I said. "But that doesn't mean I don't believe the best of you."

"Thank you." His gaze was searching for a moment. "There's more to be said, isn't there? But I expect it will keep."

"Yes," I said, relieved both that he had brought up the conversation that loomed before us and that it was to be postponed for the time being. "It will keep."

"Promise me you'll leave this murder business be, Amory."

"I can't do that," I said, meeting his gaze. "You know I can't."

"Then at least promise me you'll be careful. If something happened to you . . ."

"I'll be careful, Gil. I promise."

He nodded and released my hand. "I had better see to Emmeline."

Gil departed, and I decided to walk for a moment on the terrace to clear my thoughts. My emotions were in a greater state of turmoil than ever. I was no longer sure what was true of anyone; worse, I was no longer sure what was true of myself.

For that one sunny moment this morning as Milo kissed me, I had allowed myself to believe that, perhaps, we could make a go of it. Perhaps my leaving for the seaside without him had been enough to inspire some semblance of connubial devotion, to make him realize that he really did care for me, after all. And then, when I looked up to find Gil there, watching my husband's cleverly staged scene, I had realized, not for the first time, that Milo was always playing the game. It had left me oddly sick to my stomach.

And what of Gil? Milo had asked if I loved Gil, and though my first impulse had been to deny it, I could not pretend, even with myself, that there was not some link between us. Whether it was the bond of an old and comfortable friendship or something more, I couldn't be certain. I only knew that I saw in Gil something that Milo lacked.

One thing I could be very sure of, however. The emotional tumult I found myself in was not going to provide any assistance in finding Rupert Howe's killer. Breathing deeply of the fresh, salty air, I forced myself to focus on the task at hand.

I walked to the edge of the terrace and looked down. The seaside terrace sat empty below, the white tabletops gleaming brightly in the morning sun. The terrace had been cleaned and reopened once the police had done their part, but there was no one sitting there. I could not blame the guests for staying clear of it. It seemed ghastly to take tea on the spot where a man's life had spilled out.

My gaze dropped from the terrace to the bottom of the cliff. What had Mr. Hamilton been searching for last night? It seemed he had found it, whatever it was. My conjecture that it had been the weapon had seemed logical, but now I frowned as a thought came to me. It seemed clear to me that, if it had been the weapon that struck the fatal blow to Rupert, he would want to dispose of it. Why then, if Mr. Hamilton had discovered it among the debris at the base of the cliff, had he not flung it into the sea? That is most certainly what I would have done; yet he had put the object in his pocket. There was only one reasonable explanation for such a thing. It was something he wished to keep. It followed, then, that the object would still be in his possession. There was one logical place to look and only one way to look there.

I was going to have to find a way to sneak into Mr. Hamilton's room.

19

THERE WAS, I decided, no time like the present to begin my machinations. I was unsure of Mr. Hamilton's whereabouts at present, but I did not intend to break into his room just this moment. That would be best accomplished during lunch, when most of the others were away from their rooms. The fewer potential witnesses to my misdeeds, the better.

That meant that right now, or at least before the luncheon hour, I needed to acquire a key or some other method of ingress. Just because Milo and I were habitually negligent in locking our doors didn't mean Mr. Hamilton would be so incautious. I will admit that several ideas, some more incredible than others, crossed my mind. In the end, I decided it would be equally impossible for me to impersonate Mrs. Hamilton to the desk clerk, dress as a maid, or scale the wall to his window. I would simply have to hope he left his room open or attempt to pick the lock, an area in which I feared my skills would be woefully inadequate. I could only pray that my ventures would meet with success.

I asked the desk clerk for Mr. Hamilton's room number and learned that his wife had a separate but adjoining room. This was good news for me. It could mean another possible means of entry, yet it also meant another person to avoid in my snooping endeavors.

I spent the remainder of the morning sipping tea on the terrace and writing a long, woe-filled letter to Laurel. Sealing the envelope and bringing it to the desk to have it posted, I remembered then that I had forgotten to read the letter she had sent to me. I had never taken it from my pocket. Well, it would have to wait for later. I had no intention of returning to my room at present, since I had no desire to encounter Milo. I wished that I had insisted he keep to his own room, but it didn't seem very likely that I would be able to evict him now.

Thinking of him only made me angry, so I forced my thoughts to return to the task at hand. It had been my intention to call upon Inspector Jones, but Gil's arrival had given me pause. I suspected the inspector would not be in a cooperative mood, seeing as Gil had been released, albeit not indefinitely. I would make a trip to see Inspector Jones tomorrow, provided some insidious errand did not bring him back to the Brightwell.

I also felt it would be the proper thing for me to visit Olive Henderson in the hospital. I had not heard a recent update on her condition, and I wondered how she was faring. If I was completely honest with myself, it was not solely her welfare that interested me, though I sincerely hoped that she was all right. What I was most curious to learn was what had prompted her to cut her wrists. If, as Veronica Carter claimed, Olive had not loved Rupert, what possible motive could she have for attempting to do away with herself? It was most puzzling. I could see no reason why she should wish to confide in me, but I could try.

At last, the luncheon hour approached, and I left the terrace and entered the hotel. Crossing the lobby, I made my way toward the lift. It was my intention to sneak a surreptitious glance into the dining room to ascertain that the Hamiltons had come down before I headed upstairs to try my hand at unlawful entry. As luck would have it, the doors to the lift opened and Mr. and Mrs. Hamilton stood before me.

"Hello, Mrs. Ames," Mr. Hamilton said. He dragged his eyes over me in an appraising way. "The . . . sea air seems to have done you well. You're looking hale and hearty this afternoon."

I managed a tight smile at his unabashed reference to my moonlit rendezvous with Milo. Vulgar man.

"That's a lovely dress, Mrs. Hamilton," I said, turning to his wife, who stood silently by his side. Indeed, she looked very pretty in a gown of dusky rose. The color suited the softness of her complexion. She really was a lovely woman; I felt sorry she should be tied to so odious a man.

"Not the latest fashion, of course," Mr. Hamilton said, before she could reply. "Larissa's never had much eye for the newest things. Perhaps you could give her the name of your dressmaker. You always seem very well turned out."

She flushed, intensifying my desire to find some sort of nasty weapon in his room. If only he could be guilty. Gil would be freed, and so would Larissa Hamilton.

"Mrs. Hamilton needs no help from me," I told him coolly. I turned to her, hoping warmth and not pity showed in my smile. "In my opinion, you always look quite lovely, Mrs. Hamilton."

"Thank you," she said.

"Not having lunch?" Mr. Hamilton asked.

"Not just now. I've a headache."

"I am sorry," Mrs. Hamilton said. "I have some aspirin . . ."

"A touch too much sun, I think. I'll lie down for a while."

I entered the lift and was relieved when the doors closed behind me. I had never before encountered such a frightful excuse for a husband. Compared to Mr. Hamilton, Rupert was beginning to look like quite the gentleman, and Milo seemed on the verge of sprouting a halo and wings.

The lift stopped on the Hamiltons' floor, and I exited cautiously. My room was not on this floor, and, though most of the Brightwell guests were not likely to know that, I still did not care to be spotted. If something should go amiss, I would not want anyone remembering that they had seen me here.

Just at that moment, a gentleman exited his room and came down the hall. I resisted the urge to freeze guiltily in place as he tipped his hat to me and continued on.

I waited until he had entered the lift and then, with as much nonchalance as I could muster, I strolled down the hall and approached the door to Mrs. Hamilton's room. I put my hand on the knob and was bitterly disappointed to find it locked. Not that I really expected to find it open. Mrs. Hamilton struck me as a cautious, dependable sort of person. It seemed only natural that she would make sure that her things were in order.

I sighed. There was only one hope left now, and the odds did not seem good. If Mr. Hamilton had hidden some incriminating object in his room, it was very unlikely that he would have left the door open for any person to waltz inside.

My hand stilled for just a moment on the knob before I slowly turned it. The handle gave, and, with the slightest pressure on my part, the door swung open.

I let out a little breath I didn't know I had been holding and slid inside, shutting the door silently behind me.

Locking the door, I stood for a moment, taking stock of the room. The layout of Mr. Hamilton's room was somewhat similar to mine, though my room rested on the southeast corner facing the sea and Mr. Hamilton's was midway along the west side of the building. A large wardrobe and dressing table stood against the wall to my left. A sitting area sat near the window, and the bed rested against the wall that separated Mrs. Hamilton's room from his. A writing desk and the door to the bathroom on the wall across from the bed completed the picture. The room was surprisingly tidy. I had been expecting an ogre's den, no doubt, but everything was orderly, almost impersonal.

Before beginning my search, I moved to try the door to Mrs. Hamilton's room and found it bolted from Mr. Hamilton's side. I slid back the bolt and opened it, peering into Mrs. Hamilton's room. The layout was the mirror image of this one, her bed against the wall to his room. I closed the door but left it unlocked. Should I hear Mr. Hamilton coming back, it would be that much easier for me to slip into her room, where I could possibly make an escape. Of course, they might both arrive at their rooms together. In that case, there would be no escape. I determined that I would be gone long before they had finished lunching.

Not having a description of the item for which I was searching, I was at a loss for where to begin. The object had been small enough to fit in his pocket, which meant it could be in any number of places.

I decided to start with the obvious. I moved to the writing desk, which had two drawers. In the first, I found nothing more interesting than the hotel stationery, a few odd writing implements, a silver-handled letter opener, a gold lighter engraved with an *H* and a package of cigarettes. The second drawer contained a stack of envelopes. These were likely the letters that Mr. Hamilton had received since arriving at the Brightwell. I hesitated for only a moment.

I suppose I should have felt some sense of guilt as I sat at Mr. Hamilton's desk and began rummaging through his private correspondence, but honesty compels me to admit that I did not. If that man was a murderer, I had no qualms about proving it. If he was not a murderer, he was still a nasty man whom I disliked intensely.

Unfortunately, there was no proof to be had. A cursory inspection proved the letters to be nothing more than dull business correspondence. I did not take the time to peruse them, but they seemed to be on the up-and-up from what I could make out. It was very disappointing.

Dropping to my hands and knees, I looked beneath the bed. There was nothing to be seen there but the ivory-colored carpeting.

Sighing, I rose and walked to the wardrobe. It was a massive thing, nearly floor-to-ceiling. I opened the doors and found it mostly empty, save for a few suits of clothing and some shirts. It seemed Mr. Hamilton had packed lightly for his trip to the seaside. The clothes were expensive and well tailored, but slightly flashier than was strictly necessary.

The drawers of the dresser revealed only handkerchiefs, neckties, socks, and underthings.

I sighed again and turned to run my eyes over the room one more time. I had expected it would be difficult to search the room for a hidden object. I hadn't anticipated there would really be so few places to look. If it had been the weapon that Mr. Hamilton had scooped up, it would have to be large enough to inflict sufficient damage on a human skull. Such an object could not be swept under the rug.

Perhaps he hadn't hidden it here after all. It was possible that he had disposed of it on his way up the steps, tossed it away into the tall grass that bordered the stairway.

Not willing to admit defeat just yet, I went into the bathroom. It was no less neat than his room had been. Everything was aligned with soldierlike precision on the shelf. I found a leather shaving kit, a razor, and a bottle of pungent cologne. The medicine cabinet revealed one thing of interest: a bottle of very strong sleeping tablets. I wondered if it might have been Mr. Hamilton who had drugged me. I grudgingly admitted to myself that he was not the only person in the world with access to such medicine.

Lost in thought as I exited the bathroom, I was not prepared for what awaited me.

"What are you doing here?"

I started, barely stifling a gasp. Milo was standing in the door that separated the two rooms. He leaned casually against the door frame, as though these were our rooms and not those of two near strangers whose privacy we were invading.

"What are you doing here?" I demanded.

"I believe I asked you first."

"How did you get into Mrs. Hamilton's room?" I asked, determined not to answer his questions before he answered mine. "I tried the lock."

"But you didn't have this," he said, holding up a key.

"The key to Mrs. Hamilton's room?"

"Yes, you might have told me you were coming up here. Though it appears you had little need for my assistance."

"The door was unlocked," I said. "Wherever did you get her key?"

He smiled. "From the lady herself."

It seemed too incredible, even for Milo. "She didn't give you the key to her room . . . as an invitation?"

"No," he admitted, stepping into the room. "You may find it

hard to believe, my love, but there are women with whom my charm extends only so far. We were chatting after breakfast this morning when she mentioned the draft in the sitting room, and I offered to come up and get her shawl."

I raised a brow. "And neglected to return her key?"

"I misplaced it along the way and got another from the desk clerk. They're very obliging about their keys."

"Very clever of you," I said.

"I thought so."

I sighed. "Well, there seems to be nothing here. I can't find anything that might have been used to murder Rupert."

"Perhaps you haven't looked in the right place."

"If you think you can do better, you're certainly welcome to try," I said irritably. I was still angry with Milo, but I had decided Mr. Hamilton's bedroom was probably not the best place to have it out.

Milo ambled to the wardrobe and opened the doors. "The chap hasn't got many clothes," he noted.

"Most gentlemen don't require as many clothes as you do when traveling," I said tersely.

"You're angry with me," Milo said suddenly, turning to face me. "You weren't nearly so cross at breakfast." A satisfied smile crept across his face. "I think perhaps you didn't get enough sleep. In that case, I suppose I am to blame."

I clenched my teeth against an angry retort when I heard a most unwelcome sound. Voices were approaching in the hallway. My eyes met Milo's and we both stilled to listen.

Though I couldn't make out any words, the loud, boisterous tones left no doubt as to who stood outside the door. Mr. Hamilton had finished his lunch.

I glanced at the door to Mrs. Hamilton's room. Perhaps there was still time to slip into it and escape into the hall. That hope was quickly crushed as I heard a soft answer that must have been hers. They were both in the hallway about to enter their rooms.

I watched in utter horror as the doorknob rattled and began to turn. Mr. Hamilton was entering his room, and there was nowhere to go.

20

I HAVE OFTEN heard the expression about one's blood running cold, but I cannot say I ever truly experienced it until that moment. It seemed like an eternity that I stood frozen, my mind racing over the possible consequences of being discovered.

Fortunately, Milo took action. With smooth, rapid motions, he quietly closed the door between the two rooms and, returning to where I stood, grabbed my arm, pushing me into the wardrobe. He slipped in after me and pulled the doors closed behind us, just as I heard the door to Mr. Hamilton's room open.

The wardrobe was apparently of impressive construction, for no light slipped in the seams of the doors; it was black as pitch inside and immediately stuffy. I also couldn't help but notice that the size of the space seemed to have diminished drastically from when I had gazed in moments before. My back was against the sidewall, and Milo stood directly in front of me. He was too tall to stand up straight, so he leaned toward me, his hands on the wall on either side of me. My hand rested on his chest, and I could feel the slow, steady beat of his heart, which was in marked contrast to the mad racing of my own.

Outside the wardrobe, I could barely make out the sounds of Mr. Hamilton moving about the room. Mrs. Hamilton had apparently entered her own room, for I heard no sound of her voice. Now that the moment of crisis had passed, at least for the time being, I began to reflect on exactly how preposterous our situation was. Even if we were not caught suspiciously ensconced in Mr. Hamilton's wardrobe, I might well be stuck here for hours with Milo quite literally breathing down my neck.

As if on cue, my husband took this moment to exasperate me further.

"Rather cozy in here, isn't it?" he whispered into my ear.

"This is all your fault," I hissed.

"My fault? How is it my fault?"

"Be quiet. You're using up all the air."

We were both silent for a moment. Very few signs emanated from the room, and I was terrified Mr. Hamilton might fling the wardrobe doors open at any moment.

I wanted to cry with relief when I heard the unmistakable sound of Mr. Hamilton drawing a bath. If only he would go into the bathroom and shut the door, we could make our escape. Yet it seemed that luck was not on our side. Though the water continued to run, Mr. Hamilton could be heard whistling to himself as he moved about the room. At least the running water would help to conceal our voices.

"Good heavens," I whispered. "I hope he doesn't decide to lay out the clothes from his wardrobe before he takes a bath."

"It would be a bit awkward," Milo agreed. "We might have

talked our way out of being discovered in his room, but being discovered in his wardrobe is a different matter entirely."

"This is your fault," I said again. "If you hadn't been here . . ."

"You would have been caught."

"I would not."

The whistling faded as Mr. Hamilton presumably made his way back into the bathroom. The sound of the water did not diminish, however, so it seemed he had not yet shut the door.

"It occurs to me," Milo said after a moment, "that there may be distinct advantages to the situation in which we have found ourselves."

"Such as?"

"Use your imagination, Amory," he murmured. He leaned to kiss my neck, and I stiffened.

"Don't," I said.

His arms moved around me, and he pressed closer. "Haven't you ever wanted to be kissed in a dark wardrobe?"

"There's no need. Gil's not here to see you now."

"Ah," he said, his mouth still pressed beneath my ear. The understanding implicit in the single syllable irritated me further.

"You did it on purpose," I said, pushing against his chest.

He leaned back ever so slightly but didn't bother to deny it. "All's fair in love and war, darling."

"And which, exactly, is this, Milo?"

"It was only a kiss, Amory. It wasn't as though I ravished you in the lobby."

"You needn't feign attraction to me for Gil's sake."

"You little idiot." He kissed me in earnest then, and it was a long moment before I pushed him away.

"Stop, Milo. Listen." A series of splashes reached our ears. It seemed that Mr. Hamilton entered his bath. The water was still running, however, and it did not sound as though the door had been closed. Did the man intend to bathe with the bathroom door open? We waited.

Finally, Milo disentangled himself from me, and pushed the door open the slightest crack. A moment later, he pushed it open farther. The light shone across his face as he frowned. "Wait here a moment," he said.

"I don't . . ." He slipped out and closed the door before I could finish my sentence. I sighed into the darkness.

He was gone what seemed to be an inordinately long time. Then I heard another splash. I hoped Milo had not been discovered, but there was no sound of voices, so I waited a moment longer. I was about to step out and investigate for myself when Milo pulled the doors open. His expression was uncharacteristically solemn, and I felt that his sleeves were wet as he assisted me from the wardrobe.

"What's the matter?" I whispered.

He nodded toward the adjoining door, and I saw that water had seeped out of the room onto the carpet. And still the water was running in the bathtub.

"What . . ." My eyes met his, and suddenly I knew.

I stepped toward the bathroom.

"Amory, perhaps you'd better not."

I ignored him and went to the door, looking in to the room I had rummaged through not long before. It was just as I had feared.

Mr. Hamilton, still dressed in his undershirt and trousers, was half-submerged in the bathtub full of water. His legs hung over the edge, and his face, eyes bulging wide, stared blankly up from beneath the surface.

I stifled a gasp with my hand. I turned to Milo, my eyes wide.

"I'm afraid the plot thickens," he said.

IT WAS ALL very like some horrible bout of déjà vu.

Gazing down at the body of someone who had been alive only minutes before was awful indeed. Doing it twice in one week was utterly appalling. Though I had thoroughly disliked the man, seeing him floating in a tub like so much driftwood left me feeling shabby about my uncharitable thoughts.

"Perhaps we should pull him out," I said numbly.

"Better leave him for the police," Milo answered.

"Are you sure he's . . . dead? Perhaps we can still do something." I knew even as I spoke that it was far too late to do anything.

"I pulled his head out a moment ago to check. He's quite dead."

The nonchalance with which Milo spoke of handling the corpse made me feel a bit ill. I shuddered as I recalled the brush of his wet cuffs against my skin.

"We'd better call the police," I said.

Milo walked past me, his shoes sloshing in the water that ran across the floor. He pulled his handkerchief from his pocket and used it to turn off the water.

The room suddenly seemed very quiet. I glanced back at Mr. Hamilton. His eyes were blue; I had never noticed.

Milo made his way back to my side.

"Let's go, Amory." He took my elbow and guided me from the room.

The next few moments passed rather in a blur. Back in the

lobby, Milo told the desk clerk to call the police while I tried to collect my wits. Then we went back to our room to wait.

As Milo removed his damp shirt, I sat on the sofa, attempting to calm my nerves. I didn't know what had come over me. My hands were shaking, and my legs felt like rubber.

Milo pulled on a fresh shirt, and I watched his fingers as he deftly buttoned it. His hands were steady. If stumbling across a body in a bathtub had rattled him, he certainly didn't show it.

"How do you think it happened?" I asked at last.

"That, my dear, is a very good question," he replied, knotting his tie.

"Perhaps he fell and hit his head," I suggested, wanting desperately to believe it.

Milo smoothed his tie and regarded me with a bland expression. "Come now, Amory. You're much too clever to believe that."

He was right; I didn't believe it. Not for a moment.

"This is like a nightmare," I said, dropping my head into my hands. "It's all too horrid for words."

Milo sank onto the sofa beside me. "It's a nasty business, isn't it," he agreed as he lit a cigarette and proceeded to smoke it, relaxed as ever. Some little part of me was disappointed that he didn't pull me to him in a comforting embrace. I desperately needed a bit of reassurance at the moment.

Milo's sangfroid was not rubbing off on me. I stood, too nervous to sit, and began to pace. "Why should someone wish to kill Mr. Hamilton?"

"I haven't the faintest idea."

"It could have been anyone. He left his door unlocked."

"Yes, you got in easily enough."

"But it would have had to be timed impeccably well. How should they know that he was preparing to bathe? Only Mrs. Hamilton might have known, and she wouldn't have been able to do such a thing."

"Amory darling, do sit down. You're wearing a path in the rug."

"Perhaps they meant to kill him and just happened to take advantage of the bath," I said. "That seems more likely. But who could have done it? We didn't hear anything."

I stopped pacing as another horrible thought occurred to me. "Milo, whatever are we going to tell the police?"

He shrugged. "The truth, I suppose."

"Tell them what, exactly? That we were hiding in the wardrobe?" I asked, aghast at the suggestion. "I suppose you think Inspector Jones would applaud us for our discretion."

"I really think you should sit down. You're very pale."

"I'm perfectly well," I replied, but I dropped onto the sofa next to Milo anyway. The truth was that I didn't feel at all well. Though my hands had ceased to tremble, my insides felt all aquiver. I could not understand why I had taken this so hard. I had not been so affected by the death of Rupert. Then again, I had only seen his body from afar. Mr. Hamilton's body had been much more of a shock. The image of his staring eyes was something I was not likely to forget for a long time to come.

We sat in silence as we waited. Milo smoked with the appearance of perfect contentment as I wrung my hands, lost in thought. It just didn't make sense. Who could have killed Mr. Hamilton? Even more perplexing was the question, Who would want to?

It seemed an eternity before the officious rap sounded at our door.

Milo rose and went to open it, and I stood expectantly.

"Mr. and Mrs. Ames," Inspector Jones said as he entered, hat in hand. His tone was calm, but something about his posture seemed poised and alert, like a cat about to pounce. "I understand there has been another . . . unfortunate incident."

"Have you been to Mr. Hamilton's room yet?" I asked.

"Yes," he said. He turned to Milo. "I understand you reported the body, Mr. Ames." Inspector Jones, I had discovered, possessed the peculiar talent of being able to say a great deal without saying anything at all. Somehow, the simple question managed to convey skepticism mingled with curiosity at just what Milo had been doing in Mr. Hamilton's bathroom.

"Yes," Milo answered. "I did. Or we did, rather."

"I see."

"It was dreadful," I said.

The inspector's gaze came back to me, and I thought I saw concern flicker there. "Mrs. Ames, perhaps you should sit down."

I sighed and sat. Inspector Jones indicated the sofa, and Milo sat, too, as the inspector took a seat in one of the chairs.

"Now then," he said, pulling his notebook and pen from his jacket pocket. "How exactly was it that you discovered the body?"

I glanced at Milo. He had suggested the truth, so the truth it would be. "We were in the room when it happened," I said.

The inspector's pen stilled, and he looked up sharply. "In the room?"

"Yes . . . we were hidden."

"Hidden?" he repeated.

"Yes," Milo said, "and while we're confessing, I expect you'll find that Amory's fingerprints are scattered about the premises."

"Blast," I murmured. "I didn't think of fingerprints."

"You should have worn gloves," Milo said.

Inspector Jones's jaw clenched, and he was silent for a moment before he spoke. "May I ask why your fingerprints are scattered about Mr. Hamilton's room, Mrs. Ames?"

"I . . . I was doing a search," I said.

"A search." His jaw clenched again, and I thought he must be trying very hard to contain either extreme anger or amusement. I hoped for the latter but rather suspected the former.

I briefly explained the events that had led up to my inspection of Mr. Hamilton's room, including observing Mr. Hamilton pick up something on the beach and my suspicion that it might be the weapon. Inspector Jones, after staring inscrutably for a moment, returned to jotting methodical notes and interjecting the occasional terse question.

"I could find no sign of anything that might be a weapon in his room," I told him.

"You thought you had information regarding the murder weapon, and you didn't think this was pertinent enough to share with the police?" he asked. His eyes had taken on a decidedly hard cast, and I realized that this might not bode well for us, especially since he had yet to hear the rest of our tale.

"I didn't want to bother you with trifles," I answered. "Not until I was certain."

"Do you realize you could be arrested for breaking into someone's room?"

"The door was unlocked," I said. The inspector frowned but did not reply to this. Instead, he turned to Milo.

"And what part did you play in this, Mr. Ames? You obviously didn't try to discourage your wife from her endeavors."

"One does not dissuade Amory from anything," Milo said dryly. "But, in fact, I didn't know she was going to Mr. Hamilton's room.

I just happened to encounter her there in the course of my own investigations."

I was fairly certain I heard the inspector swear beneath his breath.

"I know this must sound frightfully far-fetched," I admitted.

Inspector Jones sighed. "Go on, Mrs. Ames."

I related how Milo and I had met up in the room and how we had heard Mr. and Mrs. Hamilton approaching. "We couldn't get out of the room. So, we ... well ..."

"We hid in the wardrobe," Milo supplied.

The inspector blinked once. "You were in the wardrobe when the incident occurred," he said slowly. "What did you hear?"

"He was whistling to himself as he filled the bathtub," I told him. "We could hear him walking around, and then he entered the bathroom."

"And after that?"

"Well, we were a bit preoccupied," Milo answered casually.

Inspector Jones digested this bit of news with perfect equanimity. I, on the other hand, was horrified.

"You needn't make it sound so sordid, Milo."

"Good heavens, darling. You're blushing like a schoolgirl."

"I am not," I replied coolly.

Inspector Jones cleared his throat. "You heard no other voices?"

"No," I answered, relieved at the change of subject. "I believe I heard Mrs. Hamilton in the hall, but I didn't hear her enter the room. There was a bit of splashing, and then nothing."

The inspector jotted this down and closed his notebook. "That should be sufficient for now."

"How is Mrs. Hamilton?" I asked.

He looked at me, his gaze suddenly sharp. "Why do you ask?"

I was startled by the question. "I assume she has taken Mr. Hamilton's death very hard. Or haven't you told her yet?"

His expression relaxed ever so slightly. "No, Mrs. Ames. We haven't told her yet. We are still hoping we will be able to."

I frowned. "What do you mean?"

"Mrs. Hamilton was drugged, heavily. The doctor is with her now. We haven't been able to wake her up."

21

SOMEHOW, I PERSUADED Inspector Jones to allow me to accompany him to the hospital. His mood was not at all agreeable, but he had not protested when I asked to ride with him.

Mrs. Hamilton had not yet regained consciousness. Though I knew it would likely be some time before I was allowed to see her, I wanted to be there when she awakened. She had no close friends here to comfort her, and I thought someone should be with her. Though Mr. Hamilton had not treated her well, I knew she would take the news hard.

The atmosphere in the inspector's car was chilly in the extreme. Disapproval rolled off him in waves larger than the ones that pounded against the shore at the base of the cliff. I had the vague suspicion that had we not developed a somewhat amiable rapport early on, he would not have been entirely opposed to arresting me for trespassing.

I glanced out the window. The wind seemed to have picked up, and there were dark clouds on the edge of the horizon.

"It seems a storm might be looming," I said.

"Indeed," he replied, and I thought that he did not mean the weather.

I felt instinctively that it would not be beneficial to allow the inspector to brood for too long. Perhaps there was still a chance to repair at least some of the damage. I adopted a soft, semirepentant tone. "I do hope you are not too angry, Inspector Jones. I understand that it was, perhaps, imprudent for me to search Mr. Hamilton's room. However, if I had come across the weapon..."

"You have no business assuming the duties of the police," he interrupted, his tone clipped.

"I didn't mean any harm by it," I replied, allowing a bit more contrition to seep into my tone. I was not really as abashed as I hoped I sounded, but I knew that it would do no good to make him angrier.

"Perhaps not," he replied, and I was pleased to note that his voice was not quite as steely as it had been a moment before. "Nevertheless, what you did was not only injudicious, it was very dangerous. Do you realize you might have been hurt yourself? What if the killer had discovered your hiding place?"

I didn't care to think about that. Then I realized the term that the inspector had chosen to employ.

"Killer," I repeated. "You think he was murdered, then?"

"I think we can safely assume Mr. Hamilton did not slip and fall while getting into his bath."

"That is, in essence, the same thing my husband said."

He glanced at me. "You seem to have patched things up with Mr. Ames."

I hesitated. Despite our recent collaborative endeavors, I was still not at all certain where things stood between Milo and me.

"He is having one of his agreeable phases," I said at last. "There is no guarantee that it will last."

"I see. And where does that leave Mr. Trent?"

I was surprised by the sudden turn our conversation had taken. The confusion I still felt regarding Milo and Gil was not something I wished to discuss with a policeman with whom I was barely acquainted. I had learned, however, that Inspector Jones always had very good reasons for the questions that he asked.

"These questions are getting rather personal, aren't they, Inspector?" I replied lightly.

"Yes, Mrs. Ames. I suppose they are." Something in his tone said that he still expected me to answer them.

I looked out the window. "I am . . . very fond of Gil. I always have been. But in the end, I married Milo. That's really all there is to it." Was it really that simple? I wasn't sure.

Inspector Jones was a very perceptive man. He must have picked up on my uncertainty. "I think, perhaps, the gentlemen in question might not find it so straightforward."

I looked at him. "Perhaps you're right. You see, I came to the seaside with Gil, in part because I have always wondered how things might have been different if . . . Gil is so very steady; with Milo it is either bliss or misery, nothing in between. So there you have it." I managed a flat smile. "You must think me a very fickle sort of woman."

"On the contrary. As evidenced by your marked proclivity for intruding where you don't belong, I find you to be a very decisive woman, and an intelligent one."

"Thank you, Inspector," I replied, pleased by the compliment despite the terms in which it had been couched.

"If I may venture a word of caution," he said, his tone still pleasant. "I should choose my allies carefully, were I you."

I looked at him sharply, surprised by the sudden warning. "That is rather a cryptic remark."

"It was not intended to be. I only mean that things are uncertain right now; watch yourself carefully."

I frowned. There was something he was not saying, and I could tell that he did not intend to explain further, at least not now.

I intended to take his advice. The danger had become all too clear today. If someone had killed Mr. Hamilton and drugged his wife . . .

I drew in a breath. I could not believe that I had not thought of it before now. It was just possible I may have had my own very narrow escape. Mr. Hamilton had been drugged and murdered. If someone had substituted my aspirin for sleeping tablets, perhaps they had meant to kill me, too.

"Inspector, there's something else . . ." I reached into my handbag and pulled out the bottle of aspirin that had been in my room. "I think someone may have tried to drug me as well."

He glanced at me sharply before returning his eyes to the road. "What do you mean?"

"It was the night Gil was arrested. I took two aspirin from this bottle, and I fell asleep almost immediately. In the morning, I was exceptionally muzzy. I'm quite certain they aren't aspirin. I know it may sound far-fetched, but . . ."

"Why didn't you mention this earlier, Mrs. Ames?" he interrupted. His voice had not lost its edge, and I rather felt like a poor pupil being reprimanded by a stern headmaster.

"Truthfully, I forgot about it. It seemed highly unlikely at the time. Really, it was only a vague suspicion on my part, but now . . ."

"Are there any tablets left?"

"Yes. There are several still in the bottle."

He held out his hand, and I gave it to him. He slipped it inside his jacket.

"I shall have them tested," he said. "It may not be as far-fetched as you think."

"But why should someone want to drug me? It doesn't make sense."

"There are a great many things that don't make sense at the moment, Mrs. Ames, but they are beginning to."

We said nothing further until we reached the hospital. I started to get out, but the inspector's hand on my arm stopped me. "A final word, Mrs. Ames." His expression was still pleasant, but I could tell by the firmness of his gaze and the officious tone of his voice that he was about to give instructions he expected to be followed.

"Thus far, I have been . . . lenient, shall we say, because I like you and, quite frankly, the frivolous prosecution of the wealthy and well connected does not sit well with my superiors. But let me warn you: if either you or your husband interferes again, I shall not hesitate to take whatever measures necessary to ensure both your safety and the success of my investigation. No more independent enquiries. Do I make myself clear?"

"As clear as crystal, Inspector," I replied.

INSPECTOR JONES WENT to look in on Mrs. Hamilton, telling me I should wait. I knew it would perhaps be a while before I could see her, so I took a seat in the area designated for waiting. I'm afraid patience is not one of my more dominant virtues, so it was not long before I rose from my seat and began to take stock of the building.

The hospital was a clean, quiet facility with long white walls. The scent of the sea mingled with the more astringent smell of disinfectant, and there was a relaxed sort of air to the place, as though people did not often get sick at the seaside. Unfortunately, that did not seem to be the case at the Brightwell Hotel. "Dropping like flies" had been Milo's succinctly inappropriate, if accurate, pronouncement.

Though it seemed impossible now that she could have had anything to do with the murders, I had intended to talk to Olive Henderson, and this seemed the ideal time to do so. I approached the solid, humorless-looking woman that sat behind the desk. "Might I see Miss Olive Henderson?" I asked.

She looked up at me with a flat expression. "Miss Henderson is no longer receiving visitors today, by the doctor's orders," she said crisply.

"Surely she's well enough for me to drop in for just a moment."

"Miss Henderson was upset by an early visitor, and the doctor specifically instructed that she receive no more visitors today."

I frowned, suddenly alert. "What visitor?"

"I'm not at liberty to divulge information. I can only tell you that Miss Henderson is currently under close observation and is not allowed to receive visitors." She began sorting papers on her desk, and I knew that I had been dismissed.

I turned from the woman, lost in thought. Who might have visited Olive Henderson today? In all likelihood, it was one of the guests from the hotel. What had upset her? It was all very mysterious.

I briefly considered sneaking into her room, but the inspector's warning was still fresh in my mind. I did not believe for an instant that his had been an idle threat, and I did not relish the thought of being locked up in some dank, dark cell.

The air in the waiting area seemed to grow more oppressive by the moment, and I stepped outside. The wind had picked up, but the sky above me was still a bright blue, dotted with wispy white clouds. Though dark clouds still showed in the distance, they did not seem to be approaching very rapidly. If rain was coming, it would likely not arrive until evening.

The hospital overlooked the sea, and I enjoyed a few moments of quiet as I gazed out at the view. Then I looked toward the village. It was not a great distance off, and it looked inviting. Inspector Jones would likely tell me when Mrs. Hamilton awakened. In the meantime, I might try a walk to calm my nerves.

I reached the village a few minutes later. I wandered around for a while, looking in the windows of various shops. Among the villagers and holiday goers, I could almost forget all the terrible things that had occurred in the past week. Almost.

A lovely little antique shop caught my attention, and I spent a few moments browsing through the crowded rows of knickknacks, ranging from cheap plaster busts to very good china. I found a set of gold cufflinks engraved with the letter *A* and purchased them on a whim. I thought Milo would like them.

I had just left the shop when I spotted Mr. and Mrs. Rodgers exiting a shop at the end of the street. They were walking quickly, their backs to me. I called out to them, but they appeared to be deep in conversation and didn't hear. A moment later, they got in a car and drove away.

I decided to head back to the hospital, but as I walked down the street, I noticed the building that the Rodgerses had exited. It was the apothecary shop. A thought occurred to me suddenly, and I stopped outside the door, hesitating for just a moment before charging ahead.

I entered the shop, and the little bell above the door jingled a greeting. A single woman stood behind the counter. She had a round, pleasant face framed with flame-colored hair. She smiled brightly as

I came in. "Good day, miss. Is there something I could help you with?"

"I just saw my friends leaving," I said, "but I didn't catch them in time and they've driven off. We're all staying up at the Brightwell. I don't suppose they purchased a bottle of aspirin for me? They may have forgotten."

"No, miss. They didn't purchase any aspirin," the woman said.

Almost before I knew what I was saying, I nodded and spoke casually. "I suppose they were picking up the sleeping tablets."

"Yes, miss. The lady said she had misplaced hers."

I kept my expression studiously neutral, but my thoughts were racing. Why should Mr. and Mrs. Rodgers come to purchase sleeping tablets immediately after Mr. and Mrs. Hamilton had been drugged? Surely they knew about Mr. Hamilton's death by now. It seemed a very odd time to make a trip to the apothecary.

I purchased a bottle of aspirin to replace the one I had given the inspector. Instead of falling into place, things only seemed to be getting more and more complicated. One thing was certain: there were enough sleeping tablets floating around the Brightwell Hotel to do away with all of us. As the woman at the counter chatted on amiably, I resolved that I would be very careful of what I ate or drank at the Brightwell from this time forward.

LOST IN THOUGHT, I arrived back at the hospital. The unhelpful woman at the desk informed me that the inspector had not yet emerged, so I took a seat. Unwelcome thoughts continued to race through my head. If someone had meant to kill me in my room after drugging me, it had been a lucky thing that Milo had decided to spend the night in my room. Yet I could think of no reason why someone should wish to murder me. I had very little to do with the whole affair. If indeed Mr. or Mrs. Rodgers had something to do with it, I could think of no conceivable reason why I should pose an impediment to them. None of it seemed to make any sense.

By the time I saw Inspector Jones coming toward me, my nerves were quite on edge. Despite my distraction, I noticed immediately that his expression was grim.

I stood, bracing myself for the worst. "Is she all right?" I asked.

"She's alive," he said, "which is not at all the same thing."

"She's taken it very hard?"

"It seems so. She's not entirely coherent. Whatever drug she was given was exceptionally strong." He paused, as though considering how much he should say, and then went on. "It's very likely that Mr. Hamilton was given the same thing. He was faceup in the water, indicating that he was probably held down until he drowned. He would have been too disoriented to struggle much."

A chill swept through me as I recalled the splashing Milo and I had heard. Mr. Hamilton had been putting up what fight he could, trying to save his life, but it had not been enough. A wave of sadness swept over me. If Milo and I had come out of the wardrobe a moment sooner, perhaps we could have done something . . .

"Are you all right, Mrs. Ames?" Inspector Jones asked. He was watching me intently, and his expression was almost kind.

"It's been a dreadful day," I said. In truth, I felt on the verge of tears.

"There is one other thing."

"Indeed?" I asked, something very like dread in my voice.

"I had one of the doctors look at those tablets you gave me. They've not yet finished analyzing them, but he is quite certain that they are sleeping tablets and not aspirin."

It was not really a surprise, but it was still something of a blow to hear my suspicions confirmed.

"Who might have had access to them?" he asked.

"I don't know. Anyone, I suppose. I'm afraid I am sometimes rather careless about locking my door. But the bottle was exactly where I left it."

"Was your husband with you that night?"

"Yes, but I can think of no reason why he would have done it. In fact, I don't understand why anyone should have done it," I said. "Surely I don't pose a threat to anyone."

"You may know more than you think," he said cryptically. "Come. I'll take you back now. You should get some rest."

I nodded. What I wanted now was to lie down in the quiet of my room and share what I had learned with Milo. When exactly he had become a source of comfort to me, I didn't know, but at the moment I found myself wanting very much to be with him.

Inspector Jones and I walked back to the car in comfortable silence.

I hesitated to tell him what I had discovered regarding Mr. and Mrs. Rodgers; he would no doubt only berate me for my underhanded tactics. However, I couldn't bring myself to keep the information quiet. Skirting around my methods, I told him what I had learned.

"Indeed," he said, and I could read nothing in his expression.

"Might the Rodgerses have any reason for killing Mr. Howe?" I asked.

"It may be nothing," he said, not answering my question. "But you did well to let me know."

At last, we reached the hotel. The car pulled to a stop, and Inspector Jones turned to me, his face grave. "I believe this will all be resolved soon. In the meantime, please be careful, Mrs. Ames," he said.

"I intend to, Inspector."

I walked toward the hotel so lost in thought that I nearly collided with Lionel Blake.

"Oh, excuse me," I said.

I looked up at him and noticed at once the tension on his features. However good of an actor he might be, he was making no attempt to hide his distress at present.

"Is it true what they are saying?" he asked me without preamble.

I nodded sadly. "I'm afraid so."

He rubbed a hand across his chin and mumbled something under his breath that I couldn't quite make out. The only word I caught was "lord." Then he seemed to catch himself, and I watched with fascination as he deliberately smoothed his features and presented me with the calm, handsome expression I had come to expect from him.

"I've been out walking around the grounds," he said, and even his tone had undergone a transformation. There was absolutely no trace of strain in his well-modulated voice now. "The hotel is beginning to seem so stifling. I will be very glad to leave this place."

"As will I."

"Do you think there will be much publicity?" he asked me suddenly.

I thought it a strange thing to ask. But perhaps as an actor he always had to consider such things. "The Brightwell and the police have done a remarkable job of keeping the press away thus far," I said. "Though I'm sure the papers are still full of sensational tales. I'd almost rather not know what they are saying..."

"I do hate to give interviews."

"I shouldn't imagine that would be necessary," I answered. "It would be entirely at your discretion to do such a thing."

He nodded. "Yes. You're right of course."

I must have glanced at the hotel, for he was immediately all contrite politeness. "Forgive me for keeping you, Mrs. Ames. I know you must be anxious to rest after . . . I do apologize."

"No apologies necessary, Mr. Blake," I said, glad nevertheless to be on my way. "I'll see you at dinner, perhaps."

"Yes."

I walked past him, and a final glance over my shoulder confirmed that he had continued his solitary walk. There was something in the encounter that nagged at me, but I was too weary at present to attempt to analyze it.

I entered the hotel feeling more tired and worn than I ever had in my life. I glanced around the people seated in the lobby, hoping to spot Milo. Instead, Mrs. Roland appeared out of nowhere, and before I could retreat, she caught sight of me and headed in my direction.

Today she was dressed in a turquoise dress bedecked with a pattern of huge magenta hibiscus, over which she had layered what seemed to be a dozen necklaces of every description: seashells, pearls, jet beads, and what appeared to be hollowed-out and intricately carved pieces of wood. She fairly clattered as she glided toward me.

"Amory darling!" she exclaimed. "You're still here! I thought you'd gone with your husband."

I was only half-listening. As much as I liked the woman, there was only so much my nerves could take at present.

"Gone where?" I asked, my gaze caught momentarily by an emerald-encrusted tortoise on a long gold chain that hung around her neck.

"Back to London, of course. I assume that's where he went."

I looked up sharply. "Milo's gone?"

"Why, yes, darling. Your charming husband left not long ago. I assumed you'd gone with him."

I felt as though I had been dealt an unexpected blow. "Surely you must be mistaken."

"Not at all, dear." She gave me an exaggerated wink. "It's impossible to mistake your husband for anyone else."

"Excuse me, Mrs. Roland. I must see to something."

"Yes, of course. You really should get some sun, Amory," she called, as I walked away. "You're looking rather pale!"

I approached the desk with as much calmness as I could muster. Surely she was mistaken. Milo would not have left without saying anything. The very idea was ridiculous.

"Have I any letters?" I asked the clerk. "Mrs. Amory Ames."

"Yes, Mrs. Ames. There's a note for you. It was left by your husband about half an hour ago. He asked that we give it to you upon your return."

I took the envelope and recognized Milo's personal stationery. Perhaps he had gone to the village and I had missed him. I opened the envelope and pulled out the note, written in his familiar bold script.

Had to dash off to London, darling. Not sure how long I shall be gone.

M.

22

I SHOULD NOT have been surprised, but I was. In fact, I was utterly astounded. I stared at the note for a long moment before crumpling it in my hand. I resisted the sudden impulse to burst into tears. Truth be told, I was too tired to cry.

This was my fault; I should have known better than to begin to rely on him. I had known, deep down, that he was capable of something like this, but I hadn't wanted to believe it. Now, I was paying for my stupidity.

"Amory . . ." Gil's voice broke into my thoughts, and I turned to find him and Emmeline emerging from the lift. I attempted to keep my feelings from showing on my face, but Gil was not easily fooled.

"Is everything all right?" he asked, a concerned frown crossing his brow.

I mastered my emotions and managed a smile. "Yes, Gil. Thank you." I turned to Emmeline. "I'm glad to see you're feeling a bit better."

"Gil insists I need some sun and fresh air," she said. "Will you take tea with us?"

"I . . . I think not today, thank you. I'm not feeling very well."

I could feel Gil's gaze on me, though I could not meet his eyes.

"Emmeline, will you wait for me in the dining room?" he asked her.

"Yes. I'll see you later, Amory?"

"Yes, Emmeline. I should like that."

She left us, and Gil turned to me. "Let's go into the sitting room a moment, shall we?"

I followed him. Finding the room empty, he turned to me. "Now then, what's wrong?"

I pushed my thoughts of Milo away for the moment. There were more important things to discuss. "I suppose you've heard about Mr. Hamilton."

He nodded. "Inspector Jones stopped by to ask me my whereabouts."

"He doesn't think that you . . ."

Gil smiled, but his eyes were dark. "It only happened after I had been released. I expect I'd hang just as easily for two murders as for one."

I felt ill at his words. "Don't say that."

"They haven't taken me back in charge, at any rate," he said. "I suppose they want to make sure that it was murder. I've telephoned Sir Andrew. It seems he will have his work cut out for him."

That reminded me of something I had been wanting to ask him. "Mr. Rodgers said that you sent for Sir Andrew before your arrest," I ventured. "Were you so certain it would happen?"

"I thought it might. I . . . you see, I'd written Rupert some pretty strongly worded letters. I was sure they would turn up."

"But they haven't."

"Not yet. I suppose it's only a matter of time. More coals heaped on the fire."

"I can't believe this is happening," I said, almost to myself.

I felt Gil's eyes on me, assessing me. "But Mr. Hamilton's death and my arrest weren't what you were thinking about when I came up to you. There's something else, isn't there?"

I smiled tiredly. "It's no good trying to hide things from you, is it, Gil? You may as well know. Milo's gone."

"Gone? Where?"

"To London. No explanation." I managed a laugh that I hoped didn't sound as forced as it felt. "It's very typical, you know."

I found I couldn't quite meet Gil's gaze and looked down at the crumbled paper in my hand instead.

"Why do you let him do it to you, Amory?" he said suddenly.

I looked up, surprised by the question, and saw that his eyes were hard and dark. I realized suddenly that he was angry—not only at Milo, but at me.

"You deserve better." His voice, though calm, held an edge. "Isn't five years of it enough?"

"I suppose this is really between Milo and me," I said, finding my own ire rising at the accusation in his tone. "After all, he is my husband."

"I would have made you a much better one."

I felt myself pale at the words, and we stared at one another. My lips parted, but I found I could think of nothing to say.

"I think perhaps I better check on Emmeline," he said after a moment of heavy silence. "Excuse me."

I watched him go, still unable to think of any sort of appropriate response.

He hadn't gone far when he stopped and turned. "Does Inspector Jones know? About Milo's leaving, I mean."

I hadn't thought of that. "I . . . I don't suppose he does."

"If you can get in touch with Milo, you'd better do it. Tell him to hurry back. It won't look well, his running off after two murders."

I SPENT THE rest of the miserable evening in my room. Gil's words echoed over and over in my head. It had been terrible, looking at the hurt and disapproval in his expression. Even worse, I wasn't sure I disagreed with him. I had made a hasty decision to marry Milo, and I was reaping the consequences. Gil might not have made life as exciting as Milo did, but he would not have made me miserable, and he would not have deserted me when I needed him the most.

I barely touched the dinner I had sent up. Perhaps Gil was right; perhaps five years was enough. As much as I had hoped Milo and I might reach some sort of harmony in our union, I needed someone I could rely on, someone who would be at my side when I needed him. Milo simply wasn't. Perhaps it was time that I simply admitted my mistake and acknowledged that we couldn't make a go of it.

The knock sounded on my door, and for a fleeting moment I thought it might be Milo. Then I realized that he probably wouldn't have knocked.

I pulled the door open and was not completely surprised to see who was standing there.

"Hello, Gil."

"I need to talk to you, Amory," he said.

I hesitated a moment before stepping back and pulling open the door. As he entered, I noticed that his gait was somewhat unsteady and that the strong scent of alcohol followed after him.

"You've been drinking," I said, surprised. Since I had known Gil, I had never known him to indulge in more than the occasional glass of wine. From the looks of things, he had had something much more substantial since our conversation this afternoon.

"I have, a little," he replied. He turned to me, his features somber. "I need to talk to you."

"Perhaps you would rather do it tomorrow, when you're feeling better."

"No. I need to tell you something."

"Would you like to sit down?"

"Not now, thank you."

We stood facing one another.

"I'm sorry about today," he said. "It seems I'm always making a mess of things."

"We're all strained at the moment. You needn't apologize."

"I shouldn't have said what I did," he went on. "It's none of my business."

"Let's just forget it, Gil."

"I knew that first night, you know," he said suddenly. "When you met him, I knew that . . . well, I had a feeling that things were going to change."

I remembered the night I met Milo as though it were yesterday. Gil and I had been at a large party given by some lord or the other. Milo had arrived late, just as we had sat down to dinner. It hadn't been cliché, locking eyes across a crowded room and all that sort of thing. I had noticed Milo when he walked into the dining room, of course; most of the women present had. I hadn't given him much thought, however. Dinner finished, Gil had gone off to speak to someone, and Milo had appeared at my side and asked me to dance. I had known who he was before he introduced himself. His reputation was wild even then, but he had been pleasant, polite. It would have been ill mannered of me to refuse. He led me to the dance floor, and, looking into those bright blue eyes, I had felt a strange sensation the first moment I was in his arms . . .

"I came back into the room, looking for you, and saw you dancing with him," Gil said. "I saw the way you looked at one another. And somehow I knew . . ."

"I'm sorry, Gil," I whispered, and I truly was. I couldn't help the way I had felt about Milo, but I could have done more to spare Gil's feelings. I had been young and inconsiderate. I regretted it now.

"I wanted you to be happy." He laughed, somewhat hoarsely. "I was almost relieved when you said you were going to marry him. At least I knew that his intentions were honorable."

"I was happy," I said. "For a while."

"I know I have no right . . . but I want to protect you, Amory. I don't want you to be hurt."

I wasn't sure if he spoke regarding Milo or the murders. Perhaps he spoke of both. I only knew that he had somehow chosen just the right thing to say.

"Thank you. That means a lot."

He swayed a little, and I reached out a hand to steady him. Somehow, he fell against me, and in the space of a moment his arms were around me. We looked at one another. Had it only been today that I had been pressed against Milo in the wardrobe? It seemed so very long ago. And now here I stood, in Gil's embrace. He was so very close; I could feel him breathing. I felt at once that I should step back, but I couldn't seem to make myself move.

"Amory," he said. "I . . ." Then he leaned down and his mouth met mine.

For just a moment, my mind flashed back to the last time he had kissed me: the night I had told him I was going to marry Milo. I had broken the news as gently as possible, and he had taken it with a grace born of refinement and his own good nature. After all had been said that there could possibly be to say, he had turned to leave me for the last time. Then he had stopped and come back to where I stood. His hand on my face, he had leaned down and kissed me.

There had been so much emotion in that gentle farewell kiss. As in love with Milo as I had been, something about it had left me heartbroken. I had wept when Gil left, utterly miserable. I felt the same thing now: a deep, aching sadness and a forlorn sort of longing that I could not precisely explain.

Then Gil's kiss deepened, his embrace drew me more tightly against him, and I was pulled back to the present. Things were different now than they had been then. Whatever my feelings, I was still married to Milo. I pulled back, my hands pressing gently against his chest, creating the smallest space between us. "We can't do this, Gil," I said softly.

He blinked, as though he was only just realizing this himself, and his hands dropped from my waist as though I were made of hot coals. "I'm sorry." He stepped back quickly, wavered, and I worried that he would fall.

"It's all right," I said, moving to take his arm. "Please, sit down. I'll have some coffee sent up."

I rang for coffee as he sank heavily into the sofa and his head dropped into his hands.

"Love makes a mess of things, doesn't it?" he said, as though he was speaking to himself. "People are always falling in love with the wrong people. It happens over and over. It would be so much simpler if ... I didn't know how she felt, you know ... I didn't think that she really meant it ..."

He wasn't talking about me any longer. Whom did he mean?

I sat on the sofa beside him. "Did you ... do you need to talk about something, Gil?" I asked him.

"I thought she was young and infatuated. I didn't realize she really meant it."

It could only be Emmeline he was referring to. But what was he trying to tell me?

He sat back and leaned his head against the sofa. "I feel terrible," he said.

"I know, dear. You'll feel better when you get some coffee."

As much as I wanted to know why he should have suddenly brought up the subject of Emmeline and her feelings for Rupert, I was silent and let Gil rest. I still didn't believe for a moment that Gil had killed Rupert, and yet it seemed very odd he should be lamenting Emmeline's grief at this particular moment. Then again, he was completely soused. I supposed it all made sense to him.

When the knock came, I answered it and took the tray from the maid, so she wouldn't see Gil in my room. Closing the door, I walked back to the sitting area and set the tray on the table in front of the sofa. "Here's the coffee," I said brightly. "It will be just the thing."

Gil didn't stir.

"Gil?"

I looked at him closely. He was sound asleep or, more likely, out cold.

I sighed. I couldn't have him moved without creating a scandal of immense proportions. He would just have to sleep it off on my sofa.

I removed his necktie and slid off his shoes before easing him into a recumbent position. Then I covered him with a spare blanket and turned out the lights. I couldn't help but think that, if anyone should find out he had spent the night in my room, I was going to have a devil of a time explaining it to Milo.

23

I HAD ALREADY dressed when Gil stirred. Despite the fact I had dimmed the lights and that the weather had turned the sky a dismal gray, he squinted as he opened his eyes. Then he caught sight of me and jerked to a sitting position, grimacing as he did so.

"What . . . Oh, no."

"Good morning, Gil," I said cheerily, trying to lessen the shock of it all. "How do you feel?"

"I kissed you last night," he said, ignoring my attempts at polite small talk.

"Yes."

He dragged a hand across his face. "I'm sorry, Amory. I don't know what to say."

"You needn't say anything."

"You must abhor me, forcing my attentions on you like a drunken . . ."

"You are never anything but a gentleman, Gil," I interrupted sternly. "And that's the last we need say about it."

"Does anyone know that I . . . spent the night here?"

"I sincerely hope not," I replied. "Did you tell anyone you were coming up to see me?"

"Not that I remember," he said ruefully. "I've never been quite that drunk before. I'm terribly embarrassed."

"Please don't be, Gil. We've all done things that we regret at one time or another."

He looked at me for a long moment, my words hanging in the space between us, and then he stood gingerly to his feet. "I'd better go, before someone sees me."

"Your shoes are under the table."

He cleaned himself up as best he could, though his hair would not be tamed and he was in need of a shave.

He paused at the door. "I wouldn't have come here like that if I hadn't been drunk," he said. "As much as I've wanted to talk about . . . things since we arrived."

"As I said, Gil, we needn't say any more about it."

"I'll talk to you later, then?"

"Yes."

I closed the door behind him and sighed heavily. I couldn't wait for this whole thing to be over so I could resume my normal life, or some variation thereof.

I SPENT THE remainder of the morning and the early part of the afternoon in my room. I had little desire for company, but that did not mean that I had given up on the murder investigation. As tumultuous as my personal life had become, I realized there were more important matters at hand. If anything was to be resolved, it was absolutely necessary that we discover who had murdered Rupert and Mr. Hamilton.

Inspector Jones's stern warning against further action had not escaped my memory. I was neither naive nor arrogant enough to dismiss his concern out of hand. He had warned me because there was a very distinct possibility of danger; the murder of Mr. Hamilton had made that abundantly clear. However, I was simply in too deeply to give up now. Someone among us had killed two people and had quite possibly attempted to kill two others, myself included. I found the very idea highly provoking. I did not intend that the killer should have another chance to harm me or anyone else.

I wondered again why someone should have given me sleeping tablets. I could not help but feel there had been something left unsaid in the inspector's admonition that I be wary, some subtle message beneath his words. Did he know something that I didn't? Did this mean he no longer truly suspected that Gil was involved? I did wish he wasn't so frightfully reticent. He had kept very quiet about his own theories, and I suspected that he was very close to revealing some vital piece of information, perhaps even the true identity of the killer. But if he knew, or even suspected, that Gil was innocent, why hadn't he acted?

I could only suppose he lacked evidence, which is why he had not yet made his move. If that was the case, I might be of help. If I were able to discover something, perhaps we could put this thing to rest. I sincerely hoped that, should I uncover something important, Inspector Jones would be willing to overlook my insubordination.

Pushing my doubts aside, I determined to focus on what I had learned thus far. My lunch tray nearly untouched, I went to the writing desk and picked up the list I had made with Milo. Obviously, Mr. Hamilton could be removed from the list of suspects. Why had he been killed? It seemed to me that, in order to discover the killer's identity, it would be necessary to determine the link be-

tween Rupert and Mr. Hamilton. It was possible they had been involved in some sort of business venture, but I thought that Inspector
Jones would have determined a link, had there been one.

No, I was fairly certain that Mr. Hamilton had been killed not
because of something in which he was involved but because of
something he knew. But what? It seemed to me that it must be connected with the item that he had found on the beach.

I had found absolutely nothing in his room that seemed a likely
murder weapon. There were a few options. Either he had disposed
of the item, or it had not been a weapon that he had found on the
beach but something else.

In order to investigate the first option, I decided to walk down the
path to the beach. I highly doubted I would be able to discover anything in the high grasses that lined the path, but it was worth a try. In
any event, I was certain I would go mad just sitting in my room.

I made my way down to the lobby, where I met Veronica Carter,
who was just about to enter the lift. She looked somewhat drawn,
her features lacking their usual chilliness.

"They've brought Mrs. Hamilton back from the hospital," she
told me in an uncertain voice. "She looks dreadful. I wanted to talk
to her . . . but it's so difficult to know what to say, isn't it?"

"Yes," I agreed, feeling another unwanted pang of sympathy for
Miss Carter. "Have they taken her to her room?"

She shook her head. "She didn't want to go back there . . . you
understand."

"Of course."

"They're preparing another room, I believe. She's in the sitting
room now." Miss Carter's composure slipped ever so slightly, and
the flash of vulnerability made her look prettier than ever, softer
somehow. "I want to go home," she said in a low voice.

"It won't be long now," I said, and I desperately hoped I was right.

I went to the sitting room to offer my sympathies and found Mrs. Hamilton alone. She was sitting in a chair, a blanket on her lap. It struck me how differently grief affects individuals. Emmeline had gone to pieces at Rupert's death, but it seemed Mrs. Hamilton was made of stronger stuff than that. She was, if possible, paler than usual, but she was very composed.

"I'm so sorry, Mrs. Hamilton," I said. "If there's anything I can do . . ."

"Thank you, Mrs. Ames," she answered softly, her eyes glistening. "I suppose it's wicked of me not to be in hysterics, but I just . . . don't feel anything. Does that make sense? I'm so numb; I think it hasn't quite sunk in."

"That's perfectly natural," I assured her, though I really had very little knowledge of such things.

"Poor Nelson . . ." Her voice trailed off as the tears that had pooled in her eyes overflowed. "I hate this place. I can't wait to get away from here. I've hated the seaside, ever since I was a child . . . You see, I had a brother that drowned in the sea."

It took the space of a moment for the quiet words to register, and when they did, I gasped, suddenly understanding so much. "How terrible," I said.

I certainly would not have pressed for details, not at a time like this, but she seemed almost unable to stop herself from going on.

"Geoffrey—my brother—and I were the very best of friends. We were twins, you see. We were inseparable. We had gone with our parents on holiday to the Yorkshire coast, our very first time to view the sea. I had loved it so then, so wide and open and beautiful. We went out to swim. I remember the water was terribly cold that day, but we didn't mind. It was a great adventure."

Her eyes were fastened on the wall behind me as she spoke, and I wondered if she were seeing the events of that day again. "My parents . . . well, I suppose they had other things on their minds. Geoffrey was right beside me, and the next moment a wave washed over us. I went under, and when I came up . . . I remember I was laughing as I did, laughing with delight . . . I realized that Geoffrey wasn't there. And then suddenly I saw him. He was being pulled out to sea. I tried to swim toward him, but it wasn't any use . . . I couldn't reach him, couldn't get to him in time."

Her blue eyes filled with tears as I sat, horrified by the story she was telling me. It was no wonder she hated the seaside and hadn't wanted to visit the Brightwell. Had Mr. Hamilton known about this? Surely he must have, and if he had, he was even crueler than I had believed him to be.

She drew in a breath and continued. "I lost a part of myself that day, Mrs. Ames. Geoffrey and I were very close, and I suppose I never really recovered from losing him . . . and now Nelson. To have water take him, too . . ."

She began to cry quietly into her handkerchief.

Milo had been right; she was afraid of something, something she had been hiding. Now, I knew what it was, why she had stared out at the sea in that dazed way, why she had steadfastly refused to go down to the beach. Milo had astutely called it an aura of tragedy, and that was precisely what it was. The Brightwell, everything about it, had brought back those horrific memories of the loss of her brother. I felt the impulse to embrace her, but I knew it would only prove awkward for both of us, so I reached out instead to clasp her cold hand.

"I'm so very sorry, Mrs. Hamilton," I said. I felt so helpless at the moment, and it was that very feeling that made me more determined than ever to find the killer.

After a moment, she dabbed at her tears and then looked up, her eyes meeting mine. "Someone killed him, didn't they?"

It took me a moment to realize that she meant Mr. Hamilton. I hesitated.

"I was given a heavy dose of sleeping tablets . . . almost a lethal dose, the doctor said," she went on.

"Did you knowingly take any tablets?" I asked, thinking of the ones that had been placed in my aspirin bottle.

"No, that's just it. The doctor said they may have been ground up and put in my coffee or some such thing. Nelson must have been drugged, too."

"I . . ." I tried to decide what I should say. The truth would come out soon enough, but I hated to be the one to tell her that her husband had been held down in his bathtub.

"But why would anyone do such a thing?" she asked, taking my silence for confirmation.

"I'm not sure, Mrs. Hamilton." I paused. She knew that he had been murdered; there was no point in denying it. "Can you think of any reason why someone might . . . view your husband as a threat?"

She shook her head, almost too quickly. "No. Certainly not."

I wondered if there was more she knew but was too afraid to tell.

"Mrs. Hamilton, if you know something . . ."

She shook her head again, a gentle but firm shake this time. "I don't know anything, Mrs. Ames. Perhaps it was an accident, after all. I may have taken something accidentally. Nelson may have slipped and fallen."

My eyes met hers, and I knew that neither of us believed it, not for a moment.

AFTER LEAVING MRS. Hamilton, I made my way to the terrace without encountering anyone else I knew, which was a relief. I was so very tired of these people. And I never again wanted to lay eyes on the Brightwell Hotel.

The wind, which had been high yesterday, had increased in velocity. The sky had taken on a leaden hue that seemed to bode ill. In fact, the seascape gave every indication that we were in for some nasty weather.

Though dusk was still hours away, the light was dim as I made my way down the wooden steps. The grasses swayed wildly in the wind, and my eyes scanned the ground as thoroughly as possible, looking for anything that might have been used to hit Rupert before he fell.

I reached the beach and found it deserted. Those guests who had not left the hotel after the murders would not find the sea welcoming today. The weather was not at all amenable to bathing. The waves crashed heavily on the shore, the sound echoing off the stone wall of the cliff. I walked to the pile of debris I had seen Mr. Hamilton inspecting. I doubted I would find anything significant, but it didn't hurt to look. There were stones and shells and bits of things that had drifted in from the sea, but I saw nothing suspicious.

A glint of something caught my eye. I reached down to pick it up. It was just a scrap of shiny glass tossed up by the sea, but its presence had caused me to remember something. Whatever Mr. Hamilton had picked up had glinted, just momentarily, in the moonlight before he had slid it into his pocket. It was unlikely, then, that it was a stone or piece of brick. Perhaps it had not been the weapon after all. But if that was the case, why had Mr. Hamilton felt it necessary to sneak about in the dark searching for it?

A droplet of rain landed on my shoulder as I stood thinking.

Then heavy drops began to hit the ground all around me. The storm that had been hovering on the horizon seemed to have made up its mind to approach. I decided to abandon my search and head back to the hotel, before I was forced to make my ascent in the pouring rain.

By the time I reached the terrace, it had begun to rain in earnest. I was more than a little wet as I entered the hotel and saw Inspector Jones. I would have avoided him, if possible, but he spotted me the moment I entered, and I had the suspicion that he had been expecting me.

He stood and waited for me to approach as I walked inside, brushing the rain from my arms.

"Ah, Mrs. Ames. Just the person I was wishing to see," he said, as though he hadn't been lurking there waiting for my return.

"That sounds ominous," I replied.

He smiled, not quite pleasantly, I thought. "I was wondering if you might tell me where your husband is."

"Milo's gone to London," I said, though I was fairly certain the inspector knew this already. I had discovered that the police seemed to enjoy asking questions to which they already knew the answers.

"Indeed," he said. "And may I enquire as to the nature of business important enough to pull him from the scene of a double homicide?"

I felt myself bristling at his officiousness. I reminded myself that he was no doubt attempting to set me on edge. Perhaps he thought I would give away something important.

"You may enquire if you wish," I replied, "but I'm afraid you'll have to enquire of Milo. If you can find him, that is. I've no idea where he went."

"And what has become of your recent camaraderie?"

I met his gaze rather coldly. "Inspector, I wonder if we might finish this conversation after I've had a chance to change my clothes. I'm very wet."

We looked at one another for a long moment before he gave a slight nod. "Of course. My apologies, Mrs. Ames. Might I come to your room in, say, half an hour?"

"If you must."

He stepped aside, and I walked past him without further comment. As much as I liked the man, almost against my will, he was severely trying my patience. In fact, I was fairly close to infuriated. He was using my uncertainty about Milo to his advantage. It was not at all a nice thing to do.

I stopped at the desk to see if I had any mail. Perhaps Milo had sent a telegram, though I knew that was unlikely. I wondered why he had set off for London so quickly. Surely he could have waited to tell me about it.

As I had expected, there was no word from Milo. There was a letter from Laurel, which reminded me of the one I had neglected to read. I determined to go to my room and read them both.

First, however, I decided I should perhaps try to locate Milo. With his usual foresight, Gil had given me good advice about warning Milo to return. Unfortunately, I had no means of doing so. As was typical, he had left no indication of where he was headed. It was possible that he would go to our London flat, but I had been hesitant to call him. I had a great aversion to being a pestering wife, but now that I knew Inspector Jones was looking for him, I felt that I should try to contact him. If I could reach him before the inspector came to my room, so much the better.

I went to my room and placed the call. As I waited for the operator to connect me to London, I retrieved Laurel's first letter, the one I had so long neglected to read.

Amory,

I thought I must warn you that I believe you may have the makings of a scandal on your hands. After you left for the seaside with Gil, I went to the post office. As I left, I saw Milo at the train station. He seemed to be waiting for the southbound train. I believe he may be following you. You naughty thing. Your love triangle is likely to be the talk of the town by the time you return.

This was not news. I would have been happy to have been warned of Milo's impending arrival, but it made very little difference now. I turned to open the letter that had arrived today.

"Hello?" I was somewhat startled to hear the soft, low voice on the other end of the line. It belonged to a woman, and we kept no staff at our London flat.

"Who is speaking, please?" I asked.

I did not imagine the hesitation. "This is Winnelda," she said at last.

I knew of absolutely no one with such a preposterous name. "Well . . . Winnelda, this is Mrs. Ames. May I ask what you are doing in my flat?"

"What am I doing in your flat?" she repeated dumbly. I could fairly hear her trembling on the other end of the line.

"Let me speak to Milo," I said at last. This really was the final straw.

"Milo?" she repeated. I wondered if she could possibly be hard of hearing.

"Is my husband there or not?" I demanded.

"No . . . no, madam," she answered. "He is out of town."

A likely story. I drew in a calming breath before I spoke. "If you should happen to see him, would you kindly inform him that Inspector Jones wishes him to return to the Brightwell Hotel. I believe he has some questions related to the recent murders."

I heard her gasp before I hung up the phone.

For just a moment, I sat completely still, digesting what had just occurred. I hadn't the faintest idea who "Winnelda" might be, but I could guess that she had been the reason for Milo's hasty departure. That was it, then. He had made the decision for me.

I determined then that I would not try to contact him again. If he chose to flee like a guilty man, he deserved the consequences. It would serve him well to spend some time in prison. At least I would know where to reach him when I began the divorce proceedings.

INSPECTOR JONES WAS, alas, punctual to the minute. If I had been disinclined to speak with him before, the idea was absolutely abhorrent now. My nerves were on edge, and it was only by the sheerest force of will that I was able to keep from breaking down in tears.

"You haven't changed your clothes," he observed as he came into my room. He was right; I had forgotten.

"Have you contacted your husband?" he asked when I failed to respond to his comment.

"I couldn't reach him."

"Mrs. Ames, I needn't tell you the implications . . ."

"No, Inspector," I interrupted, somewhat rudely. "You needn't tell me. You seemed to operate under the misconception that I have some say in what my husband does. Our marriage isn't like that."

He was watching me closely, and I hated that I could see something very like sympathy in his gaze. "I've decided not to notify the London authorities at this point. However, if you hear from him, you will let me know?"

"Yes, certainly."

He was still hesitating, and I knew that there was something else on his mind. "You don't know why he left?" he finally asked.

"I . . . He left me a note that said he had to go to London and he wasn't sure when he would return." I hesitated and then decided that I should tell him the truth. "You may as well know, Inspector. I called our London flat, and a woman answered. That probably explains his sudden absence."

Nothing showed on his features as I spoke. "I find that rather surprising, Mrs. Ames. He seemed devoted to you yesterday."

"Milo is very good at . . . exhibiting remarkable enthusiasm for whatever interests him at the moment. Unfortunately, his interest wanes very quickly . . ."

"Surely a murder investigation is sufficient to hold his attention." He was trying to speak lightly of the situation, though I sensed he was still peeved about it. "I know investigation seems to agree with you."

"It doesn't agree with me at all," I said. "When I think that we might have prevented Mr. Hamilton's death . . ." I pressed my lips together, barely managing to stifle a sob. I was suddenly unbearably miserable.

"I'm sorry," he said, and he sounded sincere. "I should have realized how difficult things have been for you. Sometimes, as a policeman, I neglect to take into account the profound effect such things can have on civilians."

"It's quite all right," I said, wiping the tears away as fast as they came. "I'm just so very tired. And I did discover both of the bodies. It's been rather a shock."

He handed me his handkerchief, and I took it, dabbing at my eyes. His sympathy only made me feel worse, and I was having a hard time stopping the steady flow of tears. I took a seat on the sofa, and he sat at the other end.

"I know it has all been very distressing," he said, "but it will be over soon enough."

Something about his tone captured my attention. I looked up at him. "Do you really think so?"

"These things have a way of working themselves out eventually."

"May I ask you a question, Inspector?" I asked suddenly.

"Certainly, Mrs. Ames."

"Do you know who the killer is?"

He watched me for a moment, as though trying to determine exactly how much he should reveal. At last, he said, "I have my suspicions."

"You don't believe that it was Gil anymore, do you?"

"I arrested Mr. Trent because of the evidence," he said carefully. "Time will tell if that arrest was premature."

"That's an evasion, Inspector. You aren't answering my question."

He smiled. "You're feeling better then, Mrs. Ames."

I returned his smile with a weary one of my own. "I haven't meant to be a bother. It's just that I am so certain Gil is innocent; I feel I must do whatever I can do to prove it."

"Do you mean that?" There it was again, the subtle indication that there was something more he was keeping just below the surface, something he was either unwilling or unable to tell me.

"Of course I do."

Still, he hesitated. I waited; perhaps if I remained silent long enough, he would choose to tell me whatever it was. My patience was rewarded.

"Mrs. Ames," he said at last. "There is something I am going to tell you that I am not at all sure I should."

My interest was immediately piqued, my emotional outburst all but forgotten. "I am intrigued."

He went on, carefully. "You told me that your husband arrived the night of the murder, and he confirmed that he came down on the afternoon train."

"Yes," I said, wondering where exactly this line of inquiry would lead.

"That information has proven to be false."

A frown flickered across my brow as I struggled to understand what he was telling me. "You mean, Milo didn't arrive on the train he said he did."

"Mr. Ames, in fact, arrived on the train directly following yours."

This newest revelation took me a moment to digest. "I don't understand," I said at last. "Milo didn't arrive until . . ." Laurel's words hit me suddenly. Milo had left immediately after I did. But he hadn't arrived at the hotel until the following night. Where had he stayed? More important, what exactly was the inspector trying to tell me?

"I didn't know," I said at last.

"No, I don't expect you did." He smiled wryly. "Your husband is an excellent liar."

Somehow, I felt that this information was not the extent of

what he was going to tell me. There was still wariness in his expression, and I sensed an unwillingness to continue.

"There's more, isn't there?"

"I'm afraid so." The hesitation vanished suddenly, as though he had made up his mind. He leaned forward slightly, as though charging ahead before he thought better of it. "You recall that there was a witness who had seen Mr. Trent on the terrace shortly before the murder."

"Yes, you wouldn't tell me who it was."

"At the time, I didn't think it wise. Now, it seems there is little choice. You see, your husband was that witness."

24

I SAT BACK in my chair, my head spinning. Milo had informed Inspector Jones that Gil had been on the terrace before the murder? It seemed almost impossible that it could be the truth, but if it was not, what reason could the inspector possibly have for saying such a thing?

"I understand why he kept it from you, of course," Inspector Jones continued in that calm, formal way of his. "It wouldn't look at all sporting of him to accuse his rival of murder."

"I'm so confused," I said, trying desperately to string together the facts that Inspector Jones was giving me into some semblance of order in my mind. "You can't mean . . . Surely you don't think Milo was attempting to implicate Gil solely on my account?"

"I'm afraid that is a possibility. At the time, I had no reason not to take his word for it. Now, other circumstances have arisen to put a different light on things. If it is the case that he gave false information, your husband may be charged with perverting the course of public justice. That is why I wish to speak with him."

"Good heavens." I breathed. "I know Milo is competitive, but I don't believe it would come to anything like this."

"I'm afraid that's the way it appears."

"I think you're mistaken," I replied. "You see, I'm simply not that important to him."

He looked at me for a long moment, and when he spoke he did not acknowledge my doubts. "I'm sorry to have to tell you this, Mrs. Ames. I know how difficult things have been for you as of late. That is why I hesitated to . . ."

"It's perfectly all right, Inspector," I said, cutting him off as smoothly as I could manage. "I'm glad you told me."

He rose, taking my cue that I would like to be alone. "If you hear from your husband, or if you have need of me, please call."

"Thank you. I shall."

After the inspector left, I changed into dry clothes as I tried to gather my thoughts. What he had suggested seemed completely illogical. I could conceive of no reason why Milo should falsely implicate Gil in Rupert's murder. It was not at all the sort of thing Milo was apt to do. He preferred direct assault to underhanded schemes, whatever Inspector Jones might believe. In any event, I was not nearly grand enough a prize to risk legal ramifications.

For that matter, I still couldn't understand why he had bothered to come to the Brightwell at all, especially if he only intended to leave again after a few days. Perhaps it had been to prove that he could still have me if he wanted me. Well, there he had succeeded admirably. I had let myself, once again, be too readily seduced. Once secure in the knowledge that I was his for the asking, he had felt it safe to leave again. Well, he would be surprised to learn that I did not intend to spend the rest of my life waiting for him to return. Five years had been long enough.

I realized I was gritting my teeth, and, in an effort to calm myself, I picked up the suspect list. Slowly and methodically, I began to read over it. There had to be something I was missing, some piece of the puzzle that had only to be discovered in order to make the entire picture clear.

My thoughts returned to poor Mr. Hamilton. He had picked up something on the beach. Somewhere along the way, he had disposed of it. I wondered if it would ever be found. I had thought it had shone momentarily in the moonlight when he picked it up, but perhaps that had been my imagination. If it had been a random rock or piece of brick, it was unlikely that it would be discovered. Even if someone should happen across it, the blood would no doubt be washed away by the torrential downpours that were beginning to fall. Then there was my suspicion that it had not been the weapon at all. If not, what could it have been?

I stared at the list, as though willing the murderer's name to appear in red letters before my eyes. I felt I was so close to discovering something, if only I could find the right link, some bit of information that would point in the right direction. At least, that was how it worked in the mystery novels.

If only I had been able to peek at the inspector's extensive dossiers on each of us. Of course, he had no doubt been poring over them, and it did not seem he had discovered anything substantial yet. Nevertheless, I had the feeling that more than one person was hiding something.

But people weren't the only aspect of this case. There were things, mysterious objects, involved, too. For instance, the sleeping pills that seemed to be haunting so many of us. They were easy enough to obtain, so that particular bit of information was not necessarily enlightening.

Four of us had been drugged: Mr. and Mrs. Hamilton, me, and Emmeline, the latter albeit by doctor's orders. I knew Mr. Hamilton had been in possession of sleeping tablets. I also knew that the Rodgerses claimed to have misplaced theirs. Whether that story had been the truth or a ruse on their part in order to cover something more nefarious had yet to be determined.

I was missing something. I felt that I had all the pieces of the puzzle, but somehow I just could not make them fit.

Suddenly weary beyond all words, I set the list aside and sat down on the sofa. My head pounding, I leaned against the cushions and closed my eyes. Perhaps if I rested for just a few moments . . .

A MOMENTOUS CRASH of lightning startled me awake, and I sat upright on the sofa, momentarily unaware of where I was. Then I recalled that I was in my room. It took me a moment to realize I must have fallen asleep.

The room was black as pitch, illuminated only by the occasional flash of lightning. Night had come upon me as I slept, and with it had come the raging storm that had been threatening for so long. The rain outside pounded against the hotel, the wind rattling the windows like something from a ghost story. I reached out to switch on the lamp and found it didn't work. The storm must have knocked out the electricity.

Rousing myself, I felt along the table and located matches. I struck one, looking around the room to see if there was a candle about. I didn't recall having seen one, and I couldn't locate one now. The match burned out, and I was about to strike a second when I heard a tap on my door. "Amory, it's Gil. Are you there?"

"Yes, Gil. I'm coming."

I felt my way to the door and opened it to find Gil, oil lamp in hand. Emmeline stood with him, her face pale in the flickering glow. They made a sort of sad little pair around the dull pool of light.

"The storm's knocked the power out," he said. "The hotel's got a few odd candles and such in the sitting room. Shall I fetch you one, or would you like to come down for a bit of company?"

"Do come down, Amory," Emmeline said. "It's so dreary in the sitting room. I couldn't bear for Gil to leave me there when he came to fetch you."

The thunder rumbled again. I had no special desire to remain cooped up in my room in the dark, in the middle of a raging storm. "Yes, I'll come down. Are the others there?"

"That's what makes it so bad," Emmeline said. "Mrs. Hamilton's there, pale as a ghost. No one seems to know what to say to her. I . . . even I can't seem to think of anything . . . and I know how she feels." Emmeline looked on the verge of tears.

"You needn't come down if you don't feel up to it," Gil interjected. "If you'd rather not speak to Mrs. Hamilton just now . . ."

"It's all right," I said. "Perhaps we can cheer her up a bit."

We ventured downstairs. The hotel was strangely quiet, save for noise of the storm and the pounding of the sea, which was audible even in the lobby. A few people sat around with candles and lanterns, talking in subdued voices. I supposed most of the guests had kept to their rooms.

Gil and I entered the sitting room. Emmeline was right. The mood in the room was strangely oppressive. Everyone was still and very quiet. It was almost eerie. Mrs. Hamilton sat near Mrs. Rodgers, neither of them saying anything.

"Perhaps we can get someone to light a fire in the fireplace," I told Gil. "It would brighten the room."

"I'll go speak to the desk clerk," he said.

"There's a windup gramophone on the table there," Anne Rodgers suggested as silence descended once again. "We don't need electricity for that."

No one responded, and she made no move toward it. Perhaps she realized none of us felt much like music.

I approached Mrs. Hamilton. "How are you feeling tonight?" I asked her.

"Not very well. The storm seems to make everything much worse." Her eyes welled with tears that glimmered in the lamp-lit room.

She reached into her purse and pulled out a handkerchief. Wiping her eyes, she also removed a cigarette case. She put a cigarette to her lips and lit it with fairly steady hands. Despite her poise, I knew she must be unnerved, for I had not seen her smoke before this.

"I couldn't sit all alone in my room in the dark," she said.

"Of course not. No one would want you to."

"I can't wait to get away from this place," Veronica Carter said suddenly, her voice loud in the room. "It's simply ghastly here."

"Yes," agreed Mrs. Rodgers, emphatically. "If it wasn't for this storm, I'd leave here tonight, that inspector be hanged."

"That's no way to talk, Anne," her husband said in that perpetually dull tone of his. "There are legal formalities to be observed."

"It's the strain," Lionel Blake replied, puffing at a cigarette. He appeared perfectly calm, as he had when we had spoken outside, but his voice sounded strange.

A sudden shriek startled us all, and a moment later Mrs. Roland flew into the room like a great bat. She was dressed head to toe in black, including the velvet turban wrapped around her head. Indeed, the long, draped sleeves of her dress flapped like bony wings as she waved her arms about. "I was almost killed coming down the stairs in the dark," she said. "The lift isn't working, and neither is the telephone. It was like wandering around in a cave." She dropped into a chair and heaved a great sigh. "A cigarette, please. Someone give me a cigarette."

Mrs. Hamilton offered her one. "What a lovely case, dear. I do so love gold things. Mr. Howe had a magnificent lighter . . . but perhaps I shouldn't speak of that now. I'm sorry if I've upset you, Emmeline. You probably bought the lighter for him."

"No, I . . ." Emmeline said, and for a moment I was afraid she was going to cry. Then she summoned up the courage to keep on talking in the same level voice. "It doesn't upset me. It was a lovely lighter. He was very proud of it. From one of the better London jewelers, Price and Lord, I think he said it was. I don't know how he acquired it . . . I should like to have it, to remember him by."

"Haven't the police given it to you?" Mrs. Roland asked, the cigarette dangling between bright red lips.

"No, it . . . it wasn't on the list of things that they found . . ." Her voice trailed off, and I knew that she meant the things that had been on the body. The poor girl. I felt it a good sign that she was able to discuss him without dissolving into tears.

"Perhaps it will turn up," I said.

"He may have put it in his little treasure box."

"Treasure box?" Mrs. Roland's heavily penciled brows rose, and I sensed that the attention of the room had suddenly shifted in our direction.

Emmeline smiled, a sad little smile that made her seem very young. "That's what I used to call it. He brought it with him when he traveled to keep his valuables in. He'd usually hide it about his room somewhere." She frowned. "The police didn't mention having seen it in his room, and I've been so upset that I didn't think of it. I shall ask them, tomorrow perhaps, when the lights come back."

"Speaking of light, has anyone a light?" Mrs. Roland asked, pulling a handkerchief from her bosom and dragging it across her face. "I'm so very flushed from my ordeal . . . I feel as though I may combust and light it myself. Humans do that sometimes, don't they? Combust, I mean. I've heard that, though it seems frightfully silly to me."

Mr. Blake supplied a match, and Mrs. Roland inhaled deeply. Then she sat back and sighed out a great cloud of smoke. "What I really need is a good stiff drink. I've had quite a fright. The lights went out, and I couldn't see a thing."

The conversation resumed, but I barely heard it, my thoughts wandering in another direction. A gold lighter was an expensive gift, especially if it hadn't come from Emmeline. Perhaps he had bought it for himself, though men like Rupert seemed very adept at getting things out of women. Unwillingly, my thoughts wandered to the gift I had bought for Milo yesterday, gold cufflinks, which had just happened to be engraved with an *A*. Engraved . . .

Mrs. Roland had seen Rupert with a gold lighter. I had found a gold lighter among Mr. Hamilton's things. It had been engraved with an *H*. Could it be that it had belonged not to Mr. Hamilton but to Rupert Howe? It was an interesting thought.

If only I could find some way to inspect the lighter again. Or, better yet, see if I could find one amid Rupert's things. Surely the police would have mentioned a "treasure box" containing Rupert's valuables to Emmeline.

Something suddenly occurred to me. Nearly all of our party was gathered here in the sitting room. What was to stop me from going to Rupert's room to look around? It would only require a key ... and I felt fairly certain I could gain hold of one.

My sense of caution, heightened by recent events, warred with the desire to attempt to gain some vital piece of information. In the end, the impulse to follow my hunch was stronger than my more practical inclination to remain quietly sitting in the lamp-lit room with the other guests. One of whom was, in all probability, a killer, I reminded myself.

"Gil was going about collecting guests," Miss Carter said to Mrs. Roland, and I realized they were still talking about the unexpected loss of power. "I'm surprised you didn't encounter him."

"He's off to find Olive, I expect," Mrs. Roland said. "Emmeline dear, you're looking thin. I've a box of very good chocolates in my room. When the lights come back on, I'll fetch them for you."

"That reminds me, I'm going to fetch something from my room," I said to no one in particular, rising in what I hoped was a passably nonchalant fashion. "I'll be back in a few moments."

I took one of the spare lights that rested on the table and set out into the lobby. The people who sat there had begun a game of cards and paid me no mind. I had hoped, because of the power outage and resulting chaos, there would be no one at the desk. Unfortunately, the desk clerk was there. I hesitated a moment in the shadows, feeling vaguely like some Victorian murderer waiting for a passing victim. If I could just create a minor distraction of some sort ...

Then a perfectly wicked thought crossed my mind, and before I had half thought it through, I dropped the oil lamp I was holding. It shattered on the marble floor, creating a small whoosh of flame as the fire hit the pool of oil, brilliantly lighting the dim foyer.

25

THE FIRE FLARED brightly, and I stood staring at it, a bit shocked by what I had done. I heard a startled gasp from one of the guests seated in the lobby.

"Oh, dear," I called to the clerk. "I'm afraid I've . . ."

"I'll get something to put it out," he said, darting from behind the desk and rushing off. I hoped he remembered that oil fires were not easily extinguished with water.

I looked down at the fire I had started. The oil was already burning itself out, and the marble floor was not going to let the fire spread. The group playing cards must have realized it as well, for they returned their attention to their game. With a quick glance around me, I slipped behind the desk and examined the rows of keys. It would only be a matter of seconds before the clerk would be back. Rupert's room was on the floor above mine. If I remembered correctly from when it had been mentioned at the inquest, it was 211. My eyes scanned the keys. It was entirely possible that the police had confiscated all the keys to Rupert's room, but no! There it was.

I grabbed the key, slipped it into my pocket, and slid quickly around the desk. A moment later, the clerk returned with a bucket of sand that he poured over the already-sputtering flames.

"I'm terribly sorry," I said, and I meant it. Though I had been almost certain the fire would not spread, I couldn't really have been absolutely sure. Had I taken a moment to think, I wouldn't have done it. I should dearly have hated to add arson to my list of sins.

"It's quite all right," he said, though he was pale. "Are you hurt, Mrs. Ames?"

"No, no. I'm fine. Is there something I can do?"

"No, I'll have someone clean up the glass. You're certain you're all right?"

"I'm terribly sorry," I said again. "I was just going upstairs and . . ."

"I think I have a torch behind the desk," he said. He moved to pull open a drawer, rummaging around for a moment before removing a torch. Flicking it on, he handed it to me, obviously relieved to give me a source of light that did not involve fire and flammable liquids.

I turned toward the stairs, the guilty weight of the key hanging heavily in my pocket. I was so lost in thought that I nearly ran headlong into Gil and Olive, neither of whom saw me, as they descended the stairs, talking in low tones. They stopped at the foot of the stairs when I approached, both of them looking vaguely embarrassed.

"Hello, Amory," Gil said. "I've just brought Olive down from upstairs."

Olive's face was pale and wan in the dim light of Gil's lamp. She was wearing long sleeves, which I imagined must cover the bandages on her wrists. Aside from an initial glance, she didn't meet my gaze.

"I didn't mean to interrupt," I said.

"Not at all," Gil said. There was something odd in his demeanor, though I couldn't quite detect what it was.

"How are you, Olive?" I asked.

"I'm all right," she answered stiffly.

As anxious as I was to search Rupert's room, I felt that perhaps now would be a good time to talk to her alone, before we were all cramped together in the sitting room. "Gil, would you mind very much if I spoke to Olive for a moment?"

Gil looked strange, drawn. He hesitated for a long moment and then nodded. He handed the light to Olive and left the two of us alone in stony silence. It seemed the best course of action would be to plunge ahead.

"Olive, I'm sorry if this question seems impertinent. In fact, I'm quite sure it will. But did you buy Rupert a gold lighter?"

She looked at me sharply, a frown creasing her smooth forehead. "I don't know why everyone thinks ... No, I didn't give him anything. I never cared for Rupert, though there was a time when we were together quite often. Aside from being a notorious flirt, he was not at all a nice man. Anyone could see that."

I was confused by her sudden denial. "Then why ..." My voice trailed off. It seemed ill mannered to ask someone exactly why they had slit their wrists with a razor blade.

Sudden understanding flashed across her face, and for a moment some of the coldness left her features. "You don't know," she said.

"Know what?"

"You think I loved *Rupert* ..."

Something flickered in her eyes, and suddenly I knew, with absolute clarity, what she meant. I was blind, utterly stupid, not to have seen it before.

"You're in love with Gil," I whispered.

Her gaze hardened again before she looked away. "I suppose you think I'm terribly foolish, behaving the way I have."

Everything began to slide into place: Olive's behavior, Gil's mysterious absences, the visit that had upset Olive in the hospital. It all seemed to make sense. I couldn't believe that I had never guessed, but perhaps I had been too involved with my own affairs to take proper notice of the affairs of others.

"I'm the one who feels foolish," I said. "I should have realized how you felt."

"He's mad about you, you know," she said. There was no bitterness in her brittle smile or in the tears that glistened in her eyes. "Whenever someone mentions you, his eyes light up and . . . I've made a perfect fool of myself trying to make him love me again. Or perhaps he never did, I don't know . . ."

Something about her words hit me forcibly, and I found that I felt on the verge of tears myself. Impulsively, I reached out and grabbed her hand. "I'm sorry, Olive . . . You see, I too know what it's like to love someone whose feelings are . . . ambiguous."

"Your husband," she said.

It was my turn to smile sadly. "I sometimes believe he married me only to prove that he could."

"I thought, when he came here, that perhaps you still loved him." There was something so blatantly hopeful in her gaze that I felt somewhat ashamed of myself.

"I . . . things are unsettled at the moment."

She nodded. "Gil will take you in an instant, if you want him. If you decide you don't, I'll still be waiting."

With that, she walked past me and toward the sitting room. Despite the desperation of her words, there was a quiet dignity about her as she walked away, and I thought that perhaps I had misjudged her.

I was glad she had gone, for I wouldn't have been able to think of an appropriate reply. It was wrong of me, I knew, to keep Gil dancing in attendance when I hadn't settled things with Milo. Yet I couldn't quite bring myself to give him up, not when it was possible he might soon be all I had left.

I made my way up the darkened staircase, shadows flickering on the walls around me. It was rather eerie. The light of the torch only extended so far, and it was not until I was nearly to the first-floor landing that I realized there was someone standing there.

I lifted the torch and stopped, startled to see Milo illuminated by the feeble beam.

"HELLO, DARLING," HE said as he approached. "Awful weather, isn't it? I was almost washed away on my way from the station." He smiled, obviously exhilarated by the wretched weather. His clothes were soaked; it seemed he must have just come in from outside.

"Have you the key to our room? I've lost mine in one of my pockets."

"I . . . yes, I have it."

We walked down the hall to our room in silence.

"I thought you'd gone to London," I said lamely as we reached my door. I was so surprised by his sudden arrival, I could think of nothing intelligent to say.

"I did. Aren't you going to kiss me?"

"No," I said. I moved past him and unlocked the door to my room. He followed me inside. With the torch, I was able to locate an oil lamp sitting on a table in the corner. I lit it and the yellow glow filled the room.

"You're angry that I left without speaking to you," he said, pulling off his dripping overcoat and tossing it over the back of a chair. "I had to catch the train, darling."

I turned to face him. "Inspector Jones told me it was you who reported seeing Gil on the terrace before the murder."

If I expected him to be abashed at this revelation, I had forgotten his unwavering self-possession. He looked at me with a perfectly unruffled expression. "Ah. He told you, did he? I expected he would."

"How could you have seen Gil talking to Rupert on the terrace before tea? You weren't even at the hotel until that evening."

"I expect he told you that, too," he said, pulling off his jacket and running his fingers through his damp hair. He had never cared for hats, even in the rain. "I came down directly after you did. I stayed at the pub. I thought it best not to drop in at the Brightwell right away."

I decided, for the moment, to let drop the subject of why he had followed me to the seaside in the first place. Instead, I asked, "Why did you tell the inspector you had seen Gil?"

"Because I did."

"Did you?" I challenged.

He smiled. "Don't you believe me?"

"Gil didn't kill Rupert, Milo."

"Perhaps not, but I thought it worth mentioning that the two of them were arguing shortly before Rupert was coshed on the head and tossed over the ledge."

Was he telling the truth? It was so difficult to tell.

"Inspector Jones was angry that you left," I told him, changing the course of the conversation yet again. I said nothing of my own anger, the hurt that had come at his jaunting off to London with barely a word.

"I expect he'll forgive me when he hears what I've learned."

He wanted me to be intrigued, so I displayed no interest whatsoever. I resisted the urge to tell him I hoped he would be arrested.

If he noticed my lack of enthusiasm, he gave no sign of it. Instead, he went to the wardrobe and pulled out a fresh suit of clothes and then went into the bathroom to dry off before changing, without so much as a word.

With a sigh, I sat down at the desk. There was so much to think about, too much happening at once. The key was still resting in my pocket, and I wanted badly to go to Rupert's room. I didn't care to have Milo tagging along when I did, so I needed to think of some way to get rid of him. I contemplated bolting from the room while he was changing, but he would only come downstairs looking for me and alert everyone to the fact that I was not in my room.

I noticed Laurel's second letter sitting on the desk. For lack of something better to do, I picked it up and slit it open with the letter knife, my eyes grazing over the words.

I've been asking around in the most casual way, and I found that it is rumored that Rupert Howe had yet to pay off a considerable gambling debt he had accrued in Monte Carlo. It was thought his hasty retreat was in rather bad taste, but I take it he was in desperate straits. I also found another interesting piece of information. You will think I have nothing to do but read gossip columns, though you know how I enjoy following the occasional piece of news. In any event, I found this article or, rather, the photograph attached to it to be very interesting. Perhaps Milo may prove of use to you after all.

Something about the note gave me a strange foreboding, and I was almost hesitant to reach into the envelope. I pulled out the slip of newspaper and looked at the photograph.

As Laurel had said, it was from one of the gossip magazines. The date indicated it had been taken in Monte Carlo about a month before. Milo, resplendent in evening dress, stood beside a roulette table. Despite the insinuation of the caption, it was not the woman in the low-cut gown clinging to his arm that caught my attention. It was the person who stood on the other side of him: Rupert.

I looked at the picture for a long moment. Milo had claimed never to have met Rupert. Yet there they stood, side by side.

I couldn't imagine why Milo should have lied about it. Unless . . . a sudden sinking feeling coursed through me as the implications of what I had discovered became apparent. One by one, the pieces of the puzzle came crashing down on me like bricks. Milo knew Rupert. Rupert had owed someone a great deal of money. Milo had arrived at the hotel before the murder but had not made his presence known.

I pulled in a deep breath, forced myself to think calmly of what I knew of the murder. Rupert Howe, surmised the police, had had an argument with someone, been struck over the head, and tossed over the cliff. We assumed that it was likely the result of some argument, a sudden conversation that had turned ugly. But perhaps it had been more than that. What if it had been deliberately planned?

Milo had arrived home suddenly from Monte Carlo, much sooner than he had originally intended. Perhaps my visit here to the seaside had just happened to coincide with one he had already planned. Perhaps he had not been following me, but Rupert . . .

"This power outage is a blasted nuisance," Milo said, coming back into the room, and I nearly jumped at the sudden sound of his voice. "Imagine, this is how our parents lived, prowling about by lamplight after dark."

"Why did you tell me you didn't know Rupert?" I asked, hoping the question would catch him off guard.

"I didn't know him," he answered easily.

I rose from my seat and handed him the photograph, watching him as I did so. Inspector Jones was right; Milo was a terribly good liar. His expression didn't so much as flicker.

"Many people play roulette," he said, handing the photograph back to me. "That doesn't mean I knew him."

"Rather a startling coincidence, isn't it?" I was watching him closely, trying to see if anything seemed amiss.

Suddenly, he smiled. A sort of dangerous amusement flickered across his features. "Why, Amory darling, do you believe I killed Rupert Howe?"

"Did you?"

He laughed. "Would you expect me to confess if I did?"

"You told me that you might kill someone, if the occasion called for it. Rumor has it that Rupert Howe owed someone quite a lot of money."

"Come now, darling. You know as well as I do that I have more money than I could ever possibly spend. It's a rather thin motive."

"But a motive nonetheless."

"And I suppose I killed Mr. Hamilton as well."

With great relief, I realized that my theory did not account for the death of Mr. Hamilton. Even if Mr. Hamilton had discovered something on the beach that might have implicated Milo, we had been in the wardrobe until . . . With a sudden sickening clarity, I recalled the splashing I had heard after Milo had left me in the wardrobe. Milo had claimed that he had pulled Mr. Hamilton out of the water to determine if he was still alive, but what if he had done exactly the opposite? I could literally feel the color draining from my face.

"You . . . you could have," I said.

His expression was still completely indecipherable. I wished desperately I knew what he was thinking.

"It's possible, I suppose," he said at last.

I wanted to reply, but I could think of absolutely nothing to say.

We stared at one another, something uncomfortable hanging in the air between us. For the first time since I had known him, I felt myself a bit afraid to be alone with him. It was not at all a sensation I relished.

"Did anyone see you return tonight?" I asked suddenly, wondering, against my will, if anyone knew that he and I were alone here.

"No, I came upstairs while you were stealing keys from behind the desk."

So he had seen that, had he? I wondered if he had inferred my motives.

"Then everyone believes you're still in London."

"I had a good reason for going to London, but I always intended to return to the scene of the crime," he said, and I felt myself grimace at his choice of words.

"I think I had better go back downstairs," I said. "They're expecting me back."

I took the slightest step toward the door, and I knew at once that he had read my unease in the movement.

"Good heavens, Amory." He stepped toward me, and, despite myself, I took a step back.

He stopped, something else entirely crossing his face. It was a look I had never seen before, something very like incredulity, completely devoid of his customary languid amusement. Then it disappeared as quickly as it had come, the familiar veil of cool indifference dropping down over his features. He swore softly. "I didn't believe you meant it. You think I killed him, both of them."

"I . . . I . . . don't . . ." My mind searched desperately, trying to think of something to say. What was there to say?

"If I had killed Howe and Hamilton, I should have done a much better job of it," he said, the slight sharp edge to his words the only indication that he was deeply angry.

I stood there stupidly, unable to form a cohesive sentence, imploring him with my eyes to try to understand my suspicion.

"And I would never harm you."

"Milo, please . . . ," I whispered. "I don't want to believe it."

"I'm going downstairs." His face was a mask, cold and hard as a marble statue. "I'll be in the sitting room with the others. Should you—or the police—wish to find me." With that, he turned and left me alone.

My heart was pounding in my ears as I listened to his footsteps echoing away. I didn't believe it of him. I couldn't. And yet everything seemed to make sense.

Should I try to reach the inspector and tell him what I had learned? Something within me revolted at the idea. I couldn't very well implicate my own husband. I needed a moment to think.

My thoughts whirled madly about in my head. Was it possible that my husband, this man I had loved and lived with for five years, was a murderer?

And more to the point: if he was, what did I intend to do about it?

26

I MUST HAVE sat in silence a full ten minutes before I attempted to pull myself together.

Things looked bad, but there was certainly some logical explanation. Unable to bear thinking about it any longer, I decided to take action. I grabbed the torch and left my room, heading toward Rupert's. One way or the other, I had to know.

I reached Rupert's room and found that it was locked, the official police sign on the door noting that unauthorized entry was prohibited. I wondered what Inspector Jones would think should he see what I was about to do.

Slipping the key into the lock, I hurried inside and shut the door behind me, locking it.

Rupert's things had obviously already been subject to a thorough search. Drawers were pulled open, their contents not replaced in a particularly orderly fashion. The police, it seemed, had left no stone unturned. But it was just possible that he had hidden his "treasure box," as Emmeline had termed it, somewhere where it hadn't been found.

I stepped toward the bureau and began looking at the items that were scattered about. I had underestimated the difficulty of searching through someone's things with only a small torch for a light. I began to despair of finding anything the police hadn't.

The things on his desk told me very little, and I assumed anything of interest had already been confiscated. I paused a moment to think. Where might Rupert hide his important papers from prying eyes? There weren't likely to be any hidden compartments in the hotel furniture. That left somewhere less conspicuous.

I searched the wardrobe, feeling in all the dark corners for something they might be concealing in their depths. My thoroughness was in vain.

Acting on a sudden inspiration, I moved to the sofa and slid my hand between the cushions. I was rewarded with a shilling and a stray seashell. The chairs yielded nothing.

Where else? Crossing the room, I dropped to my knees beside the bed. As in Mr. Hamilton's room, there was nothing to see but the expanse of rug. But perhaps . . . I shined my light along the supports, hoping that he had slipped something there. My diligence was rewarded. There, in the corner of the bed, against the white underside of the mattress, was a brown packet of some sort.

I slid my body partway under the bed and wrestled the packet from its resting place. It was made of some durable material, almost a box, as Emmeline had termed it. I pushed myself back out from under the bed and pulled the box open, examining the contents with my light. Rupert's gold lighter was not inside, but there were several sheets of paper.

With unabashed curiosity, I began sifting through them. I would notify Inspector Jones, of course, but it couldn't hurt for me to give them a cursory inspection.

There were more than a few bills. They came from his tailor, his haberdasher, a jeweler, and there was an impressive debt at a London cigar shop. None of them seem to have been paid, and my initial impression that he was interested in Emmeline for more than her sweet disposition seemed to have been confirmed.

I saw two envelopes addressed to Rupert in what I recognized as Gil's handwriting. No doubt these were the strongly worded letters Gil had mentioned. I passed them over. Whatever Gil had written to Rupert, I believed it had been done with pure motives.

Near the bottom of the stack, I came across something that was not a bill. It was a terse note scribbled in dark ink that read:

Pay what you owe or you will be sorry. —A friend.

I found the note to be something of a relief. The letter wasn't at all in Milo's style. He would have issued a much more elegant threat on vastly superior stationery.

At the very bottom of the pile, there was a small yellow envelope. Opening it, I pulled out a letter written in small, neat handwriting.

My darling,

I know you warned me not to write, but I couldn't help myself. I am not sure how much longer I can carry on. He suspects something. I'm sure of it. Even if he didn't know, pretending that we mean nothing to one another is agony. We must act as we have planned. I have waited long enough. I

want to be with you, and nothing must stand in our way. I live in antici-
pation of when our lives will be linked.

All my love,
L.

Before I could begin to make the connection, the voice behind me spoke in the darkness, startling me. "So you've found out."

So intent had I been on the contents of the letter, I had not detected the click of the lock as the door behind me opened. Who else had a key to Rupert's room? Rupert's lover, no doubt. The same person that had written the letter I now held in my hand. The person whose name began with an *L.* The realization hit me so suddenly, I felt almost dizzy with it. The note had come from the woman who stood in the doorway watching me: Larissa Hamilton.

27

I ROSE SLOWLY, the letter still in my hand. "Mrs. Hamilton."

"That's my letter, isn't it?" she asked, nodding toward the envelope. "The one I wrote to Rupert."

"I don't know," I answered. "It's not signed."

She smiled, and I thought with a sudden chill how the customary vague politeness had been replaced with a thinly veiled hostility. "I think you know that I wrote it, Mrs. Ames. You're very clever. Perhaps too clever."

My mind was working quickly. It was just possible that I had uncovered an illicit liaison and nothing more. I held the note toward her. "It was, perhaps, ill mannered of me to read it. I was hoping I could uncover something. If you'd like it back, I'll just be going back downstairs."

Her quiet smile didn't falter in the slightest as she pulled a gun from her pocket and pointed it at me. "I don't think that will be possible."

I felt a strangely numb feeling steal over me as I looked into the muzzle of her gun. I had not suspected Mrs. Hamilton, had not even had an inkling that she might have been involved. And yet it seemed foolish now to have overlooked her.

"You and Rupert were having an affair," I said. In the novels, it always seemed best to keep the suspect talking. Inevitably, help would arrive. I really held out no hope for such an opportune occurrence, but it seemed the best course of action would be to distract her until I could determine what to do.

"It wasn't as tawdry as that," she said, and her voice was wistful. "Rupert and I knew each other years ago. He was a bit younger than me, but we always got on. He knew Geoffrey, and when he was drowned, Rupert befriended me. He helped me through a very difficult time. We formed an attachment, but we were too poor to wed comfortably, and eventually we went our separate ways. It was about a year ago that I saw him again, in London."

"But you were already married."

"Yes, unfortunately. I married Hamilton six years ago, and I have been miserable ever since."

"Did you ever love your husband?" I didn't know why I had asked her that. I suppose I was just curious if there had ever been a part of Mr. Hamilton that was worth loving.

She laughed, a pretty, tinkling sound, and I realized that I had never heard her express true amusement before this. "Do you think it would be possible to love someone like Nelson? He delighted in belittling me, in making himself feel superior. No, I never loved him. He was rich, and he was the only chance I had at a better life, so I took it."

"But then Rupert came back into your life."

"Yes. We met unexpectedly at a party in London, began seeing each other. We agreed to meet here at the Brightwell. It wasn't hard to convince Nelson. One only had to make him think it was his idea, and that wasn't difficult. He knew how much I hated the sea, so it pleased him to come here." She seemed caught up in the story now, and my mind was searching for some means of extricating myself from the situation. I considered hurling my torch at her, but I was not at all confident in my aim.

"I was terribly in love with Rupert," she said softly, and I could see the anguish in her eyes as she spoke. "He was very good at making people believe what he wanted them to believe. He had Emmeline wrapped around his finger. He did the same to me."

I said nothing, waiting for her to continue.

"He made me believe that he still cared for me. He said he wanted us to be together forever, but I think he was really just interested in Nelson's money. In addition to Emmeline's fortune, he would have more money than he could ever possibly need."

"But how would that have worked, with both of you married to other people? Divorces are difficult to obtain, and surely much of the money would be lost in the proceedings."

She looked at me strangely, as though she had only just remembered that I was there. Her eyes met mine, and I was chilled at how cold they were. "No, I wasn't talking about a divorce."

I frowned, confused. "I don't understand."

"You see, we had planned to kill them all along," she said suddenly. "Nelson and Emmeline. With both of them dead, we could be together, have all the money we ever needed.

Horror coursed through me at her words. I never, in my wildest imaginings, could have concocted something like this.

She smiled, a bit sadly. "I know what you're thinking, Mrs. Ames. And you're right. It's a terrible thing. But Nelson was a terrible man."

"But what of Emmeline?"

"Emmeline is a sweet girl . . . but I've been waiting a long time for happiness."

I realized then that Mrs. Hamilton was not quite sane. She couldn't possibly be. I desperately racked my brains for some way to distract her, for something I could do to escape.

"So what happened . . . with Rupert?" I asked at last. I was genuinely curious. If I were to be murdered tonight by a deranged killer, I should hate to do it with questions still lingering in my mind.

"I'd be interested to see what you think," she replied. It was a strange request, but I took my time considering an answer.

"Your husband found out about your affair, confronted Rupert, and struck him. When you found out what he'd done, you killed your husband."

She smiled again, shaking her head. "Perhaps you're not as clever as I fancied you, Mrs. Ames. No, Nelson didn't do it. He didn't have the nerve. I killed Rupert."

This I had not anticipated. I rather expect my mouth gaped a bit.

"Gil and Rupert were on the terrace that afternoon, arguing about Emmeline, as usual."

So Milo had told the truth. Gil had been on the terrace. Their argument explained why Gil hadn't wanted to admit it; no doubt it had been a continuation of their conversation the night before.

"When Gil had gone, I went to speak to Rupert," she went on. "He said that Gil was willing to pay him to leave Emmeline alone. He had offered quite a substantial sum, and I told Rupert to take it. We could have spared Emmeline then, you see."

She looked at me as though she expected I would be impressed by her benevolence.

"But Rupert didn't want to take it." I guessed, hoping to prod her forward.

A sudden flash of anger crossed her face, harshening the normally sweet lines of her expression. "No, he didn't want to take it. Do you know what he told me?"

Even in the dim light, I could see that her grip on the gun was tightening in anger. I could guess very well what Rupert had told her, but I wasn't about to be the one to say it aloud.

"No. What?" I asked.

"He said he didn't want the money Gil had offered him, that he had suddenly discovered that he truly cared for Emmeline."

Of all the shocking truths I had learned on this dreadful little holiday, it was this salient fact that surprised me the most. "He loved Emmeline?"

"He thought he did," she replied, and though she had calmed herself, there was still some strange combination of anger and sorrow lurking in her stormy blue eyes. "He said he thought we should call it off. He said he would marry her, and perhaps we could still see each other from time to time." Her voice was growing slightly shrill, and I could imagine the hysteria that must have overcome her on the terrace as the only man she had ever loved, the man she had been prepared to kill for, told her that perhaps he didn't care so very much for her after all.

"I tried to reason with him, tried to tell him how much he meant to me, but he only smiled in that way of his and asked for a cigarette."

I knew then what she was about to say. I could see it in my head as clearly as if I had been standing with them on the terrace that day.

"I gave him a cigarette, and he lit it with his gold lighter . . . the lighter I gave him, not Emmeline. I told him one more time what he meant to me, tried to remind him what we had meant to each other . . . and then he said . . ." She paused, as though hearing the words again in her mind. "He said, 'It's run its course, Rissa. Let's be honest, you couldn't have gone through with killing your husband. You're much too weak . . . perhaps that's why our relationship can't last.'"

Suddenly she seemed to slump ever so slightly, as though all the emotion had drained out of her, and she was once again the Larissa Hamilton to whom I had grown accustomed, the pale, shrinking wife of a total boor who had married her for her looks and then quickly tired of everything but his cruelty toward her.

"And so you hit him," I supplied.

"Yes. I struck at him and hit him with my cigarette case, as hard as I could manage. Before I even really knew what was happening, he fell over the edge." Her face was ashen, and her voice trembled a little as she looked past me, no doubt reliving the scene in her mind.

"You told me that it was a stupid way to kill someone," I said, remembering our conversation on the terrace shortly after the murder.

"It was, wasn't it? With a cigarette case. So very stupid." She said vaguely, "There was so much blood on the case. It took me a very long time to clean it off."

"Then it was an accident," I said. "The police couldn't blame you for that, not really."

"Perhaps not," she answered softly. "But then, of course, I killed Nelson, too."

I had suspected this, but it was still shocking to hear it flow so calmly from her lips. My mind was reeling at the storm of revelations that were swirling around me. I felt very much as though I might welcome a good faint, but I was quite sure Mrs. Hamilton would do something ghastly to me while I was unconscious.

"In a way, I was sorry that Rupert was dead, but knowing how he felt, I mourned him very little. I was hoping the inquest would find that it had been an accident. Then I might have gone on as usual. I still planned on killing Nelson, of course. But I would have done it much later had he not begun to suspect."

"He found the lighter."

"Yes, the lighter fell with Rupert. I went down to his body, to try and take it with me, but it wasn't there. And I couldn't bring myself to go down to the shore to look for it. I couldn't bear to be so near the sea. As an afterthought, I put up the 'closed for repair' sign, hoping to buy myself a little extra time."

"You just had to hope that no one found it."

"Yes, but then Nelson dug it up on the beach somewhere. I don't know how the police overlooked it, but perhaps they only gave the beach a cursory inspection. Nelson noticed that night when we were playing bridge that my cigarette case matched Rupert's lighter, which he had used one night at dinner. He noticed stupid things like that. When he remembered the lighter, I suppose he acted on a whim and was rewarded for it. He didn't know for certain, of course, that I had killed Rupert, only that I had given him the lighter, but he was taunting me with what he had learned and said he would go to the police. He enjoyed making me afraid. And yet . . . I don't think he trusted me. He always made sure to lock the door to his room. I was surprised that day to find it open. I had expected to have to force the door from the hall."

I had left the door unlocked that day. I felt sorry for that now, though I had no doubt she could have easily entered the other way had she set her mind to it. She was, I was learning, quite a tenacious little thing.

"I took Anne Rodgers's sleeping tablets one evening when we

sat in her room looking at magazines. When Nelson and I had gone down to lunch, I put the powder in his drink. He always bathed in the afternoon, and I intended to kill him then. He had this gun, always carried it with him for some absurd reason, but I had taken it before breakfast, just in case there should be any trouble. But the gun proved unnecessary. I had only to slip into his room. He was too disoriented to struggle much."

"You drowned him," I said, "despite what happened to your brother."

Her eyes met mine, and I could detect no trace of remorse in them. "Nelson knew, of course, why I didn't want to come to the Brightwell, knew how I'd lost Geoffrey, but he said I'd had plenty of time to recover from a childhood incident." A dazed sort of smile flittered across her face. "Strange, isn't it? I've always been so very afraid of the water, but it was very useful to me this once."

She was chillingly composed as she related this to me, and I found it almost incomprehensible that this scene was actually taking place.

"That done, I went back to my room and took four sleeping tablets myself. That was a bit of a risk, as I wasn't sure of the dosage, but it turned out quite all right."

So there it was, the whole story. Now that it was revealed to me, it all made perfect sense, in a slightly insane sort of way.

And now we had come to the crux of the matter.

"And what do you intend to do to me, Larissa?" I asked. "You can't just go about leaving a trail of dead bodies. Sooner or later, they'll lead to you."

"Perhaps. But you know entirely too much. I'm afraid you can't possibly be allowed to tell what you know."

"Was that why you put sleeping tablets in my aspirin bottle?" I asked. It was one final piece of the puzzle.

To my surprise, she frowned and shook her head. "I didn't put sleeping tablets in your bottle."

It was my turn to frown. Was she telling the truth? I could see no reason why she would lie, not now when she had told me everything else.

"I had no reason to drug you. I like you, Mrs. Ames. You're a very kind woman, and I hoped it wouldn't come to this. I tried to dissuade you, even to throw suspicion in Emmeline's direction, hoping you would decide to leave the matter be, but that didn't seem to work."

She was right. Despite her story about Emmeline's overhearing Rupert and Olive planning to meet, I had never really suspected that Emmeline might have killed Rupert in a fit of jealous rage. I simply couldn't have imagined her doing any such thing. Then again, I certainly hadn't suspected Mrs. Hamilton. My instincts, it appeared, were hit-and-miss.

"Sadly, you refused to let it drop," she went on. "So you've left me with no alternative."

"You're going to shoot me?" I asked.

"I'm afraid so. If I wait until the next flash of lightning, the thunder may cover my shot," she said. "I'm sorry to have to kill you, Mrs. Ames. I'm sure your husband will be sorry to lose you; he's very fond of you, you know."

As she finished speaking, as if on cue, a brilliant flash of lightning lit the room. Almost before I knew what I was doing, I hurled my torch at her. To my everlasting gratitude, it hit her squarely in the stomach. She jerked back reflexively, and I threw myself at her. We fell to the ground, grabbling for the gun. I fell atop her, my hand clamped on her wrist. She struggled violently. For a small woman, she was remarkably strong. I was fighting for my life, however, and I had no intention of giving up.

She tried to pull her arm from my grasp, and the gun went off with a deafening boom, shattering the window. With all my strength, I pounded her arm against the floor, and the gun fell from her grasp. I grabbed for it as she heaved me off of her. She was almost on top of me when I swung the gun up and hit her across the head with it as hard as I could manage. It connected with a startling loud crack, and she slumped to the floor in a sad little heap.

I sat up, breathing heavily, a great lock of hair hanging across my face. I looked down at her. She was still breathing, and I was glad I had not done to her what she had done to Rupert. Seeing her still, crumpled form, I felt almost sorry for her. Almost, but not quite.

I heard footsteps running down the hall before the door to the room burst open. Inspector Jones rushed into the room, followed by Gil.

"Amory, are you all right?" Gil said, rushing to my side and helping me to my feet.

I brushed back the hair that had fallen across my eyes. "I'm very well, thank you." I couldn't quite hide the triumph in my tone. "And now that I've flushed out the murderer, you shall be all right, too, Gil."

28

IT WAS NOT until Inspector Jones had had his men take Larissa Hamilton away and I had given him a complete account of the evening's events that the full impact of the situation hit me. Then I felt weak with exhaustion and the dregs of fear. My head fairly spun with it.

Gil and Inspector Jones accompanied me back to my room. When I was settled in my chair, the inspector asked me a few more careful questions, jotting down the answers in his little book. He must have noticed my pallor and the trembling of my hands in my lap, however, for, after a moment, he flipped the book shut and put it into his pocket.

"I think that will do," he said. "Shall I get you a drink, Mrs. Ames?"

"Thank you, no." Against all reason, what I really wanted was Milo. I had the feeling, however, that he would not prove sympathetic to my encounter with a murderer after I had as good as accused him of the crime. "How . . . how did you know where to find me?"

"I had just arrived at the hotel," Inspector Jones explained. "I encountered Mr. Ames in the foyer, and he told me that you would no doubt want to speak to me about having caught the murderer."

Milo, ever mocking, had sent Inspector Jones along to receive my woefully erroneous theory.

"I was coming to speak to you as well ..." Gil said, his voice trailing off. I wondered if he had spoken with Olive about our conversation. "I had no answer at your room, and then I heard the shot."

"We reached Mr. Howe's room at the same time," Inspector Jones finished.

"I was hoping someone would hear the shot, though I feared they would mistake it for thunder. That was her intention."

"I knew immediately it was a gunshot." Inspector Jones smiled wryly. "Though it seemed you had the situation well under control by the time we arrived."

"I'd have never thought it was Mrs. Hamilton," Gil said. "I would never have imagined that she could do such a thing."

"I wondered when she was drugged," Inspector Jones said. "It seemed just possible that she might have done it herself. Unfortunately, several facts seemed to point to someone else."

"Me, you mean," Gil said.

Inspector Jones glanced at me. "No ..."

"Milo," I said.

The inspector nodded. "You knew that I suspected."

"I suspected him myself," I replied. "And I told him so."

"Oh, dear," I heard Gil murmur under his breath.

"That day I first interviewed you, I felt something was amiss," Inspector Jones said. "I later discovered that he had not arrived when he said he did. Then I spoke with him again the day of the inquest. That was when he reported having overheard the conversation between Mr. Trent and Mr. Howe. It all seemed too neat, somehow. Adding to the unlikely coincidences, he was in the room when you were drugged and when Mr. Hamilton was killed. When he left for London with barely a word, everything seemed to be confirmed. And I had to wonder how much you knew."

"I didn't suspect him then. It was only tonight that I thought he might have done it."

There was a moment of somewhat strained silence before Inspector Jones rose from his seat. "You were very brave tonight, Mrs. Ames," he said. "Perhaps we'll talk again tomorrow. I know you must be tired."

"Yes, thank you," I whispered. I felt myself on the verge of tears again, and I was ready to be alone.

Gil rose after Inspector Jones. He took my hand in his. "Get some rest, Amory."

"I'll try."

He nodded, releasing my hand, and turned to go. He paused at the door. "Do you want me to send Milo up?"

It was a sweet thought, and I felt the tears welling in my eyes. "I . . . don't think so, Gil. But thank you."

"I'll . . . be in my room if you need me."

I nodded, and he left. I locked the door behind him, drawing in a deep breath. So many things were spinning though my mind that I felt almost faint. What I needed was a good night's sleep, though I knew that I would not be getting one.

Still a bit shaky, I changed and went right to bed. Despite my exhaustion, my thoughts kept me awake. It was not, however, the night's events that preyed on my mind. Instead, I found myself wondering where Milo was and feeling utterly miserable that he hadn't come to me.

IF THE MURDERS had cleared the hotel of guests, Mrs. Hamilton's arrest had done its part to clear the Brightwell of the rest of our party. Mr. and Mrs. Rodgers left before dawn. They were, as I was, more than ready to leave this place behind them. Veronica Carter had departed in a sea of fur and perfume, and, though my feelings toward her had softened ever so slightly, I was glad to see her go.

I had packed my bags, leaving the rest of Milo's things untouched. He could do with them what he pleased.

I reached the lobby, when a voice called out to me. "Mrs. Ames."

I turned to see Lionel Blake approaching. "I wanted to say good-bye before you left. It was my great pleasure to meet you," he said. He held out his hand to me, and I shook it.

"It was nice to meet you, Mr. Blake. I wish you great success in your career."

Mr. Blake smiled. He seemed to hesitate for just a moment, and then he spoke. "I feel that perhaps I should apologize if I have acted mysteriously, Mrs. Ames."

"You needn't tell me anything," I said, though I was immediately curious. My nearly lethal experience with investigation had not managed to staunch my inquisitive streak.

"I was hesitant to share information with you, but I have learned of your heroic behavior last night, and I feel that I should explain. You see, I have built up a careful reputation for myself as an actor . . . an English actor. But, you see, I am not English. I am German."

I was surprised. I had thought his careful diction was a mark of his trade, not a cautious attempt to hide an accent that was still not warmly welcomed on English shores.

"You understand that things are not so easy for my people in this country as they once were. The memory of the war still hovers like a dark cloud."

This explained much. I recalled our conversation the day Mr. Hamilton had been killed, when I had encountered him outside the Brightwell. The word he had mumbled under his breath had not been "lord" but "mord," the German word for murder.

"I would not have guessed you were German," I said, thinking of the play he had been reading that morning at breakfast. "Though I did notice you read the language."

He smiled. "A clumsy mistake on my part. I should not have read that book in public. In any event, my backer is also German and has suffered because of it; he asked me to find a venue, somewhere out of the way, where he could stage a play. Luckily, we were able to find a place in London. However, I feared that if anyone found out, he would have further difficulties. That is also why I abhor undue publicity and interviews. Sometimes, under strain, my accent slips."

"I think you're quite a marvelous actor, Mr. Blake," I said with a smile. "I should like very much to see you in a play sometime."

He returned my smile. "You do understand?"

"Yes, certainly. Thank you for telling me."

"Amory darling!" I turned to see Mrs. Roland sweeping down the stairs.

Lionel Blake gripped my hand once more, leaning close to my ear. "Be careful what you tell her. She works for the gossip magazines." Then he released my hand and was gone.

I barely had time to digest this startling, though very enlightening, information before Mrs. Roland was upon me, depositing kisses on both of my cheeks. "You saved the day, I hear. How clever you are, Amory! To think of you, wrestling the black-hearted murderess to the ground . . ."

"Oh," I answered with a smile. "Nothing as dramatic as all that, though I'm glad to be putting it behind me."

"To think of it, Mrs. Hamilton drugging herself and her husband so that she could hold him down in the bathtub. It's unthinkable!" I did not know where she was getting her information, but it was astoundingly accurate.

"She must have drugged me, as well," I said, almost to myself. Though she had denied it, I could think of no other explanation for the tablets that had made their way into my bottle.

"Oh, no, I don't think so," Mrs. Roland said. "I think it must have been Veronica Carter. She was after your husband, you know. I think she thought she would have a better chance of succeeding if you were safely out of the way for the evening. A nasty trick, very much in her style."

"I . . . don't know . . ." I had seen her on my floor that day. Perhaps it had been she who put the sleeping pills in my aspirin bottle. If so, I could forgive her. Milo had spent that night in my room, after all. "I'm rather confused on that point."

"I'm sure you are, dear. And your charming husband?" she asked. "Where is he this morning?"

"I was just about to go and find him," I said. "If you'll excuse me, Mrs. Roland."

"Yes, yes, of course, dear. It was lovely seeing you."

And with that, she fluttered out the door. I watched her go for a minute, trying to take in what I had learned about her. She was really the perfect choice to work for the gossip columns. People were always telling her things without thinking anything of it. I expected this past week had given her fodder for quite a while.

I went to the desk. "Have you seen Mr. Ames this morning?" I was half-afraid that he had left again without my knowing.

"He's there, madam," the clerk said, nodding behind me. I turned to see that Milo had just emerged from the sitting room. I thought that he saw me, but he continued out onto the terrace.

Thanking the clerk, I hurried toward the doors leading out to the terrace and exited. The wind was low today, the storm having died down sometime in the night. Milo stood there, looking out at the uneasy sea. "Milo . . ."

He turned to look at me, and it was terrifying how little showed in his eyes. It was as though he had shut me out completely. And what was worse, I felt, in some ways, that I deserved it.

"Aren't you a bit afraid I'll toss you over the edge?" he asked with a humorless smile.

"I'm sorry, Milo," I said.

"I understand you captured a killer last night. I suppose you were bound to guess right eventually."

I flinched at the words and the tone in which he said them. "I didn't want to believe it was you."

"And yet you thought me capable of it."

"I didn't know what to think. You claimed you hadn't met Rupert, and then I found that photograph."

"As I told you, I didn't know Rupert Howe. We just happened to be in Monte Carlo at the same time."

"There were so many things. For one mad moment, all of the evidence seemed to point in your direction . . ."

"The evidence pointed to Trent at one point, I believe. And you never wavered in your staunch defense of him."

He was right, of course. "I'm sorry," I said again. "Can you forgive me?"

"Of course, darling. It's really of very little consequence." It was his dismissive tone, the one he used on people of whom he had tired, and when the corners of his mouth turned up it did nothing to warm his eyes.

We stood there in a tense silence. At least, I felt tense; Milo seemed almost bored. I half-expected him to walk back into the hotel at any moment. But before he did, there was one more thing I needed to know.

"I . . . there's something else I want to ask you." I hesitated to question him now, especially after all that had happened, but I had to know. Before anything else, I needed to be sure.

"Yes?" His tone held the vaguest hint of impatience, but I plunged ahead.

"Who is Winnelda, Milo?"

A cynical amusement flickered across his face. "Ah. You find I am not guilty of murder, so you adopt a lesser charge."

"She answered the telephone at the flat."

He leaned against the railing, looking back at the sea. "Winnelda is the maid."

"We haven't any permanent staff at the flat."

"We have now. She's the most horrid, clumsy little thing." He pulled a cigarette from the case in his pocket and lit it. "I had to hire her, to learn about the Hamiltons."

"What do you mean?"

"She worked for them in London. I didn't have a chance to tell you. She had some interesting things to say about Mrs. Hamilton, though it proved you had little use for my information."

"You didn't tell me where you had gone. I didn't . . ."

"It had occurred to me that I might be able to glean some interesting tidbits in London. I located this maid, and she related tales of the Hamiltons' unhappy marriage and noted that Mrs. Hamilton seemed to have a gentleman friend on the side whose description bore an uncanny resemblance to that of Rupert Howe. Winnelda is a shockingly observant girl for one so inept."

"Then you knew last night who the killer was."

"I had my suspicions."

"Why didn't you tell me?" I asked, though I knew perfectly well why he hadn't.

"It didn't seem the time," he said expressionlessly. "I intended to relate my news to the inspector. Mrs. Hamilton wasn't in the sitting room when I went down last night. I thought she had stayed in her room. It didn't occur to me that you might be in danger . . . but I suppose it didn't matter, not with the inspector and gallant Trent to the rescue . . ." He offered me a hollow smile. "All's well that ends well."

There was something in the way he said it that gave me an uneasy feeling.

"And that, my dear, explains away my unexpected jaunt to London and the mysterious Winnelda. Of course, I had to offer her a job to pry her tales from her," he went on. "Hopefully, the flat will still be standing when you get back to London." I noticed his use of "you" rather than "we" immediately. So he was not planning on coming back with me.

"I wish you had told me," I said. "You left, and then the inspector told me you had claimed to see Gil. I thought . . . it was all so confusing."

"As you know, I came down directly after you did. I arrived at the Brightwell the day of the murder and happened to overhear some of the rather heated conversation between Trent and Howe. I decided perhaps it would be best to come back later."

"Why didn't you tell me, Milo? If I had known . . ."

"It wouldn't have mattered." He blew out a stream of smoke. "It has become very apparent that you're always willing to believe the worst of me."

"You've never given me cause to doubt it," I replied. There was no malice in my tone. Only sadness. Things were not going as I had expected. "The facts seemed to implicate you. And then a strange woman answered at the flat. What would you expect me to think?"

He looked at me. "Perhaps the same thing I thought when I heard the rumor that Gil Trent spent the night in your bedroom." His voice, beneath his nonchalance, was terribly cool.

"Who told you that?" I asked softly.

"Is it true?"

"He came to talk to me, but he'd had too much to drink and passed out."

"Then it is true."

"Nothing happened, Milo."

"Nothing?" His brow went up, and I read the challenge in the gesture.

As much as I hated to, I felt compelled to tell him everything. It was harder than I imagined it would be. "He . . . I . . . we kissed. Just once."

"And?"

"And then he fell asleep and didn't wake until morning."

Something very like mockery flickered across his features. "Poor Trent. He waits five long years and then succumbs to unconsciousness once he finally has you in his arms."

"I wouldn't have done anything more . . ."

"Wouldn't you?"

"Of course not," I retorted, my ire raised. "I don't behave as you do."

He smiled, and it was a very hard smile. "You think very highly of me, don't you, my dear?"

"I'm sorry," I said with a sigh. "I shouldn't have said that. With everything that's happened, emotions are running high."

"Yes. Well," he said, "as charming as this little seaside escapade has been, I think it's time I head back to civilization."

He ground out his cigarette, and I couldn't help but feel he had just done the same with our relationship.

"Where are you going?" I asked.

"Back to Monte Carlo. Or perhaps to Switzerland. I'm not certain."

I looked down at my hands, noticing suddenly that I had never put my wedding ring back on. "When can I expect you back in London?"

"I'll drop you a line."

My eyes came up to his, and we looked at one another, neither of us willing to say what needed to be said in order to set things right.

"Good-bye then, Amory." He leaned and brushed a kiss across my cheek. His lips were warm against my wind-chilled skin.

"Good-bye, Milo," I whispered.

I longed to allow myself to lean into his arms, but I could not make myself do it. Pride is not an appealing quality, but I possessed too much of it to tell him that I didn't want him to go.

He left me then, and I turned toward the sea so I didn't have to watch him leave.

Was it my fault or his? It was really too much of a tangled mess to know. Perhaps he was right. Perhaps we should give it some time before making any rash decisions.

29

MILO GONE, I stood looking out at the sea, the tears welling in my eyes. Once again, the burden of our relationship rested on my shoulders. I would be left at home to wait until one of us made some sort of decision. I had judged him harshly, wronged him with my mistrust. I couldn't entirely blame him for being angry. Yet it had been the reputation he had earned for himself that had made me suspicious, his own actions that had made me wonder if I could trust him.

Perhaps both of us had behaved like fools.

"Amory."

I turned to see Gil, standing, somewhat hesitantly, in the doorway. "Milo . . . sent me out. He said he expected you'd be wanting to see me."

So Milo's final dig had been to send his competition in to claim me.

"He's going back to the Continent," I said.

"What does that mean?"

"I wish I knew. It seems the Brightwell Hotel is not at all a lucky place for relationships." I changed the subject, not wanting to talk about Milo any longer. "How is Emmeline?"

After the events of last night, Gil had sent her home to their mother in London on the first train this morning. It was best that she be removed from the situation, from the place that held so many haunting memories.

Gil walked out onto the terrace, his hands in his pockets. "She'll mend, I expect. But it won't be easy."

"For what it's worth, he did care for her, in his way." It was a poor comfort, I knew. But perhaps it would mean something to Emmeline. "If you could write to her, I think she would enjoy that. She will need something to distract her in the coming months."

"Of course. I should be happy to." I hesitated. "And what about Olive?"

His gaze became guarded. "She's told you that she's in love with me?"

"Yes."

"I wasn't sure she really meant it. I'm still not entirely sure."

"She's mad about you," I said, using the words Olive had used of him.

"That business with cutting her wrists, it was a dreadfully stupid thing to do." I felt that the anger that flickered in his gaze stemmed from deep concern. I knew he had been terribly worried about her. She had known it, too. It had been a foolish thing to do, but people did foolish things when they were desperate.

"I don't think she meant to do any real harm to herself."

"No," he said. "But that doesn't make it any less wretched. When did you know about Olive and me?"

"I only just realized last night. We were talking, and suddenly I realized. I was blind not to have seen it before this."

Gil walked to where I stood, not quite meeting my gaze. That he was uncomfortable was very apparent. "Did she tell you everything?"

"She didn't quite seem to know what had happened herself," I said. I felt suddenly very sorry for her.

He looked back out at the sea. "It was my fault. I treated her badly. We met and got along famously. We saw each other for quite a while. I . . . had entertained thoughts of marrying her, but then she met Rupert Howe. They seemed to take an instant liking to each other."

So many things fell into place. Apparently, Rupert had reminded Gil of Milo as well. Perhaps he had thought that she, too, would fall prey to the charms of a handsome gentleman.

"It was unfair of me," he went on, "but I thought it best to end things . . . before they went any further. So I broke it off. She took it badly, but I assumed she would recover soon enough. I went away and tried to forget about the entire thing. I didn't know she was going to be here at the Brightwell. It was devilishly awkward when I arrived with you to find her here."

"I wish you had told me."

"I thought about it, but I didn't want to place the burden of that on you. However, I was terribly afraid it was all going to come out in some sort of dreadful scene. That was one reason I didn't want you going about asking questions. Everyone knew about it, and I suspect they were all dying to say something. It was ridiculous to think I could keep it a secret."

I thought of the conversation I had had with Mr. and Mrs. Rodgers in the lobby that day, the careful way she had warned him with a hand on his leg not to say too much when the conversation turned to the changing nature of love.

"Olive was in a state all week, and, to top it off, there were those rumors going around about her and Rupert. After the murder, I was a bit afraid they might think she'd been jealous enough to . . ."

So we had all been trying to shield someone. While I'd been attempting to protect Gil, he had been hoping to protect Olive. What tangled webs we weave, indeed.

"I knew you were worried about something," I said, "and I wondered why you wouldn't confide in me."

Gil let out a sort of strangled laugh. "Yes, it's been a perfectly dreadful week, all told. First, trying to convince Rupert to leave Emmeline, and then his murder . . . and your husband's arrival. And all the time, Olive kept trying to convince me to change my mind about her . . . about our relationship. She came to my room to talk, more than once. And on the night that I was arrested, I had just come from speaking with her. We'd been hashing it out all afternoon in her room. She said she was going to tell you, and I wanted to do it first . . . but after I was released, it just didn't seem the time."

"Do you love her, Gil?" I asked.

He met my gaze. "I don't know. I thought I did. But then . . ."

But then he had come back into my life, and we had both been caught in the trap of wondering if our idealized versions of the past might be preferable to uncertain futures.

We looked into one another's eyes, and I think we both knew in that instant that the past was behind us. We could never be to each other what we had been once.

"Today, Gil," I said softly. "What do you feel for her right now, with everything in the open?"

"I . . . I do still care for her," he said, and it seemed to me that with the words there came a certain relief. He looked happy, lighter somehow.

"Then you should tell her."

"I'm not even sure she'll have me. I made a terrible mistake in not trusting her."

"She'll have you. Though you did misjudge her. She never cared for Rupert. She told me so. She's not like me, you know, not fickle in her emotions."

"Amory, don't," he said gently.

I bit my lip, tears threatening to spill over. Gil pulled me to him then, and I leaned against him, taking comfort in the embrace of a cherished friend. For a moment, I relished the security of his arms, the warm solidity of him. Then I stepped back, wiping my face, drawing in a bracing breath of sea air. "I've made such a mess of everything," I said with a humorless laugh.

He looked down at me. "None of us make the clearest decisions when we're in love. And you are still in love with him."

I sighed and nodded, admitting it to myself for the first time. "Yes. I still love him."

"I expect I've known that all along." He smiled, a bit crookedly. "I suppose I thought it was worth a chance to see what might have been."

"I'm not at all sure things will work out . . . but I need to try."

"I understand." Gil leaned against the railing as Milo had done only moments before. "You're suited, really," he said with a smile. "He needs a calming influence, and you need a little excitement. You'd have been terribly bored with me, Amory."

"I'm so sorry, Gil, for everything."

He took my hand, and we faced each another one last time. "You've nothing to be sorry for, Amory. You followed your heart. Most of the time, that's all any of us can do."

"Thank you." I drew in a deep breath, refusing to allow myself to cry again. I had already shed more tears this week than I had in the last year. "Shall I see you in London?"

"Certainly. I should always like to be your friend, Amory."

"And I yours, Gil."

He smiled and squeezed my hand. "Now, if you'll excuse me, I think I have some things I need to discuss with Olive."

"Of course. I wish you both every happiness."

He brushed a kiss across my cheek and left me alone on the terrace.

I stood there for a few moments longer, looking out at the sea. So much had happened in the short time I had been here. And yet so much had not really changed at all.

Rousing myself at last, I went back into the hotel. I would need to gather my things in order to catch the evening train. I would send a telegram to Laurel so she would meet me at the station. I didn't want to return alone to an empty house. Perhaps we could spend a few days shopping in London before I returned to the country and tried to sort out the astounding mess that was my marriage.

"I expect you will be glad to leave the Brightwell behind you, Mrs. Ames."

I turned to see Inspector Jones approaching. Though I had given him my official statement last night, I was not entirely surprised to see him. I had felt that, perhaps, he would have a few more things to say to me before I departed. I was glad to see him. Though my behavior had been trying to him, I had the feeling that he had grown rather fond of me. And I found that I admired him a great deal.

"I will indeed, Inspector. I don't think I shall ever look at a seaside holiday in the same way."

"You're going home today?"

"Yes, I was just about to leave for the station."

He didn't ask about Milo, and for that I was grateful. Insightful man that he was, I had a feeling he had a good grasp of the situation.

"You may be surprised to hear this, given my stern views on the matter, but I actually came to thank you for your help," he said grudgingly.

Despite the unwillingness of his confession, I felt flattered at the admission.

"You would have found her out," I said, and I meant it. Inspector Jones was a very clever man, and I had no doubt he would have solved the case. My continual interference had, perhaps, forced Mrs. Hamilton's hand, but she could not have eluded him forever.

"Perhaps not in time," he said gravely. "I would not have been at all surprised should she have decided Emmeline Trent would be the next to be disposed of. She had been the one to ruin all of Mrs. Hamilton's dreams, you know."

It was a dreadful thought, and one I did not care to dwell on.

"Will she hang, do you think?" I asked. As horrid as her crimes had been, I still couldn't help but feel a bit of sympathy for the quiet woman who had finally been pushed too far.

"I doubt it. From what the doctors have said, I gather she's not entirely in possession of her faculties. It's likely she'll be committed."

"Perhaps that would be best," I said.

"And what of your plans?" he asked. "Do you intend to make a habit of interfering in police investigations?" Though his expression was perfectly serious, I knew that he was teasing me.

"I think not. One murder was enough, Inspector. I plan to leave crime far behind me."

He smiled. "You say that now, but I think if something intriguing came along, you would jump at the chance to involve yourself in it."

I laughed.

The porter brought my bags down, and I willingly surrendered my room key to the clerk at the desk.

"May I drive you to the station, Mrs. Ames?" the inspector asked as we walked back out of the Brightwell and into the warm sunshine.

"Thank you, Inspector Jones." I smiled. "Given my experiences over the last week, I think a police escort would be lovely indeed."

I SAT IN my train compartment looking out at the passing landscape, the sea fading into the distance as we traveled northward. The sun had come out today, as if to signal brighter things to come, but I couldn't help feeling a bit forlorn. With all that had happened, I was terribly tired and ready to be home.

"Traveling alone?"

I looked up at the familiar voice, thinking for a moment I had imagined it. I was more than a little surprised to see Milo standing in the door of the compartment. I hadn't seen him at the station, and I certainly hadn't seen him board this train.

"I thought you'd gone on an earlier train," I said. My voice was calm, though my heart had begun racing at the sight of him. I had admitted to Gil that, despite everything, I was still in love with Milo. I hadn't wanted Milo to leave with things unsettled, and now here he was. Nevertheless, my mind refused to form any expectations; I had long ago learned that it was better not to get my hopes up.

I watched him warily as he came into the compartment and closed the doors behind him. "I've decided not to go back to the Continent just now," he said.

I was unsure of how to react, what part I should assume in this little drama that was unfolding. I had felt certain that our marriage had fallen apart this morning, and yet here he stood, as casually as if he had come into the drawing room for tea.

"Oh?" I managed to say. "What changed your mind?"

"I gave it a bit of thought, and I considered it best not to leave you alone. I don't much like the company you've been keeping lately."

"Indeed?"

"Indeed." He took the seat across from me, his expression smooth and unworried. "In fact, I'd come with the express intention of throwing Gilmore Trent off of this train."

My lips twitched at the corners, a smile coming against my will as I felt a spark of hope. "Gil isn't on this train."

Our eyes met.

"No?" he asked. I suspected then that he had already known as much, that he had waited at the station for me to make my choice, once and for all, before he took any sort of action.

"No," I said softly, and we both knew how much the simple word conveyed.

He shrugged, relaxing in his seat. "Just as well. I should have hated for your opinion of my ruthless nature to be justified."

"Milo, I . . ."

He waved a hand. "Never mind. It doesn't matter. Perhaps I did look guilty there for a while. In any event, it was interesting being the prime suspect for a moment or two."

"If only we'd confided in one another," I said. "But we've never been very good at that, have we?"

"It could be worse. At least you've never tried to drown me in my bathtub."

I let out a sound that was some cross between a laugh and a sigh. "Do be serious, Milo."

"I'm perfectly serious. There are worse marriages than ours, certainly."

"I mean it, though," I persisted, my gaze dropping to my hands. For some reason I found it impossible to look him in the face and say what needed to be said. "We're like strangers half the time. I often wonder if you still care for me at all."

I had forced myself to say it, despite the fact that I expected a flippant answer. But when I raised my eyes to his, I found that there was no amusement in his expression.

"You know perfectly well that I adore you, Amory," he said.

He was watching me intently, his eyes deep blue pools into which I could feel myself sinking. It was one of those rare moments in which he gave the impression of perfect sincerity, and I felt strongly the pull of my desire to believe him.

"Do you?" I asked softly. "I can never be sure."

He took my hand in his, his thumb caressing the finger where my rings should have been. I felt a little shiver of heat travel up my arm. He brought my hand to his mouth and brushed his lips across it, and my breath caught in my throat.

"I'd like to come home with you," he said. "I'm a bit tired of traveling at present."

I hesitated. He was always so very good at saying the right things. I wanted so much to be sure that he meant it, to be certain that he wasn't merely telling me what I needed to hear. I knew perfectly well, however, that at that moment I was willing to risk it. I was not completely certain I believed him, but, looking into his eyes as he waited for my answer, I believed that he believed himself. Perhaps that was enough. At least for now.

"Yes, Milo," I said. "I should like very much for you to come home."

He came up from his seat and sat beside me, pulling me into his arms as he leaned to kiss me.

I have never been like the silly girls in novels, for whom rational thought flees at the first brush of lovers' lips. However, I will admit that, at that particular moment, I found it very difficult to think of anything other than how much I loved this infuriating man.

A few moments later, a passing porter forced us into some semblance of propriety, and as I leaned against Milo, his arm still around me, my thoughts cleared enough for me to remember the telegram I had sent before leaving the Brightwell.

"Laurel's coming to meet my train," I said. "She won't be expecting you."

"Send her away," he replied, his lips brushing my hair. "We've much better things to do than spend the evening sipping tea with your cousin. In the meantime, the porter's gone. How much time until we reach our next stop?"

I glanced at my wristwatch, an absurd fluttery feeling in my stomach. "Nearly an hour."

"Excellent," he said, lowering his mouth again to mine. "Let's make the most of it."

And so we did.